[美国]约翰·D.莱昂斯 著　宋旸 译

# 法语文学

牛津通识读本·

French Literature

A Very Short Introduction

译林出版社

**图书在版编目（CIP）数据**

法语文学 /（美）约翰·D.莱昂斯（John D. Lyons）著；宋旸译．—南京：译林出版社，2021.2（2023.7重印）
（牛津通识读本）
书名原文：French Literature: A Very Short Introduction
ISBN 978-7-5447-8503-7

Ⅰ.①法… Ⅱ.①约… ②宋… Ⅲ.①法语－文学研究－世界 Ⅳ.①I106

中国版本图书馆 CIP 数据核字（2020）第 263708 号



著作权合同登记号 图字：10-2013-027 号

**法语文学 ［美国］约翰·D. 莱昂斯 / 著 宋 旸 / 译**

责任编辑 王 蕾
特约编辑 荆文翰
装帧设计 韦 枫
校　　对 孙玉兰
责任印制 董 虎

原文出版 Oxford University Press，2010
出版发行 译林出版社
地　　址 南京市湖南路 1 号 A 楼
邮　　箱 yilin@yilin.com
网　　址 www.yilin.com
市场热线 025-86633278
排　　版 南京展望文化发展有限公司
印　　刷 江苏扬中印刷有限公司
开　　本 890 毫米 ×1260 毫米 1/32
印　　张 8.75
插　　页 4
版　　次 2021 年 2 月第 1 版
印　　次 2023 年 7 月第 2 次印刷
书　　号 ISBN 978-7-5447-8503-7
定　　价 39.00 元

# 序 言

**刘成富**

法语文学有一千多年的辉煌历史，大致可以分为两个阶段：前五百年和后五百年。文艺复兴前五百年为中世纪文学，主要作品有《罗兰之歌》、《列那狐的故事》、《玫瑰传奇》、《特列斯丹和约瑟》以及弗朗索瓦·维庸的《小遗言集》、《大遗言集》等；后五百年则是16世纪以来的所谓“现代文学”。文艺复兴使法兰西开始步入真正意义上的文学强国，先后走出了拉伯雷、蒙田、高乃依、拉辛、莫里哀、伏尔泰、卢梭、博马舍、司汤达、巴尔扎克、雨果、大仲马、小仲马、莫泊桑、凡尔纳、波德莱尔、普鲁斯特、罗曼·罗兰、瓦莱里、加缪、萨特、昆德拉、勒·克莱齐奥等一个又一个举世瞩目的大作家，他们成功地跨越了国界，备受世界各国读者的青睐和爱戴。

法语文学可谓佳作纷呈，群星璀璨，一直闪耀着法兰西独特的思想光辉。但是，要想真正了解和把握法语文学的概貌和民族特性，其实并不是一件容易的事，最好有一部类似文学史的导读来加以引导。牛津出版社推出的《法语文学》正是出于这一构想。这部小册子的编写理念很新，不是常规意义上对名家名著的简单罗列，也不是对作家生平、作品梗概及其影响进行独立成篇的概述，而是以作品里的主人公、作者所处的时代诉求或人的天性等话题为切入点，以时代发展的顺序为主线，采用比较和串联的方式加以综合论述。这种编写的方式犹如一个多声部的、和谐统一的"交响乐"。例如，在第一章中，作者把关注的目光聚焦于"圣人"、"狼人"、"骑士"和"被诅咒的诗人"，通过对这些人物的介绍和分析，巧妙地将长达数百年的法国中世纪文学特征揭示了出来，而且围绕"忠诚"和"品格"这两个主题，凸显了那个时代的宗教色彩和备受推崇的忠君报国的崇高理想。主人公的形象生动且具体，便于读者记忆和发挥。从第二章开始，导读把我们带进了法国"现代文学"。文艺复兴是个具有划时代意义的思想运动，但也引起了法国社会的动荡不安，法国人遭遇了前所未有的内忧外患。同时，"君权神授"的思想受到了严峻挑战。作者围绕"罗马人"、"食人族"、"巨人"以及现代生活中的"女主人公"展开论述，因为这些人物分别是拉伯雷、龙萨、杜·贝莱、蒙田等人笔下人文思想的载体，极具说服力，能够集中体现16世纪法国文艺复兴的民族特性。

显然，这部《法语文学》想要回答以下几个问题：一、如果法语文学史可大致分为几个阶段，那么，各个阶段的社会主流意识是什么？二、在参与或推进社会主流意识的时候，法语作家对法国乃至世界文明进程有什么样的贡献？三、如果说过去有法国文学与法语国家文学之分，那么，法语文学又将如何进行定义呢？四、文学与历史学、社会学、哲学、法学的关系又是什么？法语文学研究的边界又在哪里？要回答好这些问题，需要的是高超的写作技巧和非同寻常的智慧和胆识。

不可否认的是，这部《法语文学》十分关注重大的历史事件，文学视野极为开阔，将文学研究纳入了文化研究的范畴。书中跨域时空的文学与史学的串联比比皆是，举不胜举，让读者从中获得了文本之外意想不到的收获。在阅读的过程中，中世纪的蒙昧主义、文艺复兴时期的人文精神、古典主义的理性原则、启蒙时代的平等思想、资产阶级的唯利是图、殖民时代的对外扩张，以及两次世界大战带来的异化和虚无主义思想，成了我们思考和关注的焦点。确实，法国作家有思想，有行动，有一种知识分子与生俱来的责任担当。第三章重点论述了高乃依和拉辛的悲剧以及莫里哀的喜剧，围绕社会政治需求，让我们发现在路易十三、路易十四时代，法国知识分子在维护王权和捍卫理性方面功不可没。社会的发展总是波浪式前进的，到了18世纪，法国社会开始动荡不安，像16世纪一样，人的天性再一次被放大。有关出身、等级和文明的“自然”基础等成了文学思辨的对象。在第四章里，作者紧扣“人的天性”将我们带进了狄德罗、伏尔泰、卢梭等人的精神世界。细心的读者会发现，牛津推出的这本小册子还为法国大革命独辟了一章，博马舍的《费加罗婚礼》似乎成了法国大革命的代名词，“阶级”、“人权”、“平等”和“自由”成了导读重点论述的对象。在这一章里，作者不仅把启蒙运动与文艺复兴联系起来，把蒙田与《法兰西组曲》的作者埃莱娜·内米洛夫斯基联系在一起，还提到了中国读者不太熟悉的杜拉斯公爵夫人的短篇小说《欧丽卡》。此外，我们还读到了撰写《人权宣言》的背景、把修道院改造成先贤祠的经过，以及《红与黑》里的主人公于连走向毁灭的深层次原因。

《法语文学》颇具启发性和拓展性思维，通过《茫茫黑夜漫游》的导读，我们对塞利纳等一批“法奸”、第二次世界大战以及纳粹集中营又有了一个新的认识。这样的导读不仅有助于我们正确把握法语文学的发展脉络，而且也有助于我们了解法兰西在不同时期的民族特质。导读将法语作家置于一个大的历史文化背景之下，有助于我们从人类文明进程的角度来对文学作品进行全方位的观照。第八章论述的是20世纪的法语文学，作者以“自我中心意识”为题，巧妙地把存在主义、荒诞派戏剧和新小说串联到了一起。作者以加缪的《局外人》为起点，然后引入萨特、波伏瓦、贝克特、尤奈斯库、罗布-格里耶、布托尔、萨洛特和杜拉斯等一批先锋作家，思路自然、清晰、流畅。创作的时代背景是不容忽视的，因为这些作家深受第二次世界大战的影响，“荒诞感”和“虚无感”无处不在，生命哲学也就成了他们文学创作的主旋律。这样的导读给人的感觉可能是，与其说萨特、加缪是文学家，倒不如说他们是哲学家。更有甚者，新小说和荒诞派戏剧不仅主题荒诞，而且形式也荒诞。典型环境里的典型人物消失了，支离破碎的故事情节走到了极端，令读者云里雾里，甚至觉得进入了疯人院。但是，导读告诉我们，这正是荒诞派戏剧所刻意追求的艺术效果。

值得注意的是，导读的最后一章论述的是近几十年的当代法国文学，但关注的核心则是“法语文学”。这一章是以疑问句“说法语的主人公无国界？”为题展开论述的，动机不言而喻，旨在更新我们对法语文学概念的认知。“法语文学”是一个新概念。“法国文学”指的是法国本土文学，而“法语国家文学”指的则是比利时、卢森堡、加拿大魁北克地区、非洲法语国家以及加勒比海等地区用法语进行的文学创作。显然,“法语文学”的概念要广得多,涵盖了移民到法国国内的外国作家,或移民到法国之外,但仍然用法语进行文学创作的人,当然也包括世界上任何一个用法语写作的人。新概念的提出自然也引入了诸多新的研究视角,例如,罗格斯中心主义、殖民文化、种族主义、文化身份、文化多样性以及世界多极化等。

这部《法语文学》短小精悍,从中世纪的英雄史诗《罗兰之歌》直至2008年获得诺贝尔文学奖的勒·克莱齐奥,几乎无所不包,区区几万字,生动地表现了法语文学的独特魅力,同时为我们开辟了一个全新的认知和思考空间。

# 目 录

# 引言：遇见法语文学

法语文学的遗产在时间和空间上都非常丰富、多变和广泛，无论对其直接受众，也就是法语阅读者而言，还是对通过翻译和改编电影接触到它的世界范围内的受众而言，都非常有吸引力。法语文学最早的杰出作品创作于11世纪的法国北部，而如今，在21世纪之初，法语文学作者遍布世界各地，从加勒比海到西非，他们的作品可以在法国，以及法语国家的书店和图书馆里找到。许多世纪以来，法语也是整个欧洲的贵族和有学养的精英使用的语言。

## 什么是“法语文学”？

“法语”和“文学”这两个词都是不确定的术语。“法语”的边界在哪里？从历史的角度说，“法语”这门语言在生活于今天的“法国”境内的人民中实际占有统治地位，仅仅始于19世纪末，当时的普及教育把巴黎和精英的语言带到了说方言的人们中间，他们有的来自布列塔尼半岛，说布列塔尼语，有的来自西

南海岸，说巴斯克语，还有人说各式各样的奥克语，比如南部的
1 加斯科涅语和普罗旺斯语，还有东北的阿尔萨斯语。此外，有很多曾经使用法语，以及现在用法语写作的重要作家并不生活在我们谓之“法国”的欧洲土地上，尽管在很多情况下他们被认为是法国公民（他们居住在马提尼克岛、瓜德罗普岛、新喀里多尼亚等地），或前法国殖民地的公民，如魁北克和塞内加尔。很多母语不是法语的作家选择用法语创作他们绝大多数的作品，比如塞缪尔·贝克特。另一些生于法国或是法国公民的作家，选择不用“法语”写作：弗雷德里克·米斯特拉尔和贝克特一样是诺贝尔文学奖获得者，他就是用普罗旺斯语写作的。至于“文学”，这个术语通行的用法始于19世纪，当时长久以来被称为“诗歌”或美文的文体与作为大学文学研究基础的回忆录和随笔混为一体。文学就是我们阅读的、并非不得不读的东西——我们不带着直接、详尽的目的阅读的东西，这样想有点轻率，但很有用。



## 从主人公开始

抓住法语文学的起承转合，在某种程度上，意味着对其传统演变的主要文本有想法，对它们如何彼此联系呼应有意识。进入这个传统，首先可能会迷失。幸运的是，不得不与陌生的社会发生关系、不得不在观察其他人的同时定义自己的位置，或许是法国传统中某些主要文本的中心议题。无论是由于选择还是环境所迫，很多法语文本的主人公都发觉自己处于矛盾的境地，或者与其社会的绝大多数成员相隔绝。这往往是作家们批评、论战、说教（公正地说，法语文学可以被称为观点文学）时的文学

策略，但它也可以是情感动荡的源泉，这种骚动比纯粹理智的洞察更能引起读者的共鸣**体验**。 2

以中心人物或主角来看待文学作品是有意义的，因为纵观历史，史诗、悲剧、短篇故事，以及诗歌，都经常以主人公的名字为作品名，无论是英语文学里的《贝奥武夫》或《哈姆雷特》，法语文学里的《囚车骑士兰斯洛特》《巨人传》《厌世者》《查特顿》《康素爱萝》《包法利夫人》《恶劣的玻璃匠》《大鼻子情圣》《娜嘉》《O的故事》等。不过即使在标题没有显示中心人物名字的作品中，对于他或她的特点、思想、行为的聚焦，也使主人公成为探索文学作品的明显的出发点。需要注意的是，“主人公”这个词也适用于主要角色是作者的某个视角的文本，例如很多诗歌或自传文本（“某个视角”意味着我们通常假设它是第一人称的叙述者的再创作，就像龙萨在他的情诗里美化或神化了“龙萨”，或卢梭在《忏悔录》里描写的自己一样）。由于文学史中的绝大多数作品都有中心人物，所以研究人物为比较一段时期内的，或不同时代的作品，提供了一条捷径。



主人公必须遇到问题。如果他们没有，那就不会有故事，不会有探索，不会有需要克服的困难，不会有有待解开的谜团，不会有需满足的欲望，也不会有要打败的敌人。此外，在法语文学传统中，中心人物往往存在这样一种独特类型的问题，以至于他们被称为“问题英雄”（男女主人公的状态和社会地位岌岌可危），甚或“反英雄”（牛津大辞典定义其为“完全不同于常规英雄”的主要人物）。选择哪一类人物作为情节的焦点，以及人物与他（她）的社会的关系，可以告诉我们有关一个文学文本及其时代的很多内容，无论这个人物是按照社会盛行的标准被描述

得非常好，还是以不可取的方式被描写得不同寻常。例如，卢梭
的《爱弥儿：论教育》中的“爱弥儿”，并不是那个时代最复杂或
3 最令人信服的角色，但是他呈现了人类天性和儿时影响的一个
革命性的范式。

在接下来的篇幅里，我们将会遇见很多主人公，在其故事初
次被讲述或出版的年代，他们往往引起争议，但现在，他们是法
语文学传统的核心，也是我们解读其时代的核心。作为比较，我
们还将看到其他一些人物，主人公们通过与他们的差异得以自
我定义。随后的章节在很大程度上对应了法语文学的传统历史
时期，在每一章都会详细讨论三到四个代表性文本，其他文本将
4 被简要提及以作对比，并建议延伸阅读。

第一章

# 圣人、狼人、骑士和被诅咒的诗人：中世纪的忠诚和品格

中世纪文本中的主角告诉我们聚焦于其上的那个时期的世界观。在11世纪，当文学以不同于拉丁语的白话，即古法语出现时，被称为法兰西的领土有着不一样的边界线，并且与我们今天所了解的国家身份或组织毫无关系。我们会将其描述为在地理上和政治上高度非中心化（“非—中心化”这个概念本身就是我们根据法国应有一个“中心”的假设逆推而来的）且社会组织个性化。在封建体系中，权力、身份、土地所有权或使用权，甚至是从一个时代到另一个时代的时间感，都取决于既定时间内既定地点的执政者。忠诚转移，权力和财富，根据个人的手腕和运气，随着统治家族一代又一代地变化。贯穿整个社会的是一个国际化的体制框架，教会，它提供了一种勾画欧洲南部和西部边界的元一认同。在这种语境中，无怪乎文学作品中的主角们（这些文学作品几近千篇一律地以诗歌的形式出现），主要展现的是他们的忠诚，这是封建社会中 5
最重要的价值。

## 圣人的生活

通常被认为是法国第一部实质性文学作品的文本，讲的是主人公决心尽忠于哪位领主。《亚勒叔一生的意义》（1050）讲述的是5世纪时罗马的一位富有贵族的独生子的故事，他年少成婚，于新婚当夜逃走，并告诉他的新娘，“现世没有完美的爱情”。他漂洋过海去往叙利亚，在那里隐姓埋名生活了十七年，进行精神上的苦修。但是由于他开始被人尊敬，所以又从居住的地方逃走，开始远航，结果天不遂人愿，又漂回了罗马。他回到家乡，无人识破，在他父亲府邸的台阶下当了超过十七年的乞丐。他的身份直到去世才通过他临终时对自己一生的记录被发现，但是我们读到的以他的视角写的《亚勒叔一生的意义》肯定与他自己的记录有显著不同。记叙体的《一生》在他去世后仍在继续，包括他的母亲、父亲和处女遗孀对他的哀悼，并指出神圣英雄主义计划，即圣洁本身的复杂性。他的母亲放声大哭，对死去的儿子说：“哦孩子，你是多么恨我！”这里，对于她是否猜测亚勒叔因为从国外来时她没有认出他而憎恨她（他没有：记叙体的《一生》向读者，而没有向他的家人，交代得很清楚，亚勒叔曾决心终其一生不被人认出）或者她是否猜测这种仇恨造成了他最初的离开，并促使他完全脱离家庭，仍存在一种模糊性。



无论如何，这首诗清楚地表明，这种类型的英雄主义需要
6 付出代价。爱圣人的那些人的情感代价要大于圣人本身，因为毕竟圣人选择了自己的优先事项。然而当家人痛苦时，整个群体却因圣人的出现而受益，圣人的灵魂直接升上天堂，与主同在：“圣亚勒叔的灵魂与肉体分离；/它径直升入天堂。”罗马的

人民、皇帝，以及教皇都在庆祝拥有了一名圣人的肉身，它从今往后将作为他们拥护主的证明。《亚勒叔一生的意义》像其他时代的很多文本一样，对多种解读，对支持和反对英雄所代表的价值的不同论据，呈开放姿态。但这并不代表《一生》的作者自己态度模糊。很明显，对作者和11世纪的绝大多数读者而言，亚勒叔代表了基督徒的胜利，超验的价值。相比大型社会单位，比如教会、城市以及帝国，家族野心和性爱是次要的。另一方面，启发性的阅读并没有阻止我们在后来的作品中看到类似的价值冲突，其主角为了对他们而言更为强烈的感召，牺牲了自己的家庭，比如高乃依《贺拉斯》（1640）中的主人公或福楼拜《包法利夫人》（1856）中的女主人公。



## 狼人——源自凯尔特人的无名英雄

狼人像圣人一样，很难有同伴，然而对狼人的忠诚是故事（也许要唱出来）的关键，出现在《亚勒叔一生的意义》之后一个多世纪的一系列叙事诗中。玛丽·德·弗朗斯（1160—1180）的《短歌故事集》借鉴了法兰西承袭至今的两种文学传统：普罗旺斯的行吟诗人和布列塔尼的凯尔特人口头叙事诗。它们可能是在英国宫廷为说法语的诺曼听众创作的。《短歌故事集》里的很多篇目都与婚姻不幸的女性有关（在先后成为法国王后和 7
英格兰王后的阿基坦女公爵埃莉诺的宫闱中，对爱情的讨论不乏诡辩），但其中有一篇脱颖而出，既因为其标题文字的独特性，《狼人之诗》（《毕斯克拉弗莱》），也因为它表现了对遭妻子背叛的丈夫的同情。

玛丽特别将《狼人之诗》这个故事的起源指向凯尔特人，同时又认识到她的听众是法国人："我不愿忘记毕斯克拉弗莱：/毕斯克拉弗莱是他的布列塔尼名字/但是诺曼人叫他狼人。"主人公（我们只知道他是"一位领主"，因此他真的无名至斯）与其他人别无二致，除了他每个星期都有几天需要摆脱人类的身份。这种变形无疑表现出凯尔特文学对于魔法，以及人类与其他生物或幻想造物之间的渗透性边界的喜爱。不过，人们时常注意到，玛丽在她复述的传统故事中将超自然的因素降至最低，在《狼人之诗》这个例子中，主人公向非人类形态的转变，可能仅仅以暴力的普通爆发，或一个人不是"他自己"的时刻的方式表现。简单地说，丈夫的反常行为就是脱光衣服，赤身裸体地在树林里到处奔跑。叙述者一开始就告诉我们，"在过去，很多人曾变成狼人"，因此，这种特征本身并没有被表述为邪恶的或必然使人惊恐的。真正的问题，在许多其他时期的文本中（比如让·德·拉封丹的《普赛克与丘比特之爱》，1669）作为主题出现的一个问题是对所爱之人的信任的缺失。他对她极尽温柔，他足够信任她，向她倾吐他是狼人的隐秘。然而她回报丈夫的只有恐惧和嫌恶。妻子偷走了他变成人时所需的衣服，他因此被困在狼的形态里，直到正义被伸张，"短歌"迎来幸福结局。显而易见的是，狼人形态的丈夫的行为，表现出的对君主的高度忠
8 诚，这是保证他胜利并回归人类身份的价值之所在。

## 中世纪法国北部方言和中世纪法国南部方言

书面的古法语于842年在"斯特拉斯堡誓言"中出现。我们所谓的古法语是现在法国北部的语言，有时被称为

"langue d'Oïl"(即"'是'的语言"),以便与南部说和写的语言(langue d'Oc或欧西坦尼亚语,其中最广为人知的是普罗旺斯语)区分开,在南部,"是"的说法是oc。普罗旺斯语是行吟诗人(在普罗旺斯语中是trobador,即吟咏或吟唱自己作品的诗人)或特罗巴里兹(女性行吟诗人)的语言。古法语与现代法语差异很大,现代法语的书写形式自17世纪以来未有大的变化。今天,许多法国读者依赖于越来越多的中世纪诗歌双语版本,这些版本将原本的古法语和现代法语翻译并排呈现。

## 史诗:武功歌

尽管《狼人之诗》中的狼人绅士是位骑士,"短歌"却并没有专注于他人形时的所作所为。不过,骑士行为是该时期另外两种主要文体,**武功歌**和**小说**的主人公的表征核心。在一个高度个人化的系统中,例如封建主义,主人公的功用和忠诚被反复考察。英雄们寻求机会去展现他们的聪慧和价值。最早、最伟大的武功歌是12世纪的《罗兰之歌》,作者已不可考。在武功歌中,首当其冲的是军事实力和对君主的忠诚。在同时代的小说(或罗曼史)中,骑士面临着在立下军功与虏获心爱的女人之间找到平衡的挑战,正如我们在克雷蒂安·德·特鲁瓦的《艾莱克与埃尼德》(约1170)中看到的那样。

《罗兰之歌》如同其他近120首幸存于世的武功歌(字面意思是"关于完成之事的歌",从拉丁语res gestae而来)一样,写的是查理大帝（768至814年间的法兰克国王，800年加冕称帝）统治时期的事件，但它是在相关事件发生三百年之后才被撰写出来的。《罗兰之歌》讲述了法兰克军队从西班牙北部撤离时发生的一场战斗，当时英雄罗兰指挥的后卫部队留下殿后，罗兰被描述为查理大帝的侄子。详细情况，包括这层亲属关系，与现今对比利牛斯山脉中那场与“异教徒”和多神教撒拉逊人的小规模战斗的历史描述大相径庭（在那场成为《罗兰之歌》基础的历史性相遇中，敌人很有可能不是穆斯林）。

在《罗兰之歌》里，通过对战斗和伤亡的大量血腥描写、对事件的重复及公式化的描述性短语，一切都被夸大了。在一个纯粹的男性社会中，角色在战斗中表现出他们的英勇，他们在荆

荆棘谷之战后，查理大帝找到了罗兰的尸首，《法国大事记》，1460

棘谷之战中肢解并杀死了大量的战士，但主人公的核心困境事实上是道德上的：是否要向主力部队求援，鉴于对战双方悬殊的兵力（二十比一），这是唯一合理的做法。尽管同伴奥利维耶不断敦促，但罗兰拒绝吹响他的号角“坳里风”向查理大帝求援。罗兰回答说：“但愿我的祖先不会因我而遭人指责/愿可爱的法兰西不会蒙受耻辱。”

这种英雄的、近乎超人的、不合常理的行为使得罗兰成为史诗中被歌颂的主体，并且值得，包括在史诗本身之中，成为皇帝和他的军队沉痛哀悼的对象。然而这种骄傲也是一种可怕的缺陷，导致了他两万名部下的死亡。这种困境的矛盾性通过奥利维耶在战斗过程中态度的转变而凸显。首先，当仍有求援的可能时，他敦促罗兰吹响“拗里风”，而当罗兰意识到失败在即时，奥利维耶转向相反的立场，说服前者不要向查理大帝救助，而应承担自己的罪责：“法兰西因你的失职而亡。”通过罗兰这个角色，佚名作者提出了在封建制度中被委以权力后的重任，在这里，生理上的强健、本领以及勇气是重要的，但对忠诚的要求、个人与集体的荣誉二者产生了相悖的需求。



11

## 罗曼史

罗曼史的主人公有其他的问题和完全不同的美德——或者，毋宁说，在一个骑士与女性的关系与他和领主以及军队同伴的关系至少是同等重要的世界里，忠诚与荣誉是以不同的方式被考察的。最初，小说（roman）仅仅是对应拉丁语（Latin）的一种指称古法语的方式，但是到了12世纪晚期，它开始指称一种故事类型，在这类故事中，孤胆英雄通过考验提升美德和自我认知，也是在这类故事中，对女性的爱慕起到了重要作用。事实上，在罗曼史传统中，女性被尊敬地描绘，并被给予极大的尊重，女性在其中的地位是罗曼史对最经典的范式引人注目的创新之一。传统上，罗曼史根据其主题分为三类：“罗马主题”（取材自古罗马，但更常涉及希腊神话和历史），“不列颠主题”（取材自凯尔特和英格兰），以及“法兰西主题”（关于查理大帝和他的骑士）。

《艾莱克与埃尼德》是克雷蒂安·德·特鲁瓦留存至今的五部罗曼史之一，作者的名字表明了他与特鲁瓦城的关系，香槟伯爵的朝廷就位于那里。当克雷蒂安在朝廷时，它基本处于香槟伯爵夫人玛丽的统治之下，她是阿基坦女公爵埃莉诺的长女。像其他四部罗曼史（《狮子骑士伊万》《囚车骑士兰斯洛特》《克里杰斯：一个罗曼蒂克的故事》《帕西瓦尔，或圣杯的故事》）一样，《艾莱克与埃尼德》属于凯尔特剧目中的亚瑟王宫廷故事，文本从布列塔尼语被翻译成英语和法语。年轻的宫廷骑士艾莱克在一次狩猎中于树林里守卫桂妮维亚王后和她的女仆，他们遇见了一位无名骑士，他身边还伴着一位女士和一个矮人。矮人用鞭子袭击了桂妮维亚的女仆，随后又打伤了艾莱克的脸和脖子。艾莱克必须反击对王后的羞辱，但他没有战斗武器。罗兰的处境在艾莱克这里得到了奇特的回应，因为后者与两位女士掉队了，并且与国王的狩猎部队失去了联系。事实上，他们掉队得太远了，连狩猎的号角也听不到，但与罗兰不同的是，艾莱克安于推迟复仇，直到他拥有了更好的装备，因为匹夫之勇不是真正的高贵。

在找到带着矮人的骑士并打败了他之后，艾莱克与埃尼德坠入爱河，埃尼德是一位贫穷贵族的女儿，这位贵族将必需的武器和盔甲借给了主人公。艾莱克幸福地与埃尼德成婚并生活在亚瑟的王宫里，他看上去拥有了一切，他的故事应该已到尾声，但这只不过是罗曼史的前三分之一，真正的挑战才刚刚开始。艾莱克沉溺于与妻子的情欲，开始失去无畏战士的声誉。告知他坏消息的责任落在了埃尼德身上："你的声誉下降了。"从某种意义上说，埃尼德因丈夫倾心于她而失去了他。她嫁的是一位令人尊敬的骑士，却发现与自己在一起的是一个愚蠢的爱人。艾莱克的解决方法是与埃尼德一同出发，寻求挑战，从而再次证明自己。接下来的一系列危险遭遇在很多方面看都像是年轻人为了成年和结婚而经历的一种启蒙考验，但在这种情况下，艾莱克有妻子陪伴在侧，他要求她不要说话。从艾莱克的角度看，这似乎是一种倒退：他想要像单身汉而不是丈夫一样历险。但是，在艾莱克每次遇险的关键时刻，埃尼德都打破沉默以给予丈夫重要信息或建议。就这样，艾莱克和埃尼德证明了他们作为一对夫妻也可以成事，并能够调和情爱与骑士精神。他们最后一次冒险遇见了一对未能找到平衡的夫妻，后者最终与周围的社会隔绝，爱情失意，也未能服务外界。 13

## 吟唱的"我"

在有关亚勒、罗兰和艾莱克与埃尼德的文本中，主人公是谁毫无疑问，尽管文本中有另一个形象，讲述故事的"我"。作者，或者作为讲述者的作者的自我代表，很早就在法语文学中出现了。法兰西的玛丽经常提醒听众，是她编写了"毕斯克拉弗莱"的故事，以及其他"短歌"中主人公的故事，如《夜莺颂》的开场白："我将要向你讲述一场奇遇。"但是这种第一人称的用法使诗人处于展示他人故事的位置。

中世纪后期，诗人以主人公的身份转移到中心位置，讲述她或他自己的故事。在某种意义上，我们可以说，诗人，讲述故事并说"我"的那个人，是中世纪欧洲最重要的文本之一的中心，这个文本就是《玫瑰传奇》，它是一部由上下两卷组成的长篇叙事诗：第一卷由让·德·洛利思于1230年左右写成，第二卷比第一卷长得多，由让·德·梅恩于1275年左右写就。但是在《玫瑰》中，诗人作为一个具体的个体，很快碎化为自己的思想和各种各样的精神力量，这些力量要么把他推向所爱的女人（即"玫瑰"），要么阻碍他的追求。这些力量变为寓言人物（懒惰、爱、恐惧、羞耻、自然、理性等等），他们的言行充满了罗曼史，因为在心灵之战（psychomachia），或"灵魂之战"的文学传统中，他们做恋人之所想，这样作者就不会在他的日常中以具体的形象出现，而是代表所有经历着爱的痛苦与困惑的一类人出现。

在《玫瑰》被创作出来的年代，诗人吕特伯夫（1245—1285）在《吕特伯夫怨歌行》等叙事作品中，把自己和自己的日常不幸作为主题，提供了一个更加具体的诗歌形象。他愿意写自己生活中的非英雄事件（例如他自己的不幸婚姻——"我近来讨了个老婆/一个既不迷人也不漂亮的女人"），他也由此创造了一种诗意的声音，讲述他那个时代在一个正在衰败的世界里发生的具体事件。吕特伯夫有两位主要的继承者，这两位诗人和他一样，他们的创作聚焦于他们自己以及一生中的事件。第一位是克里斯蒂娜·德·皮桑（1364—1434），第二位是弗朗索瓦·维庸（1431—1463）。克里斯蒂娜·德·皮桑生于威尼斯，父亲在她幼时成为查理五世的顾问，她也随之来到巴黎。她的许多作品都采用自传体的形式，比如《克里斯蒂娜的幻想》（1405），特别是《命运的突变》（1403）。对克里斯蒂娜而言（使用名或名字中的第一个词而非姓氏指称这位作家，以及早期的许多其他女性作家，如玛格丽特·德·纳瓦尔，是文学批评传统的一个特点），写作中对第一人称“我”的使用本身是一种重要的姿态，或者说行为，为女性创造一个权威的声音。这一点在《命运的突变》中得到了生动的表达，克里斯蒂娜在《命运的突变》中成为一名寡妇，她象征性地变成了一个男人，她的声音变沉，以便她能够继续职业作家的生涯。

弗朗索瓦·维庸尽管一生短暂，作品寥寥，但从15世纪起，他就在法语文学中占据了一个特别的位置，自文艺复兴以来不断重印，当时的诗人克莱芒·马罗（1496—1544）使他广受欢迎，马罗认为维庸在抒情诗和不幸这两方面都是先驱。维庸是一位典型的“poète maudit”（“被诅咒的诗人”，或噩运不断的诗人）。他神话般的生活，被极大地美化，已经成为多部电影的主题，他的诗也经常被改编成音乐——1953年，乔治·布拉桑录制了音乐版《歌昔日女子》。作为学士、诗人、盗贼以及杀人犯，维庸或许可以被称为（我们在后来的流浪汉小说中看到的）系列 15
犯罪主角的第一人。尽管很多（即使不是绝大多数）法国诗人是中产阶级或上层阶级，但边缘阶层对抒情传统仍具有持久的吸引力（也许正是为了补偿社会的僵化阶级分层）。

维庸为后来的许多法国诗歌设定了范式，在这些诗歌中，时间的流逝和死亡的来临是压倒性的主题，并与巴黎生活的具体细节相联系。主人公，诗人，将自己定义为一种造物，其短暂的在这首被称为《绞刑犯谣曲》的诗中，维庸采用了他典型的挽歌体。这是第一节。

在我们之后存世的人类兄弟，
请不要对我们铁石心肠，
只要我们受到你们怜惜，
上帝就会提前对你们恩赏。
你们看到我们五六个紧相傍：
我们的皮肉，曾保养得多鲜活
早就被吃光和烂掉剥落，
我们的骨头成了灰烬和齑粉。
没有人嘲笑我们的罪恶；
请祈求上帝，让大家宽恕我们！（郑克鲁译）



16 存在是由他周围世界的脆弱性来衡量的，这便给了世界以无所
不在的咏叹，如《歌昔日女子》中的“去日之雪今何在？”生活
在社会边缘的识字的行吟者（一种非常受像奈瓦尔、波德莱尔这
样的19世纪承袭者欢迎的人物），尽管维庸的这种自我描述具
有反英雄的性质，但这种描述与圣人的生活有很多相似之处，因
17 为圣人也生活在恒久的死亡阴影、恐惧和幻灭中。

第二章

# 最后的罗马人、“食人族”、巨人，以及现代生活中的女英雄：古典与复兴

文艺复兴时期与古代的重新接触，对法国的文化身份以及法国每个人的身份提出了挑战。对于法国和法国人而言，意大利的文化活力是其模仿和焦虑的源泉。文艺复兴时期文化的奇怪逆转意味着法国作家、画家、建筑师和音乐家的最新成就越来越被视为过时，而希腊和罗马的更为古老的文学、哲学、艺术遗产被重新发现，焕发出新鲜感。在意大利，这种转变发生得早得多，始于15世纪中叶，随着君士坦丁堡的陷落，以及希腊学者和手稿大量涌入该半岛而发生。

法国人自1494年以来就在与意大利交战。这些运动在法兰西国王弗朗索瓦一世（1515—1547年在位）治下继续进行，促进了意大利文化影响力的提升。可以说，当弗朗索瓦一世邀请莱昂纳多·达·芬奇来卢瓦尔河谷的昂布瓦兹城堡定居时，他确实给法国带来了意大利文艺复兴时期的文化。1519年，这位艺术家兼博学家在那里去世。紧随莱昂纳多其后的还有意大利的其他很多艺术家，比如切利尼、普列马提乔和塞里奥。意大利 18

对法国的影响在弗朗索瓦一世的儿子，未来的亨利二世，与凯瑟琳·德·梅第奇于1531年成婚时得到了加强，后者从佛罗伦萨带来大批随行人员。弗朗索瓦一世还建立了王家学院（也就是今天的法兰西公学院），以替代中世纪的索邦学院，并经常从国外聘请最杰出的希腊语、希伯来语和古典拉丁语学者，为法国人民提供与古代世界直接的文本交流途径。15世纪末，印刷术从德国传入法国，印刷店的迅速扩张使书籍，包括《圣经》在内，得以面向越来越多的读者。

很快就出现了两个主要的身份问题。第一是法语和法国文化本身的性质——法语能否与古代和当代意大利语相媲美，成为诗意和智识表达的载体？第二是宗教的动荡。福音运动要求直接了解《圣经》文本，由此为个体意识提出了选择的责任或重任。1529年，雅克·勒菲弗·德·埃塔普勒出版了第一部法文版《圣经》。

## 法国的薄伽丘

弗朗索瓦一世周围萦绕着机遇和革新的氛围。他的姐姐玛格丽特·德·纳瓦尔鼓励并赞助了福音运动。她还撰写（或合作撰写）了法国传统中最引人入胜的短篇小说集之一《七日谈》（于她去世后九年的1558年首印）。书名不是作者起的，而是因文集总共有七十个故事而得名。玛格丽特·德·纳瓦尔似乎打算总共完成一百个故事。每个故事都围绕一个人展开，通常是女性，据说是玛格丽特自己同时代的人。小说集中有国王、王后、公爵夫人和骑士，但是也有磨坊主、僧侣、铁匠、修女和公证
19 人。强奸、谋杀、监禁以及通奸和下流笑话比比皆是。反派通常

是天主教团体成员或是国王侍从，而带有好人光环的角色通常是（很难概括这本看似简单却又极其复杂的书）那些遵从良知并与强权斗争的人。尽管“现实主义”一词直到几个世纪之后才被用于形容文学，但玛格丽特在书的序言中声称这是对当时世界的准确再现。

玛格丽特直接有力地将这一主张与法国在意大利文艺复兴影响下界定其民族文化的意图相联系。序言为其后的故事构建了一个叙事框架：由五名女士和五位绅士组成的一群人同意讲述他们通过个人经验认为是真实的故事。以这种方式，这本书同时宣称了一种“民族主义”的文学形式，因为它承认薄伽丘的《十日谈》是其范例，但它宣称，在这本“法国的”文集中，故事都是真实的，不会因修辞而改变。这条规则是否被严格地遵守是一个存在争议的问题，但是它的陈述，以及随后故事中时间和地点的其他细节表明，它试图创建一种现实主义的本土文学范式，并与忏悔、讲真话以及主张个人正义等主题的关键性意愿密切相关，这些主题是与传统教会、家族和其他社会结构对立的。简而言之，尽管玛格丽特的作品包含的故事让人想起早期的叙事传统（中世纪的**韵文讽刺故事**），但它强调了一种作为文学环境的新的民族意识，同时也将“真实”埋入个体意识之中。虽然国王仍是国王，客栈老板仍是客栈老板，但《七日谈》中的所有人物都同样值得我们注意。

## 一种新体裁：随笔

米歇尔·蒙田作品的中心角色是他自己，这个第一人称角色，这个“我”，比我们在吕特伯夫、克里斯蒂娜·德·皮桑， 20

或维庸的作品中找到的都更详细。《随笔集》（字面意思是“尝试”）包罗万象，从消化、性功能障碍和幻想，到人类在宇宙中的位置、上帝的存在、友谊和雄辩。米歇尔·德·蒙田比玛格丽特·德·纳瓦尔（1492—1549）晚出生一个世代，从幼年起就经历了新确立的人文主义（即对古代文学的研究）的狂热。他的父亲曾在意大利的法国军队中当过士兵，并显然带回了对一种未变质的古典拉丁语（与中世纪法国大学的教会拉丁语相对）的极大热情。蒙田很有可能是最后一个母语为拉丁语的人。他在他的“论儿童的教育”一章中讲述了这种看似不可能的情况，他解释说父亲聘请了一位古典拉丁语学者，他不仅要与婴儿说话，还要教所有的家庭成员和仆人足够的拉丁语，使他们每天都能和孩子交流。在学习克雷蒂安·德·特鲁瓦的语言之前，蒙田就已经懂得了西塞罗的语言。从某种意义上说，蒙田是最后一位罗马人，是法国文艺复兴时期的象征人物，他集活跃的社会、经济和公民生活于一身［在宗教战争期间，他是波尔多的少校和政客（温和派政客）］，并且认同希腊和古拉丁语文本的智识和想象力。在“谈虚荣”一章中，蒙田回忆说，在看到卢浮宫之前，他就对罗马首都的情况很熟悉了，当他对法国名人还一无所知时，已对卢加拉斯、梅特路斯和大西庇阿有所了解了。他对罗马语言的依恋如此之深，以至于成年后，在他停止说幼时的语言后数年，看到父亲摔倒了，脱口而出的惊呼仍是拉丁语。为了完成对罗马的这一终身认同，1581年3月，他以bulla（加盖公章的证书）的形式获得了“罗马公民”的称号，或者如同他在“谈虚荣”里用法语写的那样，以bulle的形式，这个词既有证书“印
21 玺”的意思，也指“气泡”——虚荣本身的典型代表。

蒙田在他的《随笔集》（1580年出版，版本众多，有1582年版，特别是1588年版及1595年的身后版）中详尽的自我描述立刻引起了国际反响。不仅因为蒙田给了这个世界一种新的文体“随笔”（这本书于1603年被约翰·弗洛里奥翻译成英语，书名是《随笔集，或论道德、政治与军事》），也因为他帮助开创了两个在下个世纪变得非常重要的趋势：一是对自我，即moi的内省研究；二是对社会的冷静和经常是祛魅的描述。这两个趋势在17世纪被称为“劝善”文学的作品中最为明显，它们既不是蒙田的个人创作，也不完全是法国的。例如，我们可以在马基雅维利的早期作品，以及蒙田之后不久的西班牙作家葛拉西安的作品中，看到祛魅社会的观点，但《随笔集》不仅是对个人以及社会互动的分析，还展现出一种文学态度，从而吸引了读者，并为早期现代人格提供了一种范式。

蒙田的写作风格提供了一种自然的理想，如同布莱兹·帕斯卡尔日后写到的那样，你希望在这类书中找到一个作家，却为找到了一个人而惊讶和着迷。帕斯卡尔在此指出随笔作为一种体裁的新颖性。当他说没有找到一个“作家”时，是指一个话语受到尊敬的权威人物。尽管《随笔集》借鉴了很多回顾起来可以称为“随笔”（比如，普鲁塔克的《掌故清谈录》和塞涅卡的许多文本）的经典作品，但蒙田说其作品是“尝试”之合集的这一决定，标志着作家和读者关系的转变。作者对自己的作品所表现出的试探性态度，使读者更加投入，也许会有不同意见，也许会发现自己的经历与蒙田的经历有相似之处。在蒙田之后，几个世纪以来，许多法国作家都以这种形式脱颖而出。最近的包括夏尔·佩吉、保罗·瓦雷里、阿尔贝·加缪、保罗·尼赞、莫里

斯·布朗肖、罗兰·巴特、玛格丽特·尤瑟纳尔和帕斯卡尔·基
22 尼亚尔。

蒙田把自己描绘成一个多面的人物。当然，重要的是要记住，我们在《随笔集》中看到的不是一个由不同文本拼凑而成的历史人物，而是蒙田通过其写作创造的第一人称角色。他坚持自己个性的方方面面，常常表现为内与外、罗马人与法国人、“蒙田与波尔多市长”、城堡塔里的孤独读者与窗户外的家庭场景之间的对立。对他自身复杂性的这种认识，使得一种具有讽刺意味的超然态度成为可能，这种态度导致了令人惊讶的并置：关于他的消化或肾结石的评论与高涨的哲学思辨同时出现，淳朴的乡下人的活动与王子和教皇的行为一样有教益。这种讽刺性并置最令人印象深刻的例子之一出现在“论食人部落”一章的结尾处，蒙田令人难忘地表述了对文化差异的评价以及“野蛮”一词。从引用普鲁塔克的“皮洛士”开始，转到最近发现的美洲大陆及其居民、亚特兰蒂斯、占卜、斯多葛哲学，以及许多其他问题，在这一典型的曲折迂回的文本中，蒙田得出结论：新世界的“野蛮人”或“食人族”并不比法国人低等。1562年，蒙田在鲁昂遇到了这么一个美洲人，他发现后者的言谈十分睿智，带着令人愉悦的讽刺，惊叹道：“所有一切都很好。但他们偏偏不穿马裤！”



对蒙田，以及他的很多同时代的人而言，美洲新发现的民族似乎可能与被重新发现的古人极其相似。因此，对他的第一批读者来说，看到《随笔集》在希腊—罗马人的生活和当时巴西人的生活之间来回穿梭，就像他们经常做的那样，可能并不会感到如何奇怪。在这些新发现的民族身上，可以瞥见如荷马史诗

英雄，甚或可能是亚当之前的人种那般高贵而朴实的生活。过去的欧洲人和现在的美洲人之间的相似性出现在蒙田的“论车马”一章中，他在其中描述了墨西哥人对世界主要时代的概念。23
他写道，他们像我们一样，相信世界正在走向终结和腐朽。在过去，世界上有巨人，无论是比喻意义上的，还是字面意义上的。

## 拉伯雷的神秘巨人



世界上最令人难忘的两个巨人出现在医师弗朗索瓦·拉伯雷（1490—1553）的书中，他还为世界贡献了两个重要的形容词：巨大的和庞大固埃式的。高康大和庞大固埃这两个巨人并不是拉伯雷创造的——他们早就存在了，正如1532年出现的一本匿名故事抄本见证的那样，它的标题是《高康大：无比庞大的巨人高康大伟大且无可估量的事迹》——但拉伯雷在1532年至1552年出版的一系列作品中，将他们变成了文学万神殿里的重要人物，其中第一部是他化名阿尔科弗里巴·那西埃出版的。拉伯雷先是方济各会教徒，然后成为本笃会僧侣，在成为一名医生以及至少进行了三次意大利之行以前，参与了天主教内部的改革运动，并对新人文主义学问及其对教育和宗教的影响深感兴趣。

《高康大》的序言提出了该书蕴含着隐秘智慧的观点，并敦促读者吸取“骨髓”。这种对隐藏核心的比喻前有这样一句谚语：“习惯不能造就僧侣：因为一个人可能穿着僧袍，内在却完全不是僧侣。”拉伯雷的书中有写给福音派基督教支持者的隐晦信息吗？这些支持者对大学和修道院的天主教神学家深表怀疑。他们是持相反的理性主义无神论观点吗？或者，传达隐藏

居斯塔夫·多雷为拉伯雷的《高康大》(1534) 所绘插图

信息的主张仅仅是公开的喜剧素材附赠的一个笑话？争论依然
24 激烈，但很明显，对于所有正在进行的狂欢（例如，高康大到达巴
黎后撒尿淹死了几十万巴黎人）来说，在饮酒、小便和吵架的过
程中，存在着有关社会制度的重大问题。该系列书中每一本书

的不连续性和情节性将主要人物推至前台，成为主要的结构性
元素。庞大固埃是第一部的主角，随后他的父亲高康大成了第 25
二部（是倒叙，或第一部的“前篇”）的主角，而庞大固埃的朋友
班努赫鸠则是第三部的中心——班努赫鸠想要结婚，但害怕戴
绿帽子，于是尝试了很多方法预测他在婚姻中的命运。

当从现代的角度回顾拉伯雷的主人公时，我们吃惊地留意到通俗文化与教益文化、粗鄙的肉体问题与高度博学的精神问题十分轻松地融合在一起——《高康大》里的饕餮豪饮与柏拉图的《会饮篇》有明确联系。虽然下个世纪的一些作品努力保持这种特点、主题和基调的混合［例如，查尔斯·索雷尔的《弗朗西荣的滑稽故事》（1623—1633）很明显是受到了拉伯雷的启发］，在17世纪的高雅小说、喜剧和悲剧中，但大多数情况下，高康大和庞大固埃巨大的身形和饕餮胃口，以及他们的幽默都无迹可寻。在长达一个世纪的将古典人文文化融入法国（而不是意大利或意大利风格的）文化的努力中，作为典范，拉伯雷显然成功地让学识渊博、机智狡黠的法国主人公深深地扎根于法国的地理、风俗和语言中。

## 法国十四行诗

意大利的精巧诱惑以及与法式简约的对抗成为文艺复兴抒情诗的主题，尤其是在约阿希姆·杜·贝莱的《遗恨集》等作品中，第一人称的诗人角色将罗马的生活与其对家的回忆进行了比较。杜·贝莱对塑造现代法语文学的重要性超越了他在抒情诗方面的诸多成就，因为他也是创新诗人团体“七星诗社”的宣言书作者，这是一个由七位诗人组成的团体，成立于1540年代

末，其中包括皮埃尔·德·龙萨。这份宣言书，即《保卫和发扬
26 法兰西语言》（1649）主张丰富法语词汇、建立法语文化库，以使之与意大利语和古代语言相媲美。《保卫》出现在弗朗索瓦一世将法语作为官方文件语言（取代拉丁语）的维莱科特雷王家法令颁布十年之后。因此，《保卫》进一步促进了自国王而始的法国语言民族主义的兴起，并赋予专业诗人不仅限于歌颂国王和军事英雄的角色。《保卫》不仅明确了诗歌——广义上的，不仅限于抒情诗，还包括史诗、喜剧和悲剧——是一门学科，并且相比突如其来的灵感或某种情绪的简单结果，诗人作为造词者和语言建造者的工作赋予了他广泛而多样的文化使命。杜·贝莱提出了为法语创造和引进单词的各种方法，但他特别提倡一种观点——模仿主义，即法国作家应该创作古代作品的文学等价物，而不是简单地翻译。换句话说，法国应该有法国史诗、法国抒情诗等等，而非仅仅引进其他国家的作品。杜·贝莱的论战作品是记录那一时期诗人们的雄心壮志的档案，但今天我们也可以将其视为法国在面对主导全球模式的其他一切文化（无论是文艺复兴时期的罗马，还是今天的好莱坞）时，努力保持自己身份的早期表现。



遵循诸如奥维德、贺拉斯和卡图卢斯等人的范式，每一位主要诗人都在16世纪大量出现的民谣、回旋诗、诗歌书信、挽歌、墓志铭、讽刺诗（韵文描写，尤其是女性的身体部位）、悲歌、警句和颂歌中，为他或她自己塑造了独特的角色或人格。最重要的作品中，有很多采用以十行诗或十四行诗为韵文单元的形式。
27 十行诗是里昂派诗人（包括佩奈特·德·吉耶和“露易丝·拉贝”——事实上，后面这位很可能只是个虚构的身份，一群男性

诗人以此身份出版他们的作品）中的一位，莫里斯·赛福，在他的长篇密文情诗《宽恕，至高的美德》（1544）中采用的形式，这首诗有449个十行诗韵文单元。从另一方面来说，十四行诗的成功更持久，且这种形式本身印证了意大利文学的影响。16世纪最伟大的诗人，和拉伯雷一样受玛格丽特·德·纳瓦尔庇护的克莱芒·马罗，在1530年代将彼特拉克的十四行诗带到了法国。

然而，直到1550年代，十四行诗才在七星诗社的作品中取得了胜利，团体中的每一位诗人，都根据其希望创造的不同人格，赋予了这种形式以不同的调性。例如皮埃尔·龙萨，"龙萨"这个角色被描绘成各种各样饱受爱情折磨的样子，或是被描绘为一名桂冠诗人，以其超凡的语言天赋赋予垂青于他的女性以不朽。以闻名遐迩的《致海伦》（又译作《当你老了》）为例，它的开头是这样的：

当你老了，黄昏时点燃蜡烛，
在炉火旁纺着羊毛，
读起我的诗篇，哀哀叹道：
"我年轻时龙萨曾写诗赞美我。"[①]

诗人巧妙地将自己融入文本中，但不是以第一人称的形式出现，而是让一个角色谈论他，视他为天才。这篇文本是古训"及时行乐"（carpe diem）的变体，在其中，"龙萨"变成一个让人回味无穷的人物。作为"诗歌王子"，龙萨并不羞于歌颂自己的

① 译文引自《最美的诗歌》，徐翰林等编译，中国对外翻译出版公司，2006年。

才华，并隐晦地赞颂诗人超然的社会地位。在“答侮辱与诽谤”
28 中，他写到了自己在复兴古代诗歌方面的成功，并对他的批评者断言：“你们无法否认，因为我的丰盛/使你们饱足，我是你们学习的中心，/你们皆来自我的伟大。”

## 十四行诗的典范：杜·贝莱的《遗恨集》

让我们回到龙萨的同伴杜·贝莱，《遗恨集》常被认为是其最好的作品，它有助于捕捉法国作家在面对更先进的意大利文化时所感受到的竞争、激情和焦虑。诗人作为在罗马古都的幻灭冒险中的第一人称角色，突出了其民族和语言身份，表达了一个出身于卢瓦尔河谷，混迹于华丽颓废的教皇宫廷之中的谦逊、坦率之人的想法。但《遗恨集》这本书也推动了一种基于偶遇的诗歌理念——“根据此地的种种事件，/无论是好是坏，我都随机写下”。虽然这一主张在十四行诗艺术大胆、形式局限的韵文语境中确实难以持续，但它把诗意的“我”定位为当代世界的一个谦逊的观察者。这种诗意的人格，尽管多少源自维庸和鲁特伯夫，但它很晚才在法语文学传统中发展起来，直到波德莱尔和超现实主义出现，它甚至似乎预示着詹姆斯·乔伊斯的出现，因为杜·贝莱在探索罗马城时，试图将古代诗人与史诗英雄，尤其是尤利西斯相比。

《遗恨集》是一部开放式结局的、多变的作品，具有多种风格——讽刺的、挽歌式的、对话式的、描述性的，有时还有激情澎
29 湃的祝词式的（“法兰西，艺术之母，武力之母，法律之母”——他的祖国与罗马的关系发生了惊人的逆转）。它在现代法语文学中最直接的后继者可能是波德莱尔的后浪漫主义作品《恶之

花》。在《遗恨集》出版几年后，新教和天主教的不同派别之间的宗教战争深刻地改变了法国文化，并为17世纪更结构化的、往往不那么私人化的文学创造了条件。

> 旅行过的人懂得尤利西斯的幸福，
> 抢到金羊皮的人也知晓其中的乐趣，
> 然后他回到故乡，满怀知识和理性，
> 和父母共享天伦！
> 唉，我什么时候才能再见到
> 冒着炊烟的小村庄，什么季节
> 才能再见到我家门前的小花园？
> 它对我来说比一个帝国还辽阔。
> 比起张扬的罗马宫殿， 30
> 我更喜欢祖先打造的茅屋，
> 更偏爱我家房顶上薄薄的石板，而不是豪华的大理石，
> 更垂青高卢的卢瓦尔河，而不是拉丁台伯河，
> 更痴迷我的小村，而不是帕拉丁山丘，
> 更享受安茹的柔风，而不是海边大风。
>
> 摘自约阿希姆·杜·贝莱《遗恨集》 31

第三章

# 社会及其需求

## 岌岌可危的和平及新风尚

礼貌、谦逊、谨慎、自我审查、讽刺，以及对世俗生活与宗教生活仪规的高度关注，是17世纪法国的标志。今天回顾起来，我们不禁要说那是一个非常压抑且专制的社会。从那些经历过16世纪后期激烈的内战和宗教战争的人的角度来看，和平与稳定，以及少许的宗教宽容，无疑是受欢迎的。1594年波旁王朝第一位君主亨利四世的加冕礼，通过妥协给法国带来了和平。亨利，虔诚的新教徒让娜·阿尔布雷的儿子，皈依了天主教，同时，困扰瓦卢瓦王朝晚期（被指过于愿意与胡格诺派共存）的激进天主教联盟也放下了他们的武器。

1598年，亨利颁布《南特赦令》，赋予新教徒做礼拜的权利。在亨利四世和他的儿子、继承人路易十三的统治下，巴黎的面积迅速扩张，成为王室的惯常居所，贵族和富裕的中产阶级都涌向新社区——尤其是位于塞纳河右岸、卢浮宫上游不远处的玛莱

区（因其所建地的沼泽而得名）。法国上流社会变得更加城市 32
化，更加文明，但这并非一蹴而就。很多书籍、戏剧和书信证明了对如何在诙谐交谈、信件书写以及着装等方面获得适当技巧的认真讨论。这种融入并避免冒犯他人，或至少将暴力转化为创造性的语言形式的努力，暗示了肉体攻击恰恰正潜伏于表面之下。1610年，亨利四世被刺杀，正如他的前任亨利三世在1589年被刺杀一样。重新颁布的赦令并未能阻止决斗——在亨利四世的统治下，一年多达四百起。

每个人都意识到和平摇摇欲坠，整个法国都在努力推广礼貌互动的方式，避免引发新一轮的敌意。在这种氛围中，一种提倡适度、审慎甚至掩饰的理想，却又为过度、杰出和卓越所吸引的文学大行其道。就好像17世纪彬彬有礼、端庄得体的法国人依然梦想着上个世纪的殉道以及违反准则的英雄主义，同时反思确定一套规范的难度。这种文学非常强调避免极为明显的盲目和狂热，强调做一个明智的人，一个有趣的、善解人意的、乐于助人的伙伴——简而言之，一个honnête homme。这个词不容易翻译，重要的是要立即注意到它并不意味着“诚实的人”（honest man），即真诚且完全坦率地说话的人。honnête homme是一个“融入”的人，他尤其不特立独行。另一方面，17世纪的读者和作者都被主人公远悖常规、完全不“融入”且言行过火的故事迷住了。



## 莫里哀的性格喜剧

当上流社会的理想达到顶峰时，戏剧就会表明，礼貌与英雄
主义格格不入。以莫里哀《恨世者》（1666）中的喜剧主人公阿 33
尔赛斯特为例。作品全名涉及这样一个医学理论：性格基于血

液中的物质，即“情志”。由此，阿尔赛斯特是一个黑胆汁过多的恋爱中的男人。阿尔赛斯特这个角色，在首演时由剧作家亲自扮演，演绎他的目的无疑是为了博观众一笑。莫里哀以他的喜剧舞台表演技巧而闻名，他的表演有很多引人捧腹的地方。主人公坚持一个人应该在所有情况下都勇敢地说出自己的想法。他爱上了一个完全与之相反的女人，一个轻浮的年轻寡妇。赛丽曼纳精心培养了很多追求者，让每个人都以为自己是她唯一的爱人。阿尔赛斯特拒绝顺应社会常规。在涉及他全部财产的重要法律问题上，他不会屈尊奉承法官；当业余诗人给他看十四行诗时，他甚至拒绝说出客套的礼貌赞许。他意识到自己与上流社会
34 格格不入，因为在这里（如阿尔赛斯特的朋友菲兰特所说）“隐藏心中所想”的天赋是很重要的品质。因为他的真诚，阿尔赛斯特面临三个风险：失去赛丽曼纳的爱，失去财产，在决斗中失去生命或名誉。这些风险的重要性似乎很不均等，展示坦率的各种姿态及其结果之间奇怪的不平衡或许是莫里哀的喜剧意图。可能的决斗是一个严肃的问题，也是文明的脆弱性的反映，这种文明可能在几分钟内从机智巧妙的应对发展到拔剑相向。决斗遭到贵族审判委员会，即一个负责解决荣誉冲突，从而避免流血的高级法庭的干预。尽管阿尔赛斯特一再宣称他不会顺应社会，且最终将离群索居，但他似乎需要社会——仅仅是为了他自己愤怒的乐趣。在这方面，他迥异于同时期的很多其他局外人，如让·德·拉封丹《狼与狗》中的狼（《拉封丹寓言》，1668）。尽管被圈养的狗享有优渥的物质待遇，但狼确实更喜欢完全置身于社会之外。换句话说，恨世者似乎只能在他蔑视的人附近存在。



人们很容易认为阿尔赛斯特是个彻头彻尾的笑话，一个黑

佩雷勒制作的版画（1660），由路易·勒沃设计的沃子爵城堡



胆汁过多的不坚定的人，没有社交技能，没有分寸感。然而，《恨世者》通过让剧中的其他角色崇拜阿尔赛斯特，争夺他的友谊、爱情和认同，消除了这种观点。这些人物中的某些人可能自己缺乏判断力，比如十四行诗的作者奥龙特，而另一些人，比如阿尔赛斯特的朋友菲兰特和赛丽曼纳的表妹爱丽昂特，似乎对性格的判断很准确。菲兰特是17世纪honnête homme的一个很好的例子：他从来没有取得过任何属于自己的特殊成就（拉罗什富科在他1664年出版的《道德箴言录》里这样说道："真正的honnête homme是不为任何特别的事情感到自豪的人。"），他以宽容和超然的态度看待人类的不完美，他说："如欲挺身作改革世界的工作，那才是无与伦比的疯狂行为。"[1]阿尔赛斯特把菲兰

① 译文摘自赵少侯：《恨世者》，《莫里哀喜剧选》，人民文学出版社，2001年。

弗朗索瓦·肖沃制作的版画(1668),《拉封丹寓言》中的《狼与狗》



35 特描述为一个冷漠的人(情志的另一种不平衡),意思是他太平静了。这也许是阿尔赛斯特吸引周围人的关键,无论男女:他们都为他的活力、固执的坦率而神魂颠倒,而这些都反映在他肉体的躁动中:他似乎总是处在运动中,其他人追随其后。他们或许很清楚地发现,看到有人摆脱了他们每日背负的自觉和掩饰,是一件令人耳目一新的事情。

## 高乃依的超级英雄

《恨世者》中关于英雄主义的矛盾心理或许是一个喜剧范例,但它并不是孤例。我们在其中看到的,为充满活力、持异见的主人公神魂颠倒,或者对之大感震惊的社会形态,以更为严肃

的形式出现在其他作品中。我们可以看到17世纪对礼节的坚 36
持——对顺应情势的期望——是基于这样的恐惧：人们站出来，英雄般地说出他们认为可能轻易越界，引起类似不久前内战中的激烈暴力事件。《贺拉斯》(1640)是根据李维描述的发生在罗马的捍卫者贺拉斯三兄弟，与邻近城邦阿尔巴隆加的捍卫者居里亚斯三兄弟之间的斗争写成的。在这部作品中，高乃依展现了三位罗马人之一的道德困境，他必须与最好的朋友，同时也是姐夫的居里亚斯战斗。出于政治统治上速战速决以及相对牺牲较小的考虑，这场战斗被限制在两座城邦的六位战士之间。不同于居里亚斯的不情愿，贺拉斯声称，从得知对手身份的那一刻起，自己就全心全意忠于职守，不再“认识”居里亚斯：“你以阿尔巴命名，我便不再认你。”到此为止，可能不过是在恪守职责范围内的本分——或许有点冷酷，也不太礼貌，却是通往胜利之路。事实上，贺拉斯确实为罗马一方赢得了战斗，他是六个人中唯一活到最后的。

然而，正是自英雄从战场凯旋的那一刻起，贺拉斯对自己的英雄主义的态度越界成为民事暴力事件。贺拉斯的姐姐卡米耶是居里亚斯的爱人，她并没有按贺拉斯要求的那样恭敬地向他致以问候：“将你拥有的[荣耀]献给我幸运的胜利。”至少可以说，贺拉斯是无情的，只专注于自己的辉煌成就，并且，正如他之前所说的，在这种战争状态下，不愿承认任何个人的依恋或身份。但这种极端主义，甚或是狂热，他姐姐与他不相上下——很明显，它在家族中奔腾——她没有屈服或保持沉默，而是羞辱他，并将骂战上升到诅咒贺拉斯宣称是其化身的罗马的程度。她呼唤天堂的火降在这座城邦。卡米耶和弟弟的争吵是这部戏

37 在舞台表演上最激烈的部分，因为像1630年代之后的绝大部分法国戏剧中的肢体暴力场面一样，阿尔巴人和罗马人的械斗发生在舞台之外。对贺拉斯而言，第二次对战的结局很糟糕。他勃然大怒，杀死了他的姐姐。因为他所谓的“正义之举”，他被送上了法庭。随后，这出戏达到高潮，用完整的一幕来表现坚定果敢、铁石心肠的贺拉斯式的英雄主义与一个社会对法律、个人身份、职责以及政治等级的要求之间的不相容性。在高乃依笔下的罗马公民社会中，战争所要求的纯粹的男性美德不能不受约束。正如贺拉斯的首席原告瓦莱尔指出的那样，贺拉斯杀死姐姐，不仅是杀害了一名手无寸铁的女性，同时也是杀害了一位罗马公民。当暴力事件发生在城邦外且针对非罗马人时，是可以原谅的，但现在它进入了城邦，威胁着所有人。高乃依在这里展示的最主要的悖论是，和平的社会秩序建立在自相残杀（罗马针对其亲族阿尔巴城邦的战争，比如贺拉斯杀害亲姐，脱胎于罗马城创建的传奇背景——罗慕路斯杀害其兄弟雷穆斯）的基础上，这样的暴力永远不该复苏。



尽管对于英雄主义的任何思考都很重要，但勇士得胜回城的主要悖论并没有像高乃依巧妙传达的那样具有独创性，他深入处于这种境地的贺拉斯自身的体验。一代又一代的观众和读者普遍认为贺拉斯这个角色远不像其对手居里亚斯那样吸引人，但这部喜剧暗示了英雄承受的可怕痛苦。胜利的代价是牺牲不直接导向杀死既定敌人的所有感情、所有知觉。这种牺牲聚焦于某一时刻，在那之后，英雄无可避免地开始堕入一种永远与他无缘的平凡生活中去。贺拉斯要求被处死，声称“今天只有死亡才能保全我的荣耀/它本应在我胜利时就到来”。在《贺拉斯》的结尾，像《恨世者》的结局一样，观众离开时苦苦思索，这样一个宁折不弯的超级主人公如何才能重新融入平凡社会的世界。 38

## 英雄的衰落

换句话说，在特定的时刻，英雄在侧是有用的，但在漫长的征途后，他们又要尴尬地适应社会框架。按照普遍的道德标准，他们甚至不一定是“好的”。拉罗什富科写过一句令人难忘的话：“有善的也有恶的英雄。”我们只需想想高乃依的其他两个主人公，他们既是英雄，也是怪物——他的第一部悲剧《美狄亚》（1635）中的美狄亚和《罗多古娜》（1644）中的克利奥帕特拉——或拉辛后来在《布里塔尼居斯》（1669）中描绘的尼禄皇帝。当文学理论家试图将古代悲剧的遗产与基督教的现代价值观相对照时，他们对于将能够做出极端行为的人物，无论好坏，置于“英雄”的位置上有着相当的不安。高乃依的年轻对手让·拉辛引用了亚里士多德在《诗学》中关于悲剧英雄的名言，说他们应该具有一种“中等的善，也就是说，一种易受弱点影响的美德”。拉辛致力于用这种中等的善来塑造人物。拉辛避免像贺拉斯、《熙德》中的施曼娜以及《西拿》中的奥古斯特等高乃依式的主人公的惊人品质和行为，在他的大多数悲剧中，拉辛描绘了相当中庸，甚至在现代意义上“平庸”的主人公。他们是像我们自己一样的人，或者像我们在日间电视节目上看到的我们自己的翻版，但用的是夸张的诗句。《费德勒》的主人公就是这样，在这部小说中，同名的主人公是一个不幸的女人，她爱上了青春期的继子——她认为自己是一个怪物，但真正的怪物就在隔壁，后者在遭到她的拒绝后，默许了一个指控希波利特强奸她的计划。

我们可以理解为什么有人说拉辛把悲剧变成了资产阶级的情节剧。他的《安德洛玛刻》（1668）以特洛伊英雄赫克托耳的遗孀安德洛玛刻为标题，她后来成为阿喀琉斯的儿子皮洛士的奴隶。在这部悲剧中，拉辛用透彻的手法阐释了主人公的这种
39 “中等的善”的概念，甚至有人可能会想到卡尔·马克思说的：“历史重复自己，第一次是悲剧，第二次是喜剧。”这部戏的主要人物是属于后英雄时代的一代人，可能只有安德洛玛刻本人例外。他们的父母是伟大的荷马《伊利亚特》中的男女英雄阿伽门农、海伦、墨涅拉俄斯、阿喀琉斯，以及新一代的爱弥奥娜、俄瑞斯特斯，甚至皮洛士（尽管程度不那么明显）都痴迷于一种欲望，即不辜负先辈并与其竞争。爱弥奥娜回忆说，她的母亲是如此美丽，特洛伊战争是为了把她带回希腊，但她甚至不能让皮罗斯履行与她结婚的诺言。俄瑞斯特斯为他对爱弥奥娜的单恋犹豫不决，未能完成他的外交任务，即找到并杀死赫克托耳的儿子阿斯提阿那克斯，以消除特洛伊王室的一切痕迹。皮洛士本人被描述为“阿喀琉斯的儿子和对手”。但当他们的父母以史诗般的战斗震撼世界时，这群人却死于谋杀和自杀的肮脏宫廷阴谋。



然而，尽管在高乃依，甚至莫里哀笔下的大人物，与拉辛的自我意识平庸的角色之间有着明显的区别，但在英雄主义这一矛盾的主题上却有着惊人的相似之处。《安德洛玛刻》的主人公之所以走到了可怕的结局，是因为试图上演他们没有能力完成的英雄壮举，而这些壮举在任何情况下（这与17世纪法国的历史情况最为相似）都属于过去，本应留在过去。在《安德洛玛

刻》中，就像在《荷马史诗》中一样，像暴力军事英雄般行事的时代已经过去，主人公会被建议采用和平时期的技巧。一定程度的英雄主义是令人钦佩的，正如莫里哀的《老实人》中的菲林特可能会说的，但万事万物皆有其时其地。

这些主要的戏剧作品让我们对具有延续性地将文明、顺应环境和礼貌认为是理想有了一定的感知，甚至当它们从古希 40
腊—罗马被投射到法语版本时也是如此。但我们现在应该回顾一下，当时的社会环境赋予了这些理想如此的重要性，甚至是紧迫性。从16世纪的宗教战争到更稳定，甚至更官僚化的波旁王朝政权的转变一点也不容易。亨利四世遇刺是一个巨大的打击：玛丽·德·美第奇随后的摄政以她的儿子路易十三发动的政变而告终，路易十三长期在位的首相红衣主教黎塞留处决、监禁或流放了“虔诚党”的成员，而这些成员中的很大一部分来自挑战最后的瓦卢瓦王朝和亨利四世的天主教联盟。但是，彻底的内战在17世纪中叶重新爆发，这段动荡而复杂的时期被称为“投石党运动”（Fronde，法语意为“弹弓”），从1648年持续到1653年，这场战争由忠于摄政王太后奥地利的安妮的军队对抗一个由贵族和高等法院成员（巴黎立法机构成员）组成的联盟。



这场对抗在摧毁了国家大部分地区之后，通过重新确立君主制而结束。对于贵族独立英雄主义——新近例证是孔代亲王和国王的叔叔加斯东·德·奥尔良的反叛或叛国行为，他们与西班牙结盟对抗王太后——的矛盾心理只能通过这场灾难性的、浪费的冒险来加强，这给年轻的路易十四留下了深刻的印象，当时他才十岁。为了进一步集中权力，消除上层贵族一切残余的独立性，路易采取了果断的措施，使从众——至少是外在的从众——成为17世纪后半叶法国文化的核心价值观。这当然也是为什么在三大剧作家笔下的英雄地位从高乃依到拉辛呈现出显著下降的轨迹的原因之一，尽管三位都表现出英雄主义导致冲突。

英雄地位变化的另一个原因可能是，到了17世纪中叶，一
41 种幻灭的世界观的影响力上升，它与被称为杨森主义的宗教运动有关，以王家港修道院为中心，与许多有“道德主义”倾向的主要作家，如布莱兹·帕斯卡尔和弗朗索瓦·德·拉罗什富科有关。这场运动不仅仅是提倡严苛的道德（尽管有些人，如帕斯卡尔，相当禁欲），而且在很大程度上，还包括对人类社会及其动机的悲观看法，并旨在对各种关系进行冷静的分析。它认为人类绝不是英雄。



在17世纪后半叶，一种不同类型的主人公出现了，这与宫廷和城市生活的密集化、贵族的驯化以及道德家的觉醒相一致。这种新的主角是一种趋势的典型代表——或者说是一系列融合的趋势，其中有文学的“内向转向”，转向“心理分析文学”，一种被称为“公关”的社会和文化运动，以及由女性组织的社交空间“沙龙”兴起了。

### 沙龙与文学女性的崛起

“沙龙”一词现在用来形容17世纪女性接待客人的私人会议场所有些不合时宜（这个词本身在18世纪才变得突出）——这些场所的主要当代术语是ruelle、alcôve或réduit，意思是床和附近墙壁之间的狭窄空间，客人可以站

在或坐在那里与女主人交谈，而女主人仍然是躺着的。有两个这样的沙龙脱颖而出：朗布依埃侯爵夫人的蓝色房间和马德莱娜·斯屈代里的星期六。这些有教养的女性控制着她们邀请杰出男女嘉宾的空间，使沙龙成为以女性为中心的谈话场所，与男性作家可能单独见面的酒馆形成鲜明的区别。在这种环境下提倡的价值观包括免于包办婚姻和男女之间的友谊。诋毁女性的人，如布瓦洛，称她们为“女才子”，这是因莫里哀的《可笑的女才子》（1659）和《妇人学堂》（1662）而流行的一个词。 42



## 宫廷礼仪小说

在这种情况下，重点转移到对英雄，或者更确切地说是主人公的新概念（因为“英雄”一词通常不用于非军事荣誉）：在友谊和爱情方面表现得极为精致，能够特别忠于理想的人。玛丽·马德莱娜·德·拉法耶特夫人的短篇小说《克莱芙王妃》（1678年匿名出版）中的中心人物最能体现这种类型的主人公。这部作品通常被誉为最早的“心理小说”或“分析小说”之一，背景是上个世纪的瓦卢瓦宫廷。主人公是一位无辜的年轻女子，她十六岁时随守寡的母亲来到巴黎，她从母亲那里得到了关于她即将进入的世界的三条基本指令。第一条是不轻信外表：事实往往不是它展现出来的样子。第二条有点矛盾，是要从聆听法庭上其他男女的悲惨经历中吸取教训。第三条是对一个女人来说，幸福就是爱她的丈夫并得到他的爱——简而言之，她完全不同于其他女人，她们是她听到的那些故事中的典型，深陷多重的、不幸福的、通奸的情事。从故事的一开始，女主人公的目的就是要理解和区别于其他女人，并寻找那种据说只有幸福的已婚妇女才能得到的难以捉摸的幸福。

作为德·克莱芙亲王的妻子，这个年轻的女人很快就遇到
43 了德·内穆尔公爵，他是一个举世闻名的情人。接下来的爱情故事是王妃和公爵只有两次单独在一起，从未有过接触，也从未公开过对彼此的感情。尽管王室不断地窥探、好奇和八卦，但除了王妃、她的丈夫、母亲和公爵本人之外，没有人知道王妃发现了爱情和她自己本性的故事。很容易说，这是一个什么都没有发生的故事，然而，通过调整感知的尺度，我们可以看到拉法耶特夫人是如何将事件向内推移，使其进入角色的思想和情感中，在那里发生着生死搏斗，美德在与背叛抗争。主人公通过微小的、几乎不可察觉的信号互相交流。比如，公爵希望以一种除了她以外任何人都无法理解的方式来表达他对王妃的爱，于是在比赛中穿上黄色和黑色的衣服以表明身份。每个人都好奇这是为什么，因为这些颜色和他没有任何关系。然而，王妃立刻明白这是在对她示好，因为某日公爵在场的一次谈话中，她说自己喜欢黄色，但不能穿，因为她的头发是金色的。还有一次，王妃没有去参加舞会，声称自己病了（尽管她看上去身体很好）。这是另一个秘密信号，因为王妃听公爵说过，对于情人来说，最痛苦的莫过于知道他的情妇正在参加一个他自己不能出席的舞会。



战场上的英雄主义，异国的地理位置，悲剧、史诗和17世纪初长篇浪漫小说中主角之间相互争斗的非常明显的敌对行为，在这里被对眼神、衣着细节、舞会和其他社交场合的在场或不在

场的微妙解码所取代。但是，使王妃的地位等同于其他文本的主人公的，是她的问题的独特性。在她母亲最初的指导下，王妃形成然后实施了一个英雄计划：与其他所有的女人不同。宫廷的一些成员可以看到这种区别。一个王后说，王妃是唯一把一 44
切都告诉丈夫的女人。事实上，王妃私下里向丈夫承认她爱着别人，同时对那个男人的名字保密，并承诺永远不会不忠——这一表白是小说出版时最令人震惊和最具争议的方面之一。但公爵本人是小说中唯一了解她英雄般决心的人。丈夫死后（因为他不恰当地解读了一系列的表象，错误地认为妻子不忠——在这部小说中误读是致命的），在一次简短的谈话中，王妃向她的爱人承认激情是相互的，但她永远不会嫁给他。她打算，正如她告诉他的那样，按照一种“只存在于我想象中”的义务行事，不与间接和无意中导致她丈夫死亡的男人结婚。在整部小说中，尤其是在结尾部分，王妃被描述为无与伦比、独一无二、与众不同的。小说的最后一句话是：“她的生命如此短暂，留下了独一无二的美德的典范。”

在《克莱芙王妃》中，拉法耶特夫人展示了与众不同和不遵循主流行为模式的代价——在这一点上，这个故事符合我们之前在悲剧和喜剧中看到的范式，但她也展示了法国文化和女性地位的变化如何改变了值得关注并达成非凡进步的标准。对17世纪的女权主义者来说，一个女人决定独立，不再婚，并形成自己的行为理想，这至少和一个男性军事英雄的故事一样有趣。从母亲的教训开始，幸福的婚姻是女人唯一值得追求的目标，王妃以一个截然不同的成就终其一生。 45

第四章

# 天性及其可能性

## “天性”的问题

鉴于17世纪对社会及其规范强烈关注的特点，18世纪反应为部分地反对这种专一的焦点，把讨论转移到天性的问题上，也许并不奇怪。天性与文化的对立（或生理与天性的对立）由来已久，但在18世纪又焕发出新的活力。17世纪的法国思想，尤其是在文学界，对天性并不友善。似乎很显然，这个世界是有缺陷的，宗教和艺术的使命是拨乱反正，或者至少，过滤掉天性引起的错误。因为放任自流——放任脾气，由于脾气是由不平衡的情志决定的——莫里哀笔下的阿尔赛斯特结局悲惨，不容于社会。他的朋友们试图通过教他礼仪来抵消这种倾向。帕斯卡尔以更为严肃的方式告诉我们，人类的本性已经被原罪从根本上改变了，所以我们所说的“天性”只是一种反常的幻觉——在这里帕斯卡尔非常接近托马斯·霍布斯的观点，后者长期居住在巴黎，对“天然状态”没有什么好话。最后，根据“真实性”的

文学理论，法兰西学院和其他人教导说，戏剧家不应该描绘在事物的正常进程中发生的事情，而应该描绘在完美世界会发生的 46
事情。简而言之，任何一个17世纪的作家，如果以积极的方式使用“天性”一词，那就意味着与经验世界相去甚远。作家们常常称赞“天然”的说话方式，需要指出，这种风格只能通过仔细模仿最好的模特来实现。换句话说，天性是最好的人工形式。至于相对现代的观念，即人可以离开城市“走进天性”（dans la nature），这样一个未受破坏的特权空间的感觉，对路易十四的臣民来说，似乎完全是胡说八道。

这种一致蔑视天性的观念在18世纪开始改变。社会仍然处于知识和文学讨论的前沿，但现在天性以一种更为多样、更不可预测的方式成为讨论的一部分。事实上，对于启蒙运动来说，天性——人类的本性和地球上的野性力量——在广义上说，是最重要的问题的核心。天性是美好的，却被社会制度与习惯掩盖和扭曲了吗？或者说，天性对人类并无关照，甚至与人类敌对，人们应该因此停止将天性作为“善”和“权利”概念的源泉？天性是由精神和物质组成的，还是纯粹物质性的，可以通过感觉完全为我们所用？天性似乎不再是无法体验的。更早些时候，蒙田和拉伯雷更乐观的观点现在以一种非常丰富和有更好记录的方式回归了。当蒙田在他了解到的美洲土著人身上发现了很多值得称赞（以及令他震惊）的东西时，探险、商业和殖民主义带来了更多关于欧洲以外生活的信息。并不仅仅是因为巴西或南太平洋岛屿的人民更接近“自然”（从某种意义上说，他们的定居点更小，城市和技术也不那么发达），还因为大量的习俗和基本法律，这些似乎完全不言而喻的东西，被发现在不同的文化中

是如此不同，以至于法国人认为理所当然的“天性”似乎不再安
47 全。探索或重新发现天性和在这种更可靠的知识基础上重建社会，也许是启蒙运动的主要议题。

这些问题的提出并不总是为了挑战传统，因为毕竟许多法国作家主张支持既定秩序。乍一看，皮埃尔·德·马里沃（1688—1763）的戏剧和小说似乎与“天性”没有什么关系。他的风尚喜剧以其高度艺术化的调侃而闻名，他的风格是如此的独特，以至于我们可以用marivaudage（马里沃体）这个词来形容诙谐、生动的对话。然而，当我们考虑到他的戏剧——例如《爱与偶遇的游戏》（1730）——的热情观众，我们可以看到，马里沃和他的同时代人敏锐地意识到，在一个基于我们谓之“阶层”，那时谓之“条件”的社会系统中，天性与文化之间可能存在的分歧。一个年轻的女人想知道她父亲安排她嫁的那个年轻人的真实性格，乔装成自己的女仆。她完全不知道，那个年轻人为了同样的目的和他的仆人交换了身份。两对情侣组合，在这两种情况下都有真实条件都相同的一男一女，但条件并不显而易见——乔装改扮的上流社会角色彼此相爱。



这对于马里沃和他的读者来说是一个令人安心的保守结论，并且传达了一个信息：社会中的等级并不是表面的约定（就像一百年前帕斯卡尔的《思想录》中一些更大胆的段落所暗示的那样），而是有着更深的根源，无论是纯粹的继承还是基于长期的培养。整个剧本的主题都可以通过这个实验来完成的事实——实际上，不只一出戏剧，类似的问题贯穿于马里沃的作品中——意味着，在18世纪上半叶，人们对一个人的天然特征和自身条件之间的不一致的恐惧是相当普遍的。在接下来的几年

里，突出这种可能的社会失调的戏剧持续取得巨大的成功，如博 48
马舍的戏剧《塞维利亚的理发师》（1775）。至少在一定程度上是为了适应这些社会主题的更严肃和不那么保守的发展，法国戏剧在18世纪的进程中创造出新的类型，包括“感伤喜剧”（la comédie larmoyante）和“正剧”（le drame）。

## 启蒙运动与哲学家

当马里沃通过展示社会制度最终是安全的来娱乐观众时，他特别鄙视的一个群体，哲学家，提出了关于出身、等级和文明的“自然”基础的严肃问题。让-雅克·卢梭（1712—1788）发表了他的《论人类不平等的起源和基础》（1755），论证道，在私有财产、法律，以及维护不平等的社会上层建筑建立之前，人类一直快乐地处在自然的原始状态下。德尼·狄德罗（1713—1784）和让·勒朗·达朗贝尔（1717—1783）组织编写了《百科全书》（1751—1752，绝大部分是秘密出版的），他们和其他大约150名作家匿名撰写了书中的词条。哲学家，一个因争吵而分裂的异质群体，在现代意义上，甚至在笛卡尔是一位哲学家这个意义上，都不那么“哲学家”，而更像是公共知识分子，他们致力于破除迷信和无知，提倡用务实或技术官僚的方法解决社会中人类生活的问题。他们的大量工作在于促进人们更深入、更祛魅地理解物质世界，因为它可以通过感官来感知。这个方面可以在狄德罗关于感官感知的《对自然的解释》（1753—1754）中看到，但百科全书的编纂者们也促进了基于自然法则和自由体制的君主立宪制。他们的知识理论是经验主义和理性主义的，因此，他们对上帝的知识明确无误地是哲学，而不是宗教阐释。 49

在哲学家们通过具有娱乐性兼说教性的作品引起广大读者的注意的努力中，最好的例子是伏尔泰的《老实人》，一部于1759年匿名出版的当代哲学著作（哲学故事）。这个讽刺故事的直接目标是戈特弗里德·莱布尼茨的《神义论》（1710），在这部作品中，哲学家论证了上帝创造了所有可能的世界中最好的，即“最优的”世界。在这样一个系统中，没有客观的邪恶。为了描述莱布尼茨的立场，“乐观主义”一词于1737年出现在法语中。伏尔泰的故事的全称是《老实人或乐观主义，译自拉尔夫博士的德语版》。这个著名的故事（1956年伦纳德·伯恩斯坦配乐的歌剧《老实人》的基础）讲述了老实人甘迪德的冒险经历，他是一个来自威斯特伐利亚的德意志人，年轻时接受了潘格罗斯博士（希腊词根暗示他可以说任何事情，可能是在挖苦莱布尼茨的博学多产）的教育，后者传授了一种目的论的乐观主义：一切都是上帝创造出来的最好的，绝无例外。潘格罗斯的断言读者一看就觉得荒谬，但对甘迪德来说却并不荒谬：

> 万物既皆有归宿，此归宿自必为最美满的归宿。岂不见鼻子是长来戴眼镜的吗？所以我们有眼镜。身上安放两条腿是为穿长袜的，所以我们有长袜。

作为一种文学创作，甘迪德是一个非常成功的人物（character），在这个词的两个通用意义上都是：作为一个叙述性的“人”，以及某个被发挥到极致的“性格”（或个性特征）的拥有者。伏尔泰在一开始就这样描述他：“他颇识是非，头脑又简单不过；大概就因为如此，人家才叫他老实人。”因为伏尔泰讽刺了莱布尼茨式的乐观主义和所有为了避免面对不愉快的现实而坚持意识形态的人，所以我们跟随着满世界跑的人物是敏锐洞察力和非凡毅力与潘格罗斯教授的僵化教义的混合体，这一点就非常重要。伏尔泰因此得以继续积累自然灾 50
难的例子（1755年的里斯本地震），罗马天主教伪善和不容异己（葡萄牙神父为防止未来的地震而烧死三个人的火刑，大检察官的性事，巴拉圭的耶稣会王国），欧洲王国和帝国的嗜血残暴，苏里南对非洲奴隶的残害，以及各种贪赃枉法和腐败的例子，与此同时，甘迪德仅仅是在非常缓慢地放弃他那令人安心的潘格罗斯式的确信：一切都是最好的安排。尽管如此，当看到那个因为试图逃跑而被砍断一条腿以示惩罚，又被磨糖机切断一只手的奴隶时，甘迪德惊呼："哦，潘格罗斯！……你不知道这种可憎的事。就这样吧，我不得不放弃你那种乐观主义。"当被问及什么是"乐观主义"时，甘迪德回答说："这是一种在你受苦时声称一切都好的狂热。"如果莱布尼茨是伏尔泰唯一的攻击目标，如果他没有将他的英雄与恐怖的"路演"完美匹配，以制造如此滑稽的不和谐，甘迪德就不会在大众的想象中幸存下来。但是伏尔泰在这里所做的，提供了一个哲学家的缩影，他们将理性与根深蒂固的文化习惯对立起来，反对那些既扼杀判断能力、清晰感知世界的责任，又扼杀自然移情的所有制度。



## 社会表面与内在本质之间的紧张关系

皮埃尔·肖代洛·德·拉克洛的书信体小说《危险的关系》（1782）是18世纪最持久的文学成就之一，一炮打响且具

有持续广泛的吸引力（至少被改编成四部电影）。书信体形式的特点之一使得探明某条信息或某个意图变得尤为困难，因为
51 没有整体叙事的声音。这本书以不同方式被视为反贵族（这是拉克洛的许多同时代人对这本书的看法）、女权主义、反女权主义、道德主义和不道德的。作为一部主要按时间顺序排列的书信集，这部作品最初似乎提供了中立的观点，但是两位高度自觉的主导人物，瓦尔蒙子爵和梅尔特伊侯爵夫人写的信（他们不仅在书信的数量上占主导地位，尽管瓦尔蒙的信件数量多出两倍，而且在对其他写信者的巧妙操纵方面也占主导地位），基本上承担了在传统的单一叙述者的小说中叙述者的功能。他们不仅讲述发生了什么，还分析动机并预测结果。因此，我们可以认为这部小说有两个非全知的叙述者，他们互相竞争，不仅要呈现对所发生的事情的某种看法，而且要使事情发生。两人都是愤世嫉俗的理性主义者，对人性（即行为模式）有着敏锐的理解，但是理解的盲点导致了他们的毁灭。我们可以在这种心理学中看到拉罗什富科的回响；梅尔特伊明确表示，她通过阅读“最严厉的道德家”的作品来了解生活，而拉罗什富科尤其郑重地指出，人们对自己的敏感性和动机视而不见。尽管瓦尔蒙和梅尔特伊认为自己完全摆脱了宗教和道德的束缚，但他们需要修正外在表现以按照他们阶层的道德标准行事，而这套道德标准对男人和女人是不同的。对瓦尔蒙来说，作为一个风流的男性，一个成功的女性捕手的公众声誉是自豪的源泉，对他几乎没有负面影响。但对梅尔特伊而言，情况大不相同。她需要不动声色地引诱，并且总是处在这样的境遇中：需要保持其作为一个虔诚的年轻寡妇的公众声誉。即使是她勾引的

男人也必须不能让后者明白是她勾引了他们，而是必须相信是他们引诱了她。因此，社会赋予男女的不平等地位是一个重要的主题，与对腐败和游手好闲的贵族的描绘一起，代表了那个时代对社会习俗和教育的质疑。 52

在小说的结尾，瓦尔蒙和梅尔特伊的竞争（他们之间早期恋情的余烬）导致他们互相报复。梅尔特伊的报复方式更为微妙，她利用了瓦尔蒙作为公认的成功的风流诱惑者的性别自我认知，以及他对德·图尔薇夫人的真实而热情的爱之间的隔阂，后者是他迄今为止最难征服的对象。正如梅尔特伊所见，瓦尔蒙对自己的本性视而不见。他对自己的理性主义立场充满信心，认为肉体的愉悦和娴熟的诱惑是他唯一的动机。通过利用与这种男性自我形象不可分割的虚荣心，梅尔特伊激怒了瓦尔蒙，使他失去了唯一一次情感满足的机会。瓦尔蒙随后对梅尔特伊的报复更为粗鲁和容易，而且也是基于社会人为造成的性别不平衡。他干脆让那包信被发表，使她成了一个贱民。瓦尔蒙内心深处的情感和他被社会决定的虚荣心之间的差异，使**危险的关系**成为超越社会规范的价值属性，离间了人们及其更深层的、隐藏的自我。

## 动植物和“自然”

拉克洛的小说以我们或可称为心理学的形式关注人性。重要的是社交世界，而从巴黎到乡村庄园的场所变迁，只不过是在影响人群之间的互动时才被描述出来——在这方面，拉克洛的作品更接近17世纪的小说。但18世纪的许多作家表现出对非城市空间的爆炸式增长的兴趣，并将人类的行为和感知融入城市与乡村的分水岭中。到了18世纪中叶，瑞典植物学家卡尔·林奈的作品传到了法国，寻找植物标本变得越来越时髦。布封（乔治-路易·勒克莱尔，布封伯爵）于1749年出版了他的
53《自然史》的第一卷。各种不同气候下生长的动植物引起了公众的兴趣，除了重新重视植物和动物之外，与之共同生活的人也受到了关注。乡村居民不再仅仅被视为享受不到城市优势的人，因为现在田野和森林的生活似乎提供了免受城市的人为且腐败影响的保护。这是让·德·拉布吕耶尔在《品性论》（1688）中描绘的矫揉造作的巴黎和宫廷生活的无情、无灵魂的形象的一个重要延伸。拉布吕耶尔将其时代的文化描绘为矫揉造作的上层阶级的腐败和被创造出来的刻薄的形象，但并没有走那么远，直至提出在宫廷和城市之外，事物的确更加美好的地步。卢梭在《致达朗贝尔的信》（《论戏剧·致达朗贝尔的信》，1758）中，扩展了在《论人类不平等的起源和基础》中阐述过的对城市文明的批评，在这篇文章中，他谴责了腐败的巴黎剧院，支持外省小城市里“快乐的农夫”的真诚的庆典。卢梭赋予童年以新的重要性——从夏多布里昂开始，对浪漫主义者而言，童年一直是意义非凡的关注点。在自传体的《忏悔录》（1769年完成，1782年出版）中，卢梭对自己的童年给予了极大的关注。《爱弥尔》（1762）是对一种全新的教养方式的典型叙述，在其中，卢梭作为家庭教师的角色，只允许年轻的学生读一本书，即笛福的《鲁滨逊漂流记》，希望爱弥尔以自立的鲁滨逊为榜样，生活在“自然”的状态中。



1788年，也就是在凡尔赛宫召开通常被视为法国大革命开端的三级会议的前一年，卢梭的年轻朋友、工程师贝尔纳

贝尔纳丹·德·圣皮埃尔《保罗和薇吉妮》(1787)中的一幕，弗朗索瓦·热拉尔于1805年所绘的一幅版画



丹·德·圣皮埃尔（1737—1814）出版了18世纪最畅销的小说之一——《保罗和薇吉妮》。这是当时自然对抗文化的主题的 54
典范，并且创造了薇吉妮这样的女主人公，她抛弃了童年在荒野

中的简单教养方式，这直接导致了她的死亡。小说的情节发生在毛里求斯，当时是法国的一个附属岛，在那里，还是孩子的保
55 罗和薇吉妮像最好的朋友一样长大，情同兄妹。在青春期，他们的感情转变为浪漫的爱情，但薇吉妮被送到法国，与富有的姑妈一起生活。当姑妈试图强迫薇吉妮嫁人时，她拒绝了，并被送回岛上。当船接近陆地时，遇上飓风搁浅了。船上最后一个水手试图说服女主人公脱下累赘的衣服游到岸上，但她拒绝脱衣服并接受了自己的命运。作者强调了着装的问题，以及薇吉妮从她所受的欧洲教育中带来的相当不正常的谦逊。对她尸体的令人怜惜的描述，可能会让现代读者感到好笑："她闭上了眼睛；但她脸颊上死者的苍白紫色混合着谦逊的粉色。她的一只手放在衣服上，另一只手紧紧地攥在胸口……"当然，她抓着保罗的画像。

圣皮埃尔和卢梭一样，把人性和动植物意义上的天性概念结合在一起，建立了一个浪漫主义的观点，即自然以一种特殊的方式存在于某些地方，离开城市，人们就更接近"自然"，彻底离开欧洲，人们可能会发现未受破坏的自然——或者至少有可能从不同的、更佳的角度对自身和社会有一个新的理解。保罗和薇吉妮成长为正直、慷慨、直率、有点拘谨的年轻人，不仅仅是因为他们没有像同时代的欧洲人一样受到腐朽社会的影响，而且更神秘地，是因为他们与他们的热带岛屿的土地很亲近。作为一种体裁的小说的基本比喻是转喻而不是隐喻（也就是说，它通过将事物与空间的接近性而不是相似性联系起来以传达意义）的观点，有助于理解《保罗和薇吉妮》中描写手法的使用（正如后来在乔治·桑、福楼拜和巴尔扎克的小说中一样）。不仅植物

和风景的描写让人了解男女主人公的性情，而且与这些地方的
互动也塑造了这些性情。凭借卢梭的《爱弥尔》的精神，保罗可 56
以不用斧头就砍倒树，不用燧石就生着火，用棕榈芽做一顿温暖
的饭。简而言之，保罗似乎是鲁滨逊·克鲁索的化身。他的伟
大取决于他能做什么，而不是他的出身。 57

第五章

# 围绕大革命

> 因为您是位贵族，所以就认为自己是个天才？权贵、财富、阶级、影响力，这种种使一个人引以为傲！这么多的好处，您到底是怎么挣来的呢？您除了在出娘胎时使了点力气之外，其他的什么也没做。撇开这点，您不过是个平庸之人！

在皮埃尔·加隆·博马舍的杰作《疯狂一日，或费加罗的婚礼》中，费加罗，阿尔马维瓦伯爵的侍从，用这番独白形容他的主人。在经过六年的审查和曲折后，《费加罗的婚礼》最终于1784年4月27日在法兰西喜剧院上演。其后不到五年，即1789年1月，三级会议自1614年以来首次召开，我们将之视为法国大革命的导火索。

博马舍的喜剧已成为导致大革命的文化因素的象征，然而，与所有历史事件一样，选择单一的时刻作为“导火索”具有
58 一定的随意性。整个18世纪充满了对君主专制制度日益不满

的信号，越来越多的人坚信社会制度是建立在一个隐性的契约之上的，而不是基于神授君权或事物不可置疑的性质。在多才多艺的费加罗身上，博马舍创造了一位国际公认的人物，他拥有智慧、才华，并且代表了那些没有贵族头衔，但锐意进取且获得成功的tiers état（不同于贵族和教会的“第三等级”）的愤懑。费加罗曾经大胆地称自己为绅士，并解释说“如果老天乐意，我会是公侯的儿子”——他在剧中其他地方提到的偶然性清楚地表明，他和他的伯爵主人所处的实际地位，正是纯粹的偶然。

费加罗还是《塞维利亚的理发师》（1775）中风趣的理发师，在这部作品中，他是中心人物还是配角是有争议的，他是剧作的同名人物，却在为他人的利益服务，这一事实表明了文学上和更广阔的社会背景中的紧张关系。在这部早先的剧里，他帮助伯爵战胜了年迈的巴尔托洛医生的阴谋，迎娶了巴尔托洛美丽而富有的年轻的被监护人。这两部喜剧错综复杂且极其有趣的情节，以及主人公的足智多谋，至少在一定程度上使得许多作品以它们为基础，从喜剧上演两年后即推出的莫扎特的《费加罗的婚礼》，到乔治·梅里埃的早期法国电影之一《塞维利亚的理发师》（1904）。值得注意的是，这两部喜剧的题目指的都是费加罗。



费加罗是谁？《费加罗的婚礼》的结构让这个问题有点出人意料地出现在戏剧的中部，即五幕剧的第三幕，这一幕讲的是有关履行契约的一次审判。费加罗从一位年长很多的女人那里借了一大笔钱，并承诺如果他还不起钱就娶她。在将戏剧性浓缩于这一刻的时候，博马舍强调了金融、契约、法律、出身和阶级权力——所有这些都是大革命的核心主题。费加罗的雇主，伯爵，也试图引诱费加罗的未婚妻，他同时主持审判，这种安排质疑了所有公正法律的基础。费加罗能够避免这场婚姻的唯一原因就是他偶然发现自己是那个借他钱的女人失散已久的儿子。结果，费加罗的出身比他看上去的要“高”，但在等级和天赋之间仍然存在差距。费加罗的问题“这么多的好处，您到底是怎么挣来的呢”仍然成立，因为很明显，有权有势的伯爵既不比他的仆人聪明，也不比他的仆人更有活力，而且道德水准也低得多。马里沃认为一个人的智力、敏感度和天赋可能与他或她的阶级（出身）不符，但在他的戏剧中，每一种情况得出的结论都是，当一个人的真实身份确立后，他继承的特权就是正当的，对博马舍而言，情况已不再如此。



当费加罗在《费加罗的婚礼》中重新找回自己的出生身份时，博马舍不仅限于反映当时政治和社会的矛盾。他还指出文学本身也存在类似的骚动。正如几十年后维克多·雨果在《克伦威尔》的序言中指出的那样，将戏剧类型分为喜剧和悲剧似乎不再与人类社会认知的步调一致了。18世纪打破了这种继承自17世纪新亚里士多德主义的二元结构，并产生了许多被称为drames的戏剧。博马舍自己也写了一出drame，《欧仁妮》，并于1767年在法兰西喜剧院上演，与此同时他还发表了《论严肃戏剧》。他在《塞维利亚的理发师》印刷版的序言，一封“温和的信”中再次提出了这个问题。在这封通篇带有讽刺意味的信中，他指出了喜剧和悲剧之间的经典区别，以及两者之间拒斥一切
60 的传统。亚里士多德将喜剧定义为描述低于我们自身的人，而悲剧则被定义为描述高于我们自身的人。博马舍疾呼：

> 呈现不堪重负、处境悲惨的中等阶层，我呸！只应以讥笑的方式展示他们。可笑的公民和不幸的国王——这就是戏剧存在和可能的全部。

戏剧体裁的转变，随后引发可以成为中心角色，即主人公的人物类型的相应变化，例如费加罗。

## “天性”之争的一个极端

长达一个世纪的对社会秩序基础的质疑，以及对社会秩序是建立在天性（其本身是基于神圣天意）基础上之主张的日益增长的怀疑，导致了更为激进的表达。大革命的第二年，从长期监禁中被释放的萨德侯爵（1740—1814）匿名出版了《于斯丁娜，或美德遭难》（1791）。《于斯丁娜》一举成名。尽管这部小说，就像他大量作品中的绝大多数一样，因其对性行为的描写而闻名，他的性描写为我们造了一个形容词：“虐待狂的”，但萨德的作品所关注的远不止“非自然的”性行为。任何主要是为了消遣而阅读萨德的人都很可能会失望：大多数叙述都被有关永恒的邪恶以及它给作恶者带来的快感的哲学反思所打断。虽然萨德支持大革命，且尽管出身贵族却还是在1790年入选法国议会，但是，他不同于启蒙思想家，因为他不相信社会能够改善人 61
类的命运。

从启示宗教中的解放，使大革命得以建立一个基于人类理性的国家，这种解放被萨德当成在一个强者利用和摧毁弱者的世界中为快感服务的完全自由的机会。女主人公的一个迫害者冷静地解释了原始人发明超然存在来解释让他们害怕的自然现 62

拿破仑·波拿巴将萨德侯爵的一本书投入火中，这幅画被认为是P. 古斯杜里耶的作品

象的过程。在结构上，《于斯丁娜》将松散的、开放式的流浪汉情节与哥特式小说的氛围相结合。于斯丁娜是女性版的老实人，但老实人代表常识终于摆脱荒诞不经的教条，在《于斯丁娜》

中，则更大胆，宗教和传统的国家的核心原则被表现为荒谬的，而于斯丁娜徒劳地试图抗拒，她的行事代表了宗教和美德。在一封献词中，萨德将邪恶的胜利作为一种文学创新，说小说几乎总是表现出善有善报，恶有恶报，但是：

> 展示从一个灾难流落到另一个的不幸女人，一个邪恶的玩物，一切堕落的猎物，揭露了最野蛮、最饕餮的欲望[……]目标是从人类所接受的最崇高的道德教训中汲取教训——这是[……]通过一条迄今鲜有人走过的道路所达到的目标。

萨德无神论的自由主义整体上与大革命格格不入，后者强调公民的美德和平等（在萨德的小说中两者都欠缺），并且随着时间的推移越发如此。萨德在领事馆被拿破仑下令逮捕，并于波旁王朝复辟前夕在查伦顿精神病院去世。



## 从“英雄”到伟大的男人（和女人）

《人权与公民权利宣言》的第一条宣布：“在权利方面，人生来而且始终是自由平等的。社会差别只能基于公共利益。”这个被法国制宪会议采纳的简短且雄辩的官方文件显示，从1789年 63
持续到1814年的波旁王朝复辟斗争的核心问题是每个个体的人的地位（两年后，奥兰普·德古热[①]在她的《女权与女性公民权宣言》中指出妇女权利的缺失——她的文本被抵制，其本人在

① 奥兰普·德古热（1748—1793），法国女权主义者、剧作家、政治活动家，倡导女权主义和废奴主义。——译注

1793年被送上断头台）。

费加罗已经预见到了这种平等的要求，于斯丁娜作为贵族的自由主义的永久牺牲品而受难。从这些具有代表性的文学人物身上，我们前前后后可以（在博马舍的“温和的信”的帮助下）看到，所有的作品都通常是含蓄地，理所当然地，揭示了关于哪些人值得写，哪些人的故事很重要的思想。中心人物的选择可以落在一个英雄身上，比如罗兰的例子，他代表了作者所感知到的社会的最高抱负；也可以落在一个怪人身上，比如莫里哀的厌世的阿尔赛斯特；或者是一个恶棍或反英雄，某种深重罪恶的完美例子，比如在莫里哀的另一部喜剧《伪君子》中的伪君子答尔丢夫。大革命扩大了那些其故事被认为值得关注的人的范围——遵循了博马舍倡导的，但对德古热来说还不够宽广的界限——并且在接下来的几个世纪里，还将继续扩大。尽管如此，如果说法语文学只是变得更加“平均主义”，从罗兰转向费加罗，从庞大固埃转向老实人，这就过于简单化了。一直以来，代表平民的中心人物都是存在的，从精于世故、自学成才的律师皮埃尔·帕特林（《帕特林律师的玩笑》，约1464）到弗朗索瓦·德·罗塞的《我们时代的悲剧故事》（1614）中的里昂警察。然而，在一个文学反映人们终身不变的阶级（或“条件”）分配的社会中，这些人通常被描述成滑稽或令人震惊的。虽然他们可能是主角，但如果我们用“英雄”这个词来形容那些最受尊敬
64 的人，那他们就不是“英雄”。



随着启蒙运动的发展，大革命改变了这一点。1791年4月4日议会下令将刚刚建成的圣热内维耶瓦修道院教堂改造成“先贤祠”。这是一个决定性的转变，从“英雄”的旧概念转变为

1791年,在拉格莱尼之后,伏尔泰的遗骨被移入先贤祠并刻上姓名

"伟人"的新思想。此后,不仅仅是卓著的军功,非军事服务的卓越功绩也同样被承认,在社会顶端赢得一席之地。在这之前,君主出身的最高贵族,基本上是军事阶层(佩剑贵族,noblesse d'épée),诗人的最高职能之一就是歌颂军事英雄的荣耀。被称为先贤祠的实体纪念堂(今天卢梭、伏尔泰、雨果、左拉和安德烈·马尔罗都葬在那里)标志着伟大这一观念的转变的高潮,它业已表明,联系"伟人"和一个国家的先贤祠的启蒙思想先于我们今天看到后者的名字所联想到的建筑景点。 65

## 文学及其时代

波旁王朝复辟后很长一段时间里,有关大革命的文学作品仍旧继续被创作出来。在这一点上,应该观察到两个方面,一个明显,另一个不那么明显。明显的是,从1789年的三级会议到1814年路易十八登基之间的四分之一世纪里,对这些年发生的事件的描述要少于随后的几个世纪。因此，法国从接下来的时期开始有许多关于大革命的小说、戏剧和诗歌。另一个不那么明显的方面是，当我们在某个历史框架内书写无论何时的文学作品时，都很难抵制以下（错误的）观念，即过去的法国人民，他们可以得到与我们同样范围的文本。当然，在大多数情况下，他们有更多的书；他们有许多一经印刷，从未再版的书，或是当时畅销，随后便消失在法国国家图书馆深处的书。据说大革命时期有一千多出戏剧被创作出来，但是（正如维庸可能会问的那样）：昨天的戏剧在哪里？

另一方面，在某些情况下，我们拥有一些与其同时代的人看不到的作品。德古热的《女权与女性公民权宣言》于1791年出版，但当时有多少人真正看到过这个现在出现在很多高校的法国大革命课程中的提议？以萨德为例，他在巴士底狱写下的手稿《索多玛的一百二十天》在获释后丢失了，直到20世纪30年代才被广泛印刷。萨德的这部作品是应该被视为18世纪文学史的一部分，还是20世纪文学史的一部分？当然，这样的问题不仅限于这个特定时期，甚至也不限于未出版或很少流传的作品。蒙田的《随笔集》（1580年第一版，1588年和1595年修订版）通常被视为16世纪文学文化的一部分。然而，包含一些最重要章
66 节的《随笔集》的第三部，只能在16世纪的最后11年里被读到，尽管蒙田在他死后的一个世纪里成为非常重要的作家。还有伊莲娜·内米洛夫斯基的中篇小说，在奥斯维辛遇害前写成，于六十多年后才以《法兰西组曲》（2004）为名出版。它们在某种意义上属于第二次世界大战和大屠杀文化，在另一种意义上属于21世纪初的文学文化。

## 回顾大革命

因此，这场大革命继续以多种多样，有时是矛盾的方式激发文学作品的灵感，并继续将重点放在人物身上，在这场大动荡之前这些人物是无法想象出来的。杜拉斯公爵夫人的短篇小说《欧丽卡》（1823）在很多方面都表现为一部非常现代的作品，它既与奥兰普·德古热的反奴隶制及支持女性的作品有关，也与当今的女权主义和对非欧洲文化的兴趣有关。另一方面，《欧丽卡》是从一种高度保守的观点中产生的，它以谴责启蒙运动中的进步贵族和革命给解放带来了过度的希望而告终。用她自己的话来说，故事的中心人物，欧丽卡，是启蒙运动和一场不完全的大革命创造出来的怪物。她的第一人称叙事（由一位主治医生以书面形式呈现）讲述了她作为一名塞内加尔孤儿来到法国的故事，她两岁时被一位善良的殖民地总督收买为奴隶，并交给了他的姑妈，后者把她当成心爱的孩子抚养成人。欧丽卡过着幸福的生活，并接受了“完美的教育”，学习英语、意大利语、绘画，阅读最优秀的作家的作品。她知道自己是个“黑鬼”，但一点儿也不认为这是个缺点。每个人都觉得她迷人、优雅、美丽。她是一位出色的舞者。简而言之，对欧丽卡而言一切都很美好，直到有一天，她无意中听到她慷慨的赞助人和一位朋友的对话：“为了让她开心，我愿意做任何事，但当我想到她的处境时，我觉得毫无希望。可怜的欧丽卡！我看她是孤独的，终生孤独！” 67

从那时起，欧丽卡意识到她的种族使她无法在一个只有婚姻才能赋予地位、尊严和体面关系的社会里结婚。用故事中一个人物的话说，欧丽卡的成长过程“违反了自然秩序”。她只能 68

嫁给一个“为了钱也许会同意生黑人孩子”的劣等的、贪财的男人。欧丽卡最后来到了一座修道院，既为在海地起义的非洲奴隶，也为在法国大革命中被处决和上法庭的非洲奴隶而感到羞耻。除了修道院，她在任何地方都格格不入，既不适于旧法国

让-巴蒂斯特·卡珀克斯制作的胸像，题为“为什么生而为奴？”(1868)

的、她在其中被抚养成人的白人贵族秩序，也不适于她的祖国塞内加尔，也不适于被认为是平等的民主社会。杜拉斯公爵夫人在复辟时期主持了一个非常有影响力的巴黎沙龙，她在《欧丽卡》里展示了法国浪漫主义保守或反动的一面。这个简短的故事融合了卢梭和圣皮埃尔关于社会的有害影响和自然秩序的一些观点——欧丽卡就像一个塞内加尔的维吉尼亚人，在被运到欧洲时迷失了方向。但杜拉斯公爵夫人的“自然秩序”的观点是反革命的，属于结束流亡归国的复辟贵族的世界。

这些流亡贵族中的许多人都怀着对旧秩序的坚定的怀旧之情来写作，他们的背景往往可以追溯到遥远的过去，或者继续18世纪对异域风情的探索，但带有反启蒙的、基督教的色彩，就像非常有影响力的《基督教真谛》（1802）一书的作者，弗朗索瓦·勒内·德·夏多布里昂呈现出的那样。他的中篇小说《勒内》最初作为这部较长作品的一部分出版，在《勒内》中，他描绘了一个陷入困境的主人公勒内，一个孤独、痛苦、以自我为中心的贵族，他被对妹妹的乱伦之爱所困扰（这里再一次坚持违反自然秩序的悲剧后果），妹妹在北美印第安人中找到了真相。勒内前往路易斯安那州可能是受到安托万·弗朗索瓦·普雷沃斯特早先创作的极受欢迎的《曼侬·莱斯戈》（1731）的影响，在这部作品中，妓女曼侬——后来很多“悲剧女性”的原型——和她的情人在法国殖民地寻求平静的生活，但曼侬在荒凉的荒野中死于暴晒和疲惫。夏多布里昂在某种程度上是卢梭的自相矛盾 69
的追随者，他把新世界作为批判现代人类的有利条件：异化、自大、缺乏屈从于传统的谦卑。在夏多布里昂看来，“现代”和进步的概念，其含义与大革命之前大相径庭。启蒙运动在很大程度上接受了从17世纪起对古典主义的推崇，这种推崇远高于古典主义产生于其间的中世纪。夏多布里昂接受了进步的观点，但将其归因于基督教，因此将重点从古代转向基督教统治的世纪。他与重要的理论家、批评家，《论文学与社会建制的关系》（1800）的作者斯塔尔夫人（除此以外她还有其他许多作品）进行了一场公开的争论。在争论中，他强烈反对任何不以基督教为基础的现代性的积极概念。在19世纪，他对中世纪古典世界观的颠覆拥趸甚众。

大革命引起的政治与文化分歧的另一边是司汤达（玛里-亨利·贝尔的笔名，1783—1842），他曾在拿破仑的军队服役，他在于连·索雷尔，《红与黑》（1830）的主人公身上创造了反勒内的类型。于连是一个雄心勃勃的年轻人，出身非常低微，受拿破仑的鼓舞，却生活在波旁王朝的压迫之下。青少年时期，他最喜欢的书是卢梭的《忏悔录》和《圣赫勒拿岛回忆录》，后者是拿破仑在滑铁卢战败后，作为阶下囚的最后几年的谈话录。司汤达被认为是“现实主义”小说的先驱，他既创造了一个令人着迷的复杂角色，又唤起了大革命后直到七月革命的长期的社会紧张和动荡（如同司汤达1830年的小说）。尽管于连的两个主要特征是虚伪和野心，但他周围的女人和男人都爱他，在他向上流社
70 会升迁的过程中帮助他，随后便是他的惊人罪行和死刑。他的英雄抱负——无论他采取何种反英雄的手段来实现它们——与他周围社会的庸俗、自命不凡和贪婪之间的对比，是之后不久在阿尔弗雷德·德·维尼的戏剧《查铁敦》（1835）和随后几十年
71 的许多作品中发现的英雄浪漫主义概念的典范。

第六章

# 驼背人、家庭主妇和漫步者

正如司汤达的小说所显示的那样，19世纪早期的法国在政治和文化上是分裂的，一方面是与传统机制（如罗马天主教会、君主制、市郊和乡村）重新连接的愿望，传统机制让人觉得每个人在社会秩序中都有一个相对固定的位置，另一方面是对人类潜能、自由和普遍权利理想的渴望。这种二分法具体的表现形式通常为巴黎与外省（法国的其他任何地方；重要的是，在法语中，这是一个单数名词的表达，既指地点，也指条件）之间的对立。

## 怀旧与历史

法国大革命的余震与反革命的反应一直持续到19世纪末——德雷福斯事件和左拉1898年振聋发聩的社论《我控诉！》揭露了法国贵族特权的持续存在，但另一场革命，工业革命，起到了影响法国社会以及对时间、地点、人际关系和人类创造的观念的作用。对古代制度和基督教文化遗产的迷恋，以夏

72 多布里昂为例，成为一种趋势，并通过如儒勒·米什莱的历史学家、如圣伯夫的文学史学家、如维奥莱·勒·杜克这样的建筑师等人的作品而具有更大的历史分量。杜克（以现在人们通常认为的比历史上准确的方式更具幻想性的方式）负责重建巴黎圣母院大教堂、圣米歇尔山和卡尔卡松城堡。继夏多布里昂和斯塔尔夫人的作品之后，维克多·雨果在其戏剧《克伦威尔》（1827）的序言中有力地提出了一个有关社会和审美进步的理论，它以人类社会三个时代的概念——原始、古代或古典、现代——为历史框架，这与文学类型的发展顺序相对应：抒情诗、史诗和戏剧。

对雨果而言，"现代"阶段相当宽泛，因为他将其等同于基督教在欧洲的统治地位。戏剧诞生于基督教对人类说下面这番话的那一天：



> "你是双重的，你由两个造物组成，一个易腐，另一个不朽；一个是肉体，另一个虚无缥缈；一个被欲望、需求和激情束缚，另一个在热情和遐想的翅膀上诞生；一个总是俯向地球，它的母亲，另一个总是跃向天堂，它的家园。"这就是戏剧诞生的日子。

从这种双重性概念出发，雨果坚持所有现代艺术的混合特征，即既应描绘卑劣的，也应描绘崇高的；既应描绘琐碎的，也要描绘重要的。雨果拒斥17世纪和18世纪的戏剧，他［如同司汤达在《拉辛与莎士比亚》（1823—1824）中指出的一样］认为英国剧作家优于法国悲剧作家，因为莎士比亚除了崇高，还包含

卢克–奥利维耶·默尔森版画（1881），灵感来自维克多·雨果的小说《巴黎圣母院》（1831） 74

了忧郁、粗俗和怪诞。雨果指责法兰西学院及其新亚里士多德诗学扼杀了科内尔的创造力，他尤其称赞《熙德》的作者是“一个完全现代的天才，受中世纪和西班牙的激发，却不得不自欺欺
73 人，投身于古典”。

## 怪诞英雄

怪诞与中世纪之间的联系出现在雨果的《巴黎圣母院》（1831，早于修复这座摇摇欲坠的历史建筑十四年，修复部分是由于雨果作品的影响）里——这部小说更广为人知的英语名是《圣母院的驼背人》。尽管雨果并不赞同英文书名，因为对他而言，大教堂本身才是中心角色，但小说中15世纪晚期的敲钟人卡西莫多集畸形的躯体和慷慨的精神于一体，提供了一个双重性的典范，作者是如此珍之重之。驼背人第一次出现在小说中，是节日狂欢的人群决定根据最丑的鬼脸选出自己的“傻瓜教皇”。参赛者依次把脸伸进教堂墙壁上的一扇破圆窗户里——这样，实际上，鬼脸和石头结合起来，暗示了哥特式的怪人或石像。最后，一个众人皆赞的脑袋出现了。它是完美的：“这时惊讶和赞叹达到了顶点，原来那副怪样正是他的本来面目啊。或者可以说，他的全身都是一副怪样。”[①]这就是卡西莫多，他在转喻和隐喻层面都与大教堂本身联系在一起：他经常出现在教堂里，同时与这座建筑的哥特式美学相似。



但这种怪诞的双重性最著名的戏剧范例是阿尔弗雷德·德·缪塞的戏剧《洛伦佐传》，在雨果为《克伦威尔》作序

① 译文摘自《巴黎圣母院》，陈敬容译，人民文学出版社，2019年5月。——译注

七年后出版。《克伦威尔》和《洛伦佐传》在其作者的有生之年都没有上演过，按照当时的审查标准，两者都过于具有煽动性，而且以其出版形式，都被认为是不可能上演的——缪塞的戏剧似乎需要六十到一百名演员和群众演员。缪塞的《洛伦佐传》部分参考其情人乔治·桑（阿芒丁娜·奥洛尔·吕西·杜班，杜德旺男爵夫人）的文本，一出名为《1537年密约》的历史剧。缪 75
塞的作品聚焦于主人公的道德特点，一开始无论是对观众，还是对剧中几乎所有同时代的人而言，都似乎是完全邪恶的。洛伦佐完全沉浸在酒精和性的快感中，为他的主人和表兄佛罗伦萨公爵亚历山大充当皮条客，为了后者，他迅速而熟练地通过威胁、许诺和金钱获得城中妇女的性服务。他是个胆小鬼，从不佩剑，当有人向洛伦佐发起决斗时，他吓晕了，连公爵也称其为“软蛋”。随着剧情的展开，洛朗札齐奥（佛罗伦萨人给他的蔑称）被视为恶霸、间谍、马屁精和懦夫，似乎值得所有人的鄙视。但接着，洛朗札齐奥的角色看上去被故意设置成以杀死亚历山大为目标——这样一来，洛伦佐只不过是一个非常成功的演员，隐藏了统一而高尚的自我。然而，洛朗札齐奥让缪塞着迷的是某些更阴暗的东西：洛伦佐，原本纯洁、好学、理想主义的古罗马学者，以杀死塔克文的卢修斯·尤尼乌斯·布鲁图斯为榜样，他不仅仅是假装恶毒，毋宁说是真的成了洛朗札齐奥。

雨果的双面人的概念，既可怕又崇高，在缪塞的主人公身上得到了实现，后者确实沉迷于粗野放荡的生活，同时仍然渴望一种政治与人格都纯洁的英雄姿态。我们被引导去假设，在第一幕中看到的洛朗札齐奥不仅仅是一个假象，而是他自身欲望的真实表达：

> 对于行家来说，还有什么比幼儿的放荡更令人好奇的
> 呢？在一个十五岁的孩子身上看到未来的荡妇；在友情建
> 76 议的幌子下，慈父般地研究，播种，渗透恶行神秘的脉络。

洛朗札齐奥在佛罗伦萨的家庭中传播腐败，他自己也在堕落，变得如此愤世嫉俗，或者说如此现实，以至于在人性方面，他的将杀死亚历山大的孤胆密谋坚持到底的意图，与佛罗伦萨某些家庭群体的反暴政没有任何关联。在表现佛罗伦萨人——毫无疑问，通过他们，也表现了他19世纪的同代时人——的性格时，缪塞指出那些表面上“高贵”并迅速捍卫自己荣誉的人是无能的。洛朗札齐奥，表面上卑鄙，却设法杀死了亚历山大公爵，虽然这确实改变不了什么。在这出戏的结尾，与开始时一样，佛罗伦萨人抱怨、密谋，生活照旧继续。



## 外省生活

英勇奋斗是徒劳的，资产阶级粗俗的、享乐主义的、保守的常识总是会战胜那些在生活之外寻求更多东西的人，这种恼怒的感觉常常体现在快速变化、时尚的巴黎与乏味的、乡村的、无趣的外省生活的对比中。巴尔扎克写下体量惊人的小说集，在其创作过程中，他决定称之为人间喜剧，小说集分为多个系列和子系列，反映了巴黎—外省的区别的重要性，例如“外省生活场景”、“巴黎生活场景”和“乡村生活场景”。然而，与外省生活的牢笼进行抗争的最伟大的英雄是爱玛·包法利，她是福楼拜的小说《包法利夫人》里的主人公。

1856年，当这部作品第一次以连载的形式出现在《巴黎评

论》上时，它有一个非常重要的原标题，《包法利夫人，外省风俗》。爱玛，一个比她周围的任何人都聪明的女人，尽管她只受过修道院的教育，对她而言，最强大的魔法存在于以下句子中，“巴黎就这样做！”[①]这几个字足以把她推进第二个情人的怀抱。 77
对她来说，巴黎是她的终极梦想之地，尽管没有理想的角色或人物形象，这个地方不够宽敞。福楼拜的小说充满了对推动行动的表现与因素的效果的表现。爱玛喜欢那些从修女、小说、杂志，甚至餐盘所讲述的故事里走向她的女主人公！作为修道院里的孩子，他们“用彩绘的盘子吃晚饭，盘子上画着德·拉瓦利埃尔小姐（路易十四的年轻情妇，曾经从宫廷流落到修道院）的故事”。在偏远的诺曼村庄，爱玛收取从巴黎寄来的杂志，还阅读乔治·桑和巴尔扎克的小说。她的婆婆一度试图阻止她阅读小说——暗示爱玛是她那个时代的堂吉诃德，因为阅读而发疯。她的生活在能量强烈的情感冲动和挣扎着实现自我之间循环往复，随之而来的是周期性的昏睡和生病。这种交替变化，在季节周期上如此规律，似乎古来有之，从未改变过，它与外省的乏味生活形成了鲜明对比。尽管爱玛在她的阶层中——福楼拜由此以狄更斯式的敏锐塑造出众多栩栩如生的人物——鹤立鸡群，但她既不十分聪明，也不极为考究。她的不幸印证了雨果在《巴黎圣母院》中说过的一句话：“一个独眼人和完全的瞎子比起来缺点更严重，因为他知道他缺什么。”[②]



福楼拜传达的对外省的看法（同司汤达和巴尔扎克的小说一样）表明，卢梭和贝尔纳丹·德·圣皮埃尔的追随者如此珍视

① 译文摘自《包法利夫人》，李健吾译，人民文学出版社，2015年7月。——译注
② 译文摘自《巴黎圣母院》，陈敬容译，人民文学出版社，2019年5月。——译注

的对自然和乡村生活的崇拜，在19世纪中叶遭到了抵制。在福楼拜的作品中，放牛并没有什么振奋人心和高尚的地方，鲜花盛开的田园景色没有给爱玛带来任何慰藉。事实上，通过爱玛烂俗的想象，福楼拜戏仿了遁世乡村的田园诗的浪漫观念，爱玛幻想着和鲁道夫私奔到"一个渔村，沿着峭壁和茅屋，迎风晾着一
78 些棕色的渔网。他们就在这里待下来，在海边港湾深处，住在一所棕榈树的浓荫覆盖下的平顶矮房"。[①]这特别滑稽，也非常可悲，住在乡下的爱玛已经将她对城市居民的幻想内化了。



由于爱玛是福楼拜的朋友和同为小说家的乔治·桑的读者，很难不将爱玛的性格与桑的早期作品《康素爱萝》（1842）中的女主人公相比较，这是一部宏大的历史小说，背景设在18世纪，其结构几乎是流浪汉小说式的，但在风格上却不尽相同。《康素爱萝》追述了康素爱萝的一生，从威尼斯的贫穷的童年到最终与半疯的鲁多尔施塔特的波希米亚（捷克）贵族阿尔伯特的婚姻。逐一对照，这两部小说完全相反：爱玛被困在一个平淡无奇的法国村庄里，而康素爱萝的生活几乎是一部奥匈帝国游记；爱玛向往贵族生活，向往城市和剧院的精致，而康素爱萝则花费大量的时间逃离这些。爱玛周围的生活似乎非常无聊，但她试图给它注入激情，而康素爱萝的生活则充满罗曼蒂克的氛围，以及在有地下通道和幽暗森林的中世纪城堡里的冒险。但最重要的是，女主角的性情是截然相反的。康素爱萝本身就是善，她总是耐心、慷慨、足智多谋、关心他人，对财富和名望无动于衷，不需要逃进异国情调。

① 译文摘自《包法利夫人》，李健吾译，人民文学出版社，2015年7月。——译注

## 城市流亡者

“世界之外的任何地方”是夏尔·波德莱尔对人类愿望的判断，爱玛·包法利如此出色地诠释了这一点，而它对康素爱萝而言却是如此陌生。这个表达，在英语中，是散文集《巴黎的忧郁》（1869）中一篇散文诗的标题。在《世界之外的任何地方》中，他
唤醒了永恒的“别处”的力量：“今生是一所医院，每个病人都被 79
换床位的欲望所困扰。”这种对世界其他地方正在发生的事情的兴趣是一个有趣的悖论的关键，福楼拜、巴尔扎克、桑、司汤达，以及其他人，可以用外省人的故事来娱乐见多识广的读者，他们被认为过着令人窒息的生活，继而表现为终其一生向往巴黎（或者渴望乡村生活，如果他们是巴黎人的话）。一个不幸的外省家庭主妇的生活中又有什么能使像波德莱尔这样的巴黎人感兴趣的呢？

波德莱尔是福楼拜的小说的众多崇拜者之一。在他关于《包法利夫人》的评论文章中——这篇文章发表于宣判福楼拜侮辱公众和宗教道德的罪行不成立后的几个月——波德莱尔将这部小说描述为写作力量的胜利，这种力量如此伟大，以至于几乎不需要主题。波德莱尔知道或是凭直觉得出福楼拜在五年前写给情人露易丝·科莱的一封信中的著名表述，说他的梦想是有朝一日写一本“无关任何的书……几乎没有主题，或者至少几乎看不出主题”（1852）。波德莱尔在《包法利夫人》中发现了这种艺术挑战的胜利：选取最平庸的主题，通奸，在愚蠢和偏狭大行其道的地方，外省，创造一个女主人公，以男性的方式面对这种“天才的完全缺席”。这位女主人公，包法利夫人本人，“在她

的同类中，在她狭隘的阶层中，面对她的渺小前景，是非常崇高的”。波德莱尔在赞美福楼拜的小说及其女主人公的同时，似乎有时会自我认同于她，尽管他们所处的地方截然不同。

波德莱尔是典型的巴黎诗人，几乎无法想象他在其他地方，但这并不是说他为巴黎唱赞歌。波德莱尔吸收了雨果关于怪诞和人类双重性的教义，对丑陋和崇高以及所有不可预测和格格不入的东西着迷。作为一个百分之百的巴黎人，波德莱尔既是
80 诗人，又是他诗歌的主题，他像爱玛·包法利一样，培养了错位的意识。关于爱玛，他写道，在她的修道院学校里，她为自己创造了一个“未来和机遇之神”，对波德莱尔而言，首都最重要的价值之一就是它能够制造产生抒情诗的随机相遇。



19世纪中叶，大都会可能提供的自由和机会，是法国的其他任何城市望尘莫及的，因为它正在爆炸式增长，这很容易理解。1801年，巴黎的人口几乎与17世纪末相同，在不到14平方千米的土地上大约有50万居民。到19世纪末，人口增加了五倍，巴黎吞并了附近的城镇和村庄，使城市面积扩大了八倍。这样的环境有利于波德莱尔归于爱玛·包法利的“机会之神”，他也为自己抓住了一个恰逢其时的诗意人物形象，漫步者的形象，他在一篇关于画家康斯坦丁·盖斯的文章《现代生活的画家》中如此描述这个角色：“对如假包换的漫步者而言，对于充满激情的观察者来说，置身于人群、起伏、迁移、跳动和无限之中是一种极大的乐趣。”十四行诗《致一位过路的女子》（收于《恶之花》中）描绘了诗人—漫步者在这座巨大的、行色匆匆的现代城市中所珍视的相遇的密集度和偶然性。两段四行诗句，没有指向，描述了一个拥挤的街道场景，然后是一个引人注目的女性形象。诗

句首先提及女人的目光，随后诗人直接对这个女人说话。闪电般的一瞥将诗人的思绪从这次邂逅转向了未来不可能的邂逅，并将这首十四行诗转向了爱玛·包法利和她的读者所熟知的主题：对充满爱的他地他时的渴望。唯一的斜体字*jamais*（永诀）——波德莱尔几乎从未用过斜体字——强调了此时的世俗特征，即今生可能不会出现。令人伤逝的女人，实际上可能是**死亡**，但她也可能只是人群中的一个女人，她稍纵即逝的形象滋养 81
了诗人的想象力，诗人在这种精神交流中赋予了她一个相应的角色。这首诗的标题暗示了极端，城市生活的充实，人们在城市中快速迁移，彼此擦肩而过（人们在村庄里不会这样），也暗示着超越生命的人的行动的最终缺席——生与死本身压缩成了黑暗紧随其后的光明的对立面。



**致一位过路的女子**[①]

喧闹的街巷在我周围叫喊。
颀长苗条，一身哀愁，庄重苦楚，
一个女人走过，她那灵动的手
提起又摆动衣衫的彩色花边。

轻盈而高贵，一双腿宛若雕塑。
我紧张如迷途的人，在她眼中，
那暗淡的、孕育着风暴的天空

① 译文摘自《恶之花》，郭宏安译，广西师范大学出版社，2002年。

啜饮迷人的温情，销魂的快乐。

电光一闪……复归黑暗！——美人已去，
你的目光一瞥突然使我复活，
难道我从此只能会你于来世？

远远地走了！晚了！也许是**永诀**！
我不知你何往，你不知我何去，
82 啊我可能爱上你，啊你该知悉！



作为雨果的双面人的一个变体，漫步者非常巧妙地适应了时代，特别是对逝去的过去和未遂事件的不和谐。他生动地生活在现在、过去的巴黎和别处。在《天鹅》（献给维克多，雨果，1860）这首诗中，波德莱尔以巴黎的另一次偶然邂逅为主题，巴黎正在经历奥斯曼在1853年至1870年间进行的巨大变革，他创造了拥有我们今天所知的宽阔林荫大道和标准建筑高度的城市。在此过程中，中世纪的巴黎几近消失，从而赋予中世纪的遗迹一种新的、怀旧的价值。

在《天鹅》中，波德莱尔创造了不同时刻的巧妙的镶嵌画，特别是这三个：现在，他正在穿越杜伊勒里宫和卢浮宫之间新建的卡胡赛尔广场；一个过去时刻，那里曾经有一个动物园；古希腊的想象时刻，特洛伊王子赫克托耳的遗孀，成为皮洛士的奴
83 隶的安德洛玛刻，俯身向她英勇丈夫的纪念碑。波德莱尔将这些时刻聚集在“缺席”的主题轴上：在穿越卡胡赛尔时，他看到

马克西姆·拉兰（1827—1886），《为建造圣日耳曼大道而进行的拆除工程》，奥斯曼重建巴黎的一幕

动物园已经不在那里了。在那个动物园里，一只天鹅从笼子里逃出来，徒劳地从干燥的人行道上找水。诗人想象天鹅回忆起逝去的青春之湖，然后想象安德洛玛刻回忆起赫克托耳。这首 84

诗的最后三段四行诗唤起了无数其他失去了东西的人，特别是那些失去处所的人，比如“瘦弱憔悴的黑女人……找寻……骄傲非洲失落的棕榈树”。如此，城市诗人可以用漫步者的形式来丰富他对叙事人物的体验，因为他将逐一自我代入他们：安德洛玛刻、天鹅、非洲女人，甚至可能还有《罗兰之歌》中即将死去的英雄：“一桩古老的记忆又把猎角狂吹。”

在波德莱尔看来，巴黎唯一恒久不变的可能就是无穷无尽的变化，这种变化在《天鹅》之后的十年里加速了。1870年至1871年的普法战争终结了第二帝国，带来了被称为巴黎公社的起义及对其的血腥镇压。19世纪后半叶，巴黎的面积几乎增加了两倍，以首都为中心的铁路网的持续发展带来了更多的工人。

85 克劳德·莫奈，《圣拉扎尔火车站》(1877)

这种变化的一面反映在埃米尔·左拉（1840—1902）的自然主义小说中，它们关注的是这个繁荣时期，即法国殖民帝国的全盛时期真实的底层。这些作品包括《小酒店》（1877）和《人兽》（1890），都是关于酗酒对工人阶级家庭的伤害。但是，作为对小说和戏剧对自然主义的反应，象征主义出现了，波德莱尔是其发轫，而斯特凡纳·马拉美则是其最伟大的代表。马拉美的绝大多数诗歌，表面上轻浮、偶然（例如，关于女性的扇子、发型的系列等），涉及死亡和纪念，特别以诗人为典范。除了龙萨和雨果，马拉美可能是最积极地倡导用语言本身的力量来挑战死亡的诗人。因此，马拉美的主人公通常是诗人，在一系列“墓穴”十四行诗中被颂扬，比如《爱伦坡之墓》（1876），但最终，马拉美在身后出版的、创作于1870年左右的《伊吉杜尔，或埃尔比农的疯狂》中达到了抽象的顶峰，散文诗的主人公名字就叫伊吉杜尔（拉丁文“因此”的意思）。主人公在用掷骰子挑战虚无之后，在坟墓中死去：“这个人物，相信唯一绝对的存在，在梦中想象自己无处不在［……］认为行动是无用的。”这个文本可能是马拉美在将近三十年后出版的伟大的神秘主义诗歌《骰子一掷永远取消不了偶然》（1897）的最初形式，在后者中，我们似乎又一次撞见伊吉杜尔掷骰子。在它的图形布局上，外形上以不同的字形和字体撒落于纸面，这是法语文学中最具创造性的文本之一，对接下来的一个世纪至关重要。 86

*LE NOMBRE*

**EXISTÂT-IL**
**autrement qu'hallucination éparse d'agonie**

**COMMENÇÂT-IL ET CESSÂT-IL**
**sourdant que nié et clos quand apparu**
**enfin**
**par quelque profusion répandue en rareté**
**SE CHIFFRÂT-IL**

**évidence de la somme pour peu qu'une**
**ILLUMINÂT-IL**

# LE HASARD

*Choit*
*la plume*
*rythmique suspens du sinistre*
*s'ensevelir*
*aux écumes originelles*
*naguères d'où sursauta son délire jusqu'à une cime*
*flétrie*
*par la neutralité identique du gouffre*

87 斯特凡纳·马拉美的诗歌《骰子一掷永远取消不了偶然》(1897) 中的一页

第七章

# 从马塞尔到萝丝·瑟拉薇

## 普鲁斯特小说的世界

马拉美的抒情诗中令人陶醉的形而上学的抱负，有时似乎准备抛开语言和书页，它起初似乎与卷帙浩繁的意识流长河小说、标志着20世纪开端的马塞尔·普鲁斯特（1871—1922）的《追忆似水年华》（1913—1917）没有什么共同之处。然而，这两位“美丽年代”（这个称谓是第一次世界大战之后取的，指代大战前从1870年普法战争结束到1914年的和平年代）的作家有着相同的、受到当时哲学运动滋养的冒险精神。人们很容易把普鲁斯特的小说看作是一部教育小说［（Bildungsroman）或者是它的变体，艺术家成长小说（Kunstlerroman）——艺术家的教育］，但在这部小说中，这种形式通常的线性已让位于经验时刻与后来的诠释时刻之间极为复杂的相互作用。这种复杂性因篇幅、基于对正确使用遗物的不同看法的版本比较，以及标题各异的不同英文译本而更加复杂。《追忆似水年华》目前在法国七星文

库的版本（附有大量注释）篇幅超过7 000页，由七部加了标题
88 的子小说组成。其中的第一部（1913年由作者自费出版）《在斯万家那边》包含了以下章节：“贡布雷”、“斯万之恋”和“地名：那个姓氏”。七部子小说中的最后一部《时光重现》出版于1927年，也就是普鲁斯特去世后五年。小说的时间跨度从最早的贡布雷的童年记忆，一直延伸到该系列最后一部小说《时光重现》（*Le temps Retrouvé*，字面意思是“重新找回的时间”）中战后巴黎的场景。

第一章，贡布雷，以叙事者关于睡觉和醒来的叙述开头——令人吃惊的第一句是“在很长一段时间里，我都是早早就躺下了”。[①]读者无法知道是谁在发表这一声明——事实上，主人公的名字在组成整部作品的七部子作品中很少被提及，但很快就清楚了，关于这个“我”存在某种非常大胆和神秘的东西。在看书时睡着了，他写道，有时候在半小时后醒来时，仍想着之前正在读的那本书。但是这些想法往往有一种特殊的形式：“我总觉得书里说的事，什么教堂呀，四重奏呀，弗朗索瓦一世和查理五世争强斗胜呀，全都同我直接有关。”叙述者用了几页的篇幅，对意识觉醒时的内容进行了调查，并对思维主体与一系列完全不同的客体的认同进行了评论。大脑起初并未将它们当作是客体，而仅仅是将之视为自身的一部分，对于读者而言，这个事实最令人吃惊。叙述者继续追踪分离阶段，思考者重新回到清醒的世界，并且不再理解最初看起来如此天真地显而易见的梦中
89 的想法。



① 《追忆似水年华》的译文均引自《追忆似水年华》（全七册），译林出版社，2012年6月。下同。——译注

这部小说的开头几页，以其对自我边界的彻底质疑，深深地扎根于法语文学的传统。蒙田在《随笔集》“论实践”一章的一个著名段落中叙述了他在一次摔倒后恢复意识的经历，卢梭在他的《孤独漫步者的遐想》中也这样做过。笛卡尔在《方法论》中也曾试图剥离自我意识，回归简单的存在意识，后者先于任何有关思考自我的性质的现有认识。在普鲁斯特的时代，弗朗茨·布伦塔诺和他的两位杰出的学生，埃德蒙·胡塞尔和西格蒙德·弗洛伊德的教导，使这种笛卡尔式的质疑重新流行。普鲁斯特当然知道亨利·柏格森的作品，他关于时间意识的著作经常被拿来与普鲁斯特的作品相比较。尽管普鲁斯特可能是自主地对自我清醒的现象学产生了兴趣，但不可否认，他为意识、感觉和记忆的探索带来了新的活力和具体性。

他还重新凸显了童年。关于上床睡觉和醒来的开场冥想引出了在贡布雷的暑假期间的家庭就寝仪式。为了让孩子从睡前必须与母亲分离的痛苦中分心，他的家人让他在自己卧室的墙上投射一盏幻灯投影，在那里，用图像展现的传奇故事中的英雄戈洛，展示了他根据被投射于其上的物体——门把手、窗帘、墙壁——自我变形的能力：“戈洛的身体……能对付一切物质的障碍，遇到阻挡，他都能用来作为赖以附体的依凭，即使遇到门上
的把手。”如此，作为一个成人叙述者，马塞尔能够将清醒的自我 90
想象成一座教堂或国王与皇帝之间的较量，这一能力在孩子对幻灯展示英雄形象的体验中得到了预体现，因为这种体验超越了时间和地点，成为他本身。弗洛伊德用另一种方法教授童年经历的长期影响，而普鲁斯特则用这种延绵不断的叙事模式以及人们确认——以及与之认同——主人公角色的能力，把童年

和成年紧密地联系在一起。

这种能力出现在叙述者对斯万的描述中，斯万是年轻的马塞尔家族的一位成年朋友，巴黎人，他和马塞尔的父母一样，在贡布雷有一座乡村别墅。作为孩子，马塞尔害怕斯万来参加晚宴，因为这意味着他的就寝仪式将受到干扰，他的母亲将忙于履行女主人的职责。简而言之，斯万似乎是由于爱人的缺席而造成可怕痛苦的原因。然而，作为一个成年人，马塞尔认为，斯万比任何人都更清楚这种痛苦是什么样的，因为他也因为爱奥黛特·德克雷西而遭受痛苦。对斯万的这种处理仅仅是马塞尔作为叙述者——但同时也是主人公——聚焦他人的广泛维度的特征塑性的一个典型例子，他随着年龄的增长，发现人们的不同侧面。早期对“戈洛”可以是他自己，也可以是一个门把手的意识，其中产生的魅力是一种为后续意识提供价值的力量，他后续意识到最初看起来完全不同且不相容的人、态度、行为和地点，实际上是一体的。例如，贡布雷通往斯万家（即通往“在斯万家那边”）的小路一开始似乎与通往盖尔曼城堡的道路完全相反，斯万和贵族盖尔曼家族似乎毫不相关，但后来证明他们有关联。然而，甚至正如他对空间组织的感知所显示的那样，叙述者最伟大的才华在于创造出令人难忘的人物。因此，《追忆似水年华》
91 的任何一位读者都有可能在脑海中上演一出保留剧目，剧中演员有厨师弗朗索瓦、坦特·莱奥尼、查卢斯男爵、圣卢普、阿尔贝蒂、画家埃尔斯蒂尔等人。这些都是从叙述者自己的“自我”中流淌出的，他成了一个超级人物，储藏了他所叙述的整个世界。小说最动人的篇章是收尾部分《时光重现》，他意识到过去从未过去，它仍然活在他身上。

## 马拉美的遗产

普鲁斯特同时代的保罗·瓦雷里（1871—1945）有着截然不同的审美气质。与前者的长篇小说以及众所周知的冗长晦涩的句子（有些句子长达好几页）形成鲜明对比的是，瓦雷里的文本无论是散文还是诗歌篇幅都非常小。在法语文学中比较不寻常的主人公有他的泰斯特先生，他是一系列文本的主人公——我们可以称之为散文诗或随笔，在这些文本中，瓦雷里以第二自我的形式探索自己的智识，他的名字能让人联想到“头”（古法语中的tête或teste）和“文本”。同样，在他的诗歌中，瓦雷里展现了一个自我，一个moi，接近形而上学的自我。瓦雷里是马拉美最近的继承人，也是最后一位伟大的象征主义诗人，他最伟大的诗歌成就是《海滨墓园》（1920）。就像许多当代绘画（你可能会想到康定斯基）一样，这首24节诗唤起了一个事件或场景，然后萃取其精华，提炼到几乎瞥不见有形事件的程度。在《海滨墓园》里，诗人似乎在描述一种顿悟，这种顿悟是当他从墓园眺望地中海时，在数小时的思考中产生的。他思考的问题是躯体、思想和时间之间的关系（也贯穿《泰斯特先生》的文本的主题），以及对躯体的最终接受，以及肉体生活的需求和乐趣。更
容易理解的是出版于《海滨墓园》一年后的短诗《脚步》。 92

**脚步**

你的脚步圣洁，缓慢，<br>
是我的寂静孕育而成，

一步步走向我警醒的床边，
脉脉含情，而又冷凝如冰。

纯真的人啊，神圣的影，
你的脚步多么轻柔而拘束！
我能猜想的一切天福
向我走来时，都是这双赤足！

这样，你的芳唇步步移向
我这一腔思绪里的房客，
准备了一个吻作为食粮
以便平息他的饥渴。

不，不必加快这爱的行动
这生的甜蜜和死的幸福，
因为我生活在等待中，
93 我的心啊，就是你的脚步。

《脚步》很好地诠释了瓦雷里在他的诸多诗歌中，在物质和形而上学的边界上起舞的方式。这首诗是写给一个“纯真的人”的。是女人还是精神？“神圣的影”是真的神圣，还是夸张？这些脚步是指真正的脚步，还是诗歌本身的韵脚？或者，pas是诗人的心跳（他说他的心就是这些pas），他能听到是因为周围的一切都寂静无声？当这些pas停止时，诗人，以及诗歌，似乎都将结束。这些是瓦雷里的诗歌所引发的各种问题，它们为耐心的冥想创造了机会，对于瓦雷里来说，这是相比19世纪的小说，诗歌明显的优越性。

## 超现实主义

瓦雷里的相识安德烈·布勒东也反对作为一种体裁的小说，《娜嘉》（1928年初版，1962年修订版）是他提出的一种替代。布勒东的作品意义重大是因为他是超现实主义者的领袖，这一运动反映了欧洲大陆对新事物的渴望，渴望新事物取代19世纪的文学和艺术，以及导致第一次世界大战杀戮的社会秩序。法国超现实主义是在其他运动的背景下出现的，如意大利的未来主义（战争之前已经发起，但在其后的几十年里产生了重大影响）、英国的漩涡派、苏联的结构主义、德国的包豪斯风格，以及瑞士和法国的达达主义。安德烈·布勒东是两篇《超现实主义宣言》（1924和1929）的作者，因此成为这些运动中最重要的公 94
众领袖（这里所说的“运动”是指一群自称超现实主义者并倡导一套美学和社会教义的作家）。布勒东主张想象的生活优先，并认为大多数人都知道，“现实”生活只是一个更真实的（surréel，“高于现实”）生活的苍白反映，而更真实的生活是在推翻狭隘的理性主义思想形式、拒绝成人生活的有限选择的基础上实现的。在这样一个有限的、普通的、被实际问题支配的人身上：

> 他所有的姿态都将是畏缩的，他的想法都将是狭隘的。他只能根据发生在他身上和可能发生在他身上的事情，想象这件事与大量类似事件之间的联系，那些他没有参与过

的事件，错过的事件。

我们大多数人都已失去的想象的生活，充满了残酷的可能性。在一个撇号中，布勒东感叹道，“亲爱的想象力，我最爱你的，是你不原谅”。对布勒东来说，想象的世界并不在传统小说家和诗人精心、悉心锤炼的创作中，而是在我们周围的日常世界中，而我们并没有意识到这一点。布勒东是西格蒙德·弗洛伊德早期和热心的读者[正如我们可以从“错过的事件”一词看到的那样——这个词是根据我们称为失言或“弗洛伊德口误”的法语术语的模式创造的]，他是阿尔弗雷德·雅里的《愚比王》（1896）和洛特雷阿蒙的《马尔多罗之歌》（1868年印行，但直到20世纪20年代才为人所知）的崇拜者，他倡导“自动写作”的概
95 念，作为一种突破传统形式和理性主义思维的方法，首次在诗歌散文集《磁场》（1919，与菲利普·苏波合著）中实践。

鉴于布勒东的写作倾向于避免任何形式的预先构思、道德审查和对传统体裁的尊重，他非常重视生活中偶然性的创造作
96 用也就不足为奇了。这一点在他的文本《娜嘉》中得到了体现，这部作品有时被称为“小说”，尽管布勒东抨击小说传统，并声称前者只是对真实事件的记录，以他与一个自称娜嘉（尽管她明确表示这不是她的真名）的年轻女子的偶然相遇为中心。他从娜嘉身上感受到了各种超心理学的力量，在回答他的问题“你是谁”时，她回答，“我是游荡的灵魂”。他见过她几次，通常是偶遇，当他们在巴黎漫步时，每个地点都因为半未言明的解释而变得沉重，这表明娜嘉至少以前曾来过这其中的某些地方。他们在多芬广场用餐，后来又发现他们偶然地身处一间名为“多芬”

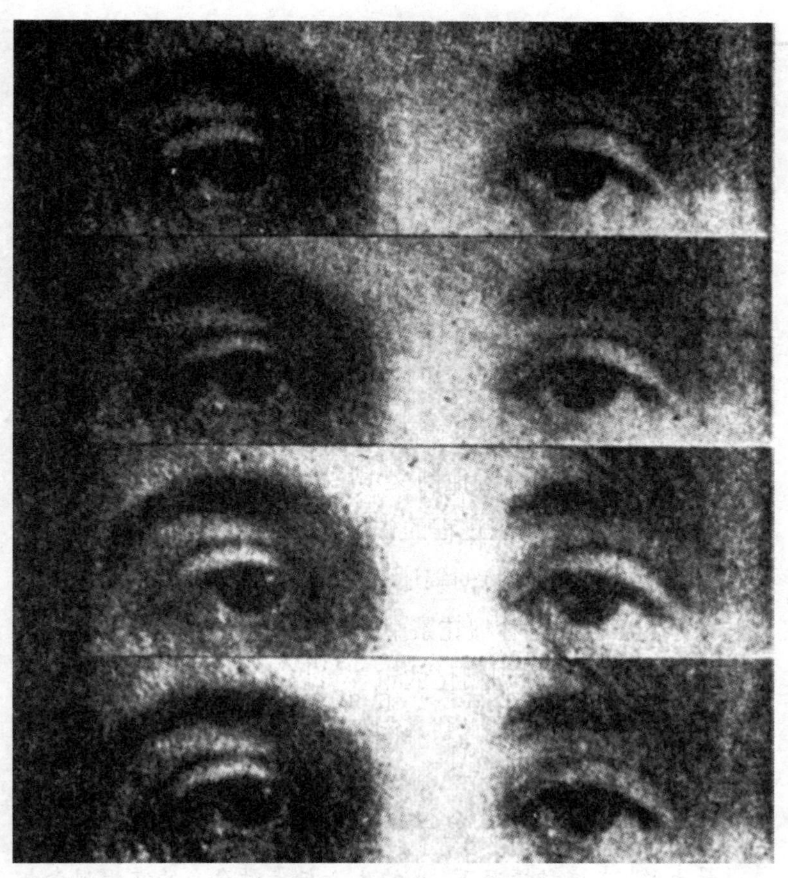

"人字形的眼睛",安德烈·布勒东《娜嘉》的摄影剪辑插图



的咖啡馆；布勒东解释说，它经常被认为是同名的海洋哺乳动物海豚。布勒东对巴黎这些地点的真实性的尊重可以从文本中插入的48张照片看出，其中一些翻拍了娜嘉的画作，但大多数都代表了地点，比如先贤祠广场上的伟人酒店、多芬广场、人文书店、圣图安跳蚤市场等。这些照片表面上是为了避免冗长的描述，这些描述典型地是19世纪现实主义和自然主义小说的一部分，

但是，既然布勒东也用文字描述事物和人，那么它们似乎还有另一个目的，或至少效果，那就是保存那些对作者来说几乎具有护身符意义的物品。

布勒东的这部薄薄的作品就体量而言，相比绝大多数小说，更接近于一本小册子——与普鲁斯特枝枝蔓蔓的作品至少有一个共同点。两位作者都认为日常世界是巨大的魅力源泉，并继续在可以被认为值得描写和叙述的东西上不断扩展更大的包容性。普鲁斯特将芦笋、柴油机尾气和同性恋妓院与哥特式教堂和室内音乐相提并论，而布勒东则认为跳蚤市场、系列电影和广
97 告很重要，并将其囊括进他的文本中。更重要的是这些作者在审美创造中赋予无意识过程的作用。在《追忆似水年华》的一个著名段落中，普鲁斯特的叙述者马塞尔，将童年事件的重新发现归因于品尝浸在一杯椴花茶中的玛德莱娜小点心时突然闪现的回忆。这种对无意识回忆的审美可以与布勒东在《娜嘉》中表现的意图相媲美，他如此讲述自己的人生：



> 在某种程度上，它受到偶然事件的影响，从最小的到最大的，在这种情况下，我的生活与我对存在的常规观念相悖，生活把我带进了一个几乎被禁的世界，一个充满突然的联系、石化的巧合和阻止其他精神活动的本能反应的世界。

## 右翼的创新小说

并非所有写作的伟大转变都来自宣言和自我标榜的运动。在散文风格方面，路易·费迪南·塞利纳（1894—1961，原名为路易·费迪南·戴都什）的《茫茫黑夜漫游》在1932年出版后

的几十年里，对小说的措辞产生了巨大的影响。除了对风格的影响外，它还使得主人公对崇高意义上的“英雄”地位的要求缩水。在这部以第一次世界大战为开篇的第一人称小说中，强硬、尖刻、来自工人阶级的年轻叙述者费迪南·巴尔达缪［与作者同名，并成为塞利纳后来的小说《死缓》（1936）中主人公的名字］，他很快就认定战争是一场毫无意义的屠杀，并因为精神疾病，主要是因为恐惧，住院治疗。简而言之，他绝不是英雄，因为他所看到的身边的英雄主义的例子似乎是从想象力的缺乏或单纯的愚蠢中骤然产生的。发现自己身处一家军事医院，院长的治疗理念是向病人灌输爱国情怀，于是巴尔达缪假装顺从，甚至讲述了一些故事，这些故事成为他在法兰西喜剧院细数其“英 98
勇”冒险的基础。从佛兰德斯游荡到巴黎，再到西非，再从那里到美国，最后回到巴黎，他在那里成为一名医学博士，巴尔达缪是没有背负被强加的哲学枷锁的老实人。事实上，他对几乎每一个宏大的价值观免疫，这是在二十年后成为公认趋势的“荒诞”文学的先驱。他就像伏尔泰的角色一样，是一个批判的透镜，通过他谴责美国资本主义、法国军事和殖民阶级，以及作为英雄主义载体的文学本身。在精神科医生夸耀自己的方法得到认可中存在某种潘格罗斯式的东西——“我说，令人钦佩的是，在我领导的这家医院里，在我们每只眼睛的见证下，诗人和我们的一位英雄之间令人难忘地达成了一项崇高的、创造性的合作”——但是，巴尔达缪，毕竟是这个故事的叙述者，他是第一个看穿这番胡言乱语的人。塞利纳的叙述者破坏性的、一语双关的描述，通过将宏大淹没在琐碎或粗俗中，达到了祛魅的目的。在他看来，曼哈顿的银行就像是安静的教堂，出纳员的窗口就像忏悔室的铁栅，仅仅在几段之后，巴尔达缪描述了一间公共厕所里“拉屎工”的辛勤劳动。

塞利纳对俚语和流行节奏的运用，工人阶级的演讲与一种窄焦点叙事顺序相匹配，这种顺序使巴尔达缪的注意力集中在小细节上，同时激发读者从所有这些中提取这种附加评论的意识形态意义。塞利纳的创新，在不同的方面，对他同时代的年轻人，如（《局外人》中的）阿尔贝·加缪，以及多年后的作家，如（《母猪女郎》中的）玛丽·达里耶塞克都产生了巨大的影响。
99 塞利纳的反犹主义以及后来与亲纳粹的维希政权的关系（战后他被宣布为“国耻”）并没有削弱《茫茫黑夜漫游》的巨大而持久的声誉。然而，民粹主义英雄巴尔达缪曾宣称“战争是我们所不理解的一切”，对于广大读者来说，他比同时代的另一部有关第一次世界大战的小说，罗杰·马丁·杜加尔的《1914年夏天》（1936，长篇小说《蒂博一家》的一部分，1922—1940）中的反战英雄更具有生命力，马丁·杜加尔因这部作品于1937年获得诺贝尔文学奖。也许，除了塞利纳作品的创造性和辛辣的黑色幽默之外，反战小说的这种持久的成功是由于巴尔达缪的泛犬儒主义之死，相比马丁·杜加尔笔下的理想和平主义的雅克·蒂博，前者似乎更接近于对现实的普遍看法。



## 第二次世界大战与集中营

虽然塞利纳在第二次世界大战后继续写作，但他的声望主要有赖于《茫茫黑夜漫游》和《死缓》，因为在战争期间和战后，阿尔贝·加缪和让-保罗·萨特开始占据民粹主义批评的一些相同的阵地，并为贯穿塞利纳作品的难以预测的怀疑和愤

马塞尔·杜尚装扮的萝丝·瑟拉薇，1920—1921，曼雷摄影

怒提供了连贯的哲学语境。战争本身，以及德国集中营，了结了许多作家的生命，改变了其他作家的生活。它有助于形成像午夜出版社这样持久的机构，午夜出版社在战争期间秘密地出版作品，并成为战后的主要出版社。这场战争结束了两次大战

之间的许多有趣和实验性的东西，罗贝尔·德斯诺斯（1900—1945，在特雷津集中营死于斑疹伤寒）可能是最好的例子。1924年至1929年，德斯诺斯任《超现实主义革命》评论编辑，他出版了大量作品，借鉴了巴黎的流行文化和低俗的系列犯罪片《方托马斯》。

在超现实主义的圈子里，一个思想以笑话的方式流传开来
100 的示例是萝丝·瑟拉薇这个人物，她出现在德斯诺斯1939年
的作品《萝丝·瑟拉薇：精确的眼影、络腮胡和各种拳打脚踢》
以及其他地方。1920年，多媒体艺术家马塞尔·杜尚创造“萝
丝·瑟拉薇”作为第二自我。杜尚被曼雷拍成了女装的“萝
101 丝”，随后德斯诺斯让“她”成为贯穿于他的一些诗中的人物，甚
至直到1944年6月，也就是他去世前一年。在《春天》（1944年6
月）中，我们看到了以前俏皮的形象，现在被当作属于以前时代
的想象而为人所记住，或者属于将要到来的时代，在诗人死于战
争的舞台之后。



**春天**

你，萝丝·瑟拉薇，在这些流浪的界限之外
在一个为爱的汗液
为绽放于塔楼墙壁上的玫瑰的香气，
为水与泥土的发酵所苦的春天里。

鲜血淋漓，斜坡上的玫瑰，舞者，石头的躯体
102 出现在田地中的剧场里。

一个又哑又瞎又聋的民族
为她的舞蹈和春天的死亡欢呼。

好吧。但烟灰中的话语
在雨的指尖下随风而逝
但我们听见并听从了它。

洗衣间里水像云彩一般流淌过
肥皂，暴风雨大作，停歇
当太阳绽放于灌木丛的那一刻。 103

第八章

# 自我中心意识

《局外人》（1942）出版于第二次世界大战期间，与随笔《西绪福斯神话》和戏剧《卡利古拉》一并被其作者阿尔贝·加缪（1913—1960）称为“荒诞三部曲”。简单地看一下这三部作品的标题就可以看出，它们凸显的是那些与他们的社会中的正面英雄地位格格不入的中心人物，他们是局外人、失败者、怪物——或者兼而有之。在20世纪中叶，法语文学本身当然没有被边缘化。第二次世界大战期间作为成年人生活的一代作家中产生了六位诺贝尔文学奖获得者（弗朗索瓦·莫里亚克，1952；阿尔贝·加缪，1957；圣-琼·佩斯，1960；让-保罗·萨特，1964；塞缪尔·贝克特，1969；克劳德·西蒙，1985）。很明显，这是一个法国作家吸引了全世界目光的时代。在某些程度上，他们都或者自己是局外人（其中四人出生于法国本土之外），或者写的是令人难忘的局外人（莫里亚克的《寂寞的心灵》，1927；萨特的《恶心》，1938）。

## 非典型的英雄

《局外人》的书名指的是主人公默而索，一个条件和受教育情况中等的年轻人，在阿尔及尔的一个办公室工作，他无缘无故
地射杀了一个年轻的阿拉伯人。这个故事以第一人称单数的简 104
单语言叙述，展示了默而索逐渐意识到自己与周围社会的隔阂。这个文本不是正式的日记，但似乎是不定时写就的，有时记录刚刚发生的事情，有时呈现主人公打算做什么。默而索有一种相当漠然的特质，尤其是在开头，尽管与其说是缺乏情感本身，不如说是缺乏惯常社会形式下的约定俗成的戏剧化和情绪表达。第一句话就是很好的例子：



> 今天，妈妈死了。也许是昨天，我不知道。我收到养老院的一封电报，说："母死。明日葬。专此通知。"这说明不了什么。可能是昨天死的。[①]

在简单陈述句中，对细节，尤其是感觉倾注了大量的注意力，几乎没有解释。我们从默而索类似于老实人的视角看世界，像塞利纳的巴尔达缪一样，没有哲学可循或者去对抗（默而索的叙述确实让人疑惑伏尔泰的故事如果用第一人称叙事会是什么样子）。默而索喜欢游泳、抽烟、日光浴、和他的女朋友玛丽做爱。一次出游，在海滩上，默而索充当和事佬，从一个朋友那里拿过一把左轮手枪，朋友威胁要杀死一个和他起过冲突的阿拉

① 《局外人》译文摘自《局外人》，郭宏安译，译林出版社，2011年6月。下同。——译注

伯人，但后来默而索开枪射中了阿拉伯人。他的叙述并不让人感到恐惧或敌意，而是联想到炎热，联想到炽热的阳光。

小说中最非凡的时刻是默而索在临行刑前的自我发现。在
105 整个叙述中，主人公—叙述者似乎不假思索地记录下发生的事情。他对世界的看法是如此中立和缺乏感情，以至于他自己有时似乎是一个不在场的人，几乎是一个记录仪。但是他的监禁和审判——他更多地因为自己是谁而被审判，而不是因为阿拉伯人的死——使他意识到自己与其他人的不同，在他的反抗中，他变成了重要的人，一个自我："即便是坐在被告席上，听见大家谈论自己也总是很有意思的。"他在"世界的动人的冷漠"中发现了自己的存在，他最后希望当他被送上断头台时会有很多观众，他们会用仇恨的喊叫声来迎接他。一个几乎没有特征的人物最终以英雄的维度自我想象。

## 只有等待的戏剧

如果说默而索只是通过肯定自己的局外人身份而得以英雄化，那么塞缪尔·贝克特笔下的主人公显然从一开始就占据了局外人的位置。然而，贝克特（一位真正的爱尔兰—法国双国籍、双语作家）与加缪不同的是，他的人物与日常社会的世界保持距离。通常，缺乏同情心的中心人物和他们的意识构成了整个文本，就像小说《无名氏》（1953）里的声音。在贝克特的作品中，最容易理解和最著名的无疑是他的两幕剧《等待戈多》（1952）以及剧中悲剧性的流浪汉或小丑，对一些评论家来说，这是典型的"荒诞派戏剧"，这一术语也适用于贝克特的同代人欧仁·尤奈斯库（1909—1994）的戏剧，他是《秃头歌女》（1950）

和《椅子》（1952）的作者。两个男人在一棵树旁的瘠薄风景中等待某个从未谋面的“戈多”的到来，贝克特成功地完成了以此创作出一部引人入胜的戏剧的壮举。这一切发生在哪里？是否可以简单地将这两个人物描述为寄居于作者的意识中？ 106

整部作品都有一种贫瘠和荒凉的氛围，这种氛围又被语言的简洁所加强。贝克特说，他用外语写作是为了使自己“贫瘠”和“规训”，从而文本不会有风格和诗意。无论这是不是

1956年巴黎电影制作公司的一张照片，吕西安·兰布尔和皮埃尔·拉图尔在塞缪尔·贝克特的《等待戈多》中，摄影罗杰·布林

贝克特用法语而非用英语写作的真正原因，可以推论出，纵观历史，诗歌本身不同于普通话语的地方正是在于接受了语言的限制。在长达千年的法语文学的大部分时间里，抒情诗都是
107 以“规训”了作者的诗体长度和押韵的固定形式写成的。同样地，中世纪的《玫瑰传奇》等重要的作品，从其人物形象中剥离了具体的次要特征，聚焦于对故事而言最核心和最具普遍性的东西。尽管《等待戈多》的演员不能被轻易地解读为寓言性的抽象概念——比如用“希望”“绝望”“理性”等来形容——但他们的对话传达了一个简化为最具示意性的人类存在的黑色幽默的版本。



弗拉季米尔和爱斯特拉冈，被称为狄狄和戈戈，前一天可能在同一个地点，在一起或不在一起，等待同一个人，不知道是否该等，想办法打发时间，并试图决定第二天他们要做什么。等待时，为了消磨时间，他们讨论在树上上吊——弗拉季米尔认为这会给他们带来性快感。在一场关于如何做到这一点的荒谬讨论之后，他们什么也没做——什么都不做是首要原则。在两幕剧的每一幕结束的时候，他们都决定离开，但舞台指示显示“他们站着不动”。[1]在每一幕的当中，另一对角色出现：波卓和他的仆人或奴隶幸运儿。弗拉季米尔和爱斯特拉冈的小丑形象中马戏团的魅力被这对新角色加强了，因为挥舞着鞭子的波卓似乎是一个能让他的人，由他牵着绳子绕圈的幸运儿，表演特技的马戏团领班——至少在第一幕里。到了第二幕，波卓是瞎子，不记得前一天发生的任何事。幸运儿在第一

① 引自施咸荣译本。下同。——译注

幕中表演了一段冗长的、不带喘气的、毫无意义的演讲（也许暗示着学习，甚至包括体育在内的所有人类成就的无用），在第二幕中却缄口不言。

在一个如此神秘、如此简练的文本中，寻找舞台上发生的事情与生活和思想世界之间某种联系的任务落在了观众的肩上。读者和评论家不厌其烦地抓住剧本最细微的方面作为诠释的基础。最明显的问题是“戈多”的含义：他是“上帝”吗，如果是 108
的话，后缀“-ot”的意思又是什么？它是一个小词吗？它表示蔑视吗？每一幕接近尾声时，都有一个男孩来带口信：“戈多先生”今天不会来，而是第二天来。每一次，男孩都坚持说他以前没来过。弗拉季米尔和爱斯特拉冈听从了戈多要求他们等他来的请求，他们是否已经失去了行动能力，并把自己锁在了等待的监牢里？或者，认为戈多有朝一日会来的想法是弗拉季米尔和爱斯特拉冈唯一的慰藉？否则还有什么？



这出戏充满了几乎是警句形式的、令人难忘的黑色幽默——无论我们赋予其什么含义。爱斯特拉冈对弗拉季米尔说：“咱们老是想出办法来证明自己还存在，是不是，狄狄？”就戏剧中虚构的角色而言，这是一个非同寻常的问题。毕竟，有关角色存在的问题，如果有的话，传统上是由观众提出的，通常是诸如这样的问题“这个角色可信吗？”也就是说，“这样的角色可能存在吗？”这就是17世纪有关高乃依的主人公和女主人公的争论。后来，在博马舍的《费加罗》中，人物似乎要跃出他的角色之外，将等级制度抛到一边，通过过剩的想象、活动和欲望而占据他值得拥有的一席之地。在某种程度上——18世纪70年代末的王家审查员心中也很清楚——危险在于，费加罗或类似的人，会变得过于真实，不再只是舞台上有趣的人物，而是出现在巴黎街头，要求他们的权利。因此，有一部戏剧的中心人物，如爱斯特拉冈，远非评论意义上的“英雄”，唤起了人们对自身存在意义之渺小的关注，是非同寻常的。

## 角色的崩塌与重塑

这不是时代的异类。在第二次世界大战后的三十年里，角
109 色的概念，与文学传统中许多其他概念或实践一样，遭到了激烈的质疑。质疑有多种方式和多种体裁。例如，在尤奈斯库的《秃头歌女》中，角色的身份被分解成一小串名字。史密斯先生和史密斯夫人谈论某个叫“勃比·华特森”的人，或者说最初似乎如此，因为“勃比·华特森”越来越多。史密斯夫人说，她不是在想勃比·华特森，而是：



> 我想到是他妻子。她同她丈夫勃比一样，也叫勃比·华特森。因为他们俩同名同姓，见到他们俩在一起，你就分不清谁是谁了。直到男的死了，这才真知道谁是谁了。

表面上看，这是一出取笑英国中产阶级的戏剧，也取笑法国人对英国中产阶级的看法。但是，在法国存在主义（尤奈斯库通常与之没有关联）影响力的巅峰时期，也可从中窥见对个人身份的更广泛的焦虑，以及在被引用的段落中，对女性存在的焦虑。如果只有在丈夫勃比·华特森死后，女性的勃比·华特森才能与之区分开来，那么其原因可能就在此前一年出版的一本大获成功的书中：西蒙娜·德·波伏瓦的《第二性》（1949）。

德·波伏瓦（1908—1986）凭借这本书吸引了大量的读者，书中分析了女性在特定角色中的文化神话：少女、女同性恋、已婚妇女、母亲等。

同时，在文学理论和文学批评以及政治和社会思潮中，人物或角色或代理人或中心叙事人物的概念成为小说大量讨论和 110
实验的对象。小说这一体裁在19世纪末似乎已经僵化为一种“经典的”形式，几十年来一直受到攻击。诗人和文学哲学家保罗·瓦雷里曾在1923年批评小说缺乏严谨，结构松垮。在一个引人注目的阐述中，他抱怨普鲁斯特道，小说作为一种体裁，与梦异曲同工，即它们拒绝对自己的结构承担任何责任：“所有它们远离的都属于它们。”



## 关于小说的小说

在瓦雷里对这部小说发表尖刻评论的两年后，安德烈·纪德（1869—1951）写了一本关于写作小说的小说《伪币制造者》（1925）。主人公爱德华正在写一部与纪德的小说同名的小说，这个书名本身就宣告了对现实主义小说的批判。这种文本自我映射的结构，就好像一系列套盒，在法语中的术语为嵌套式结构（mise en abyme，字面意思是“置于裂隙中”），起源于纹章学，现已广为人知。这种文本对文本的映射批判在战争前几年和20世纪60年代变得很普遍。在让-保罗·萨特（1905—1980）的《恶心》（1938）中，第一人称叙述者，一位历史学家，长时间地反思了写作与存在之间的关系，并在叙事结束时决定停止写历史并改写一本小说——或许就是一本类似我们现在正在阅读的小说的小说。

小说中映射的影响深远的早期例子是被称为新小说的形式实验的主要运动的背景，这一术语由阿兰·罗布-格里耶在1963年的随笔《为了一部新小说》中广为宣扬。据知，“新小说”一词是埃米尔·昂里奥在对罗布-格里耶的小说《嫉妒》（1957；这个
111 词也有百叶窗的意思）的负面评论中首次用来描述这类创作的。《嫉妒》阐述了新小说对中心人物的概念提出质疑的方式，以及其他许多被归于传统小说的惯例。

《嫉妒》是由一个无名的人物叙述的。事实上，动词“叙述”在这种情况下可能会产生误导，因为整个故事从未被真正讲述，而是可能由读者从看似重叠、有时重复、有时矛盾的片段拼凑出来的，这些片段更像是描述（它们是现在时态）而不是讲故事。在《嫉妒》中有姓名的人是A...、弗兰克和后者的妻子克里斯蒂娜。作品逐渐揭晓叙述者假设A...和弗兰克之间有绯闻。我们可以推断——从记录告诉我们的餐桌上设了四个位子，但克里斯蒂娜不会来等——这个叙述者是个嫉妒的丈夫。这个文本充分证明了“凝视派”这一术语的合理性，它也被用来指新小说。下面是一个典型的段落：

> 在他们身后的香蕉种植园里，一个梯形一直延伸到山上，自从种植了树根之后，还没有收获过一丛香蕉，梅花形栽法的规则依然是绝对的。

所描述的对象和事件故意是平庸的：餐桌的设置、卡车爬坡的声音、被碾碎的千足虫在墙上留下的污点、窗户、放在桌上的手。

尽管这些描述的来源从未确定，但它——或者更确切地说，他，丈夫——并非没有实体，因为在这个观点上存在强烈的坚 112
持，从字面意义上说，鉴于文本中指定的距离、角度和光照条件，某些事物是可见或不可见的。叙述者的特征也可以从他所注意到的东西，从他的描述的用词和准确性，从他对某个时刻以及他所注意到的A...的某些特质的强迫回归推断出来。然而，除了通过这种对物质世界的描述的努力，我们无法接触到任何角色的想法，只有一系列线索。一个中心人物既无处不在，却又明明白白地哪儿都不在，这一矛盾的境况显示了作者在更新中心人物的表现形式方面极尽努力，这个中心人物远非“英雄”，但却是小说本身存在的根本。



这种对主人公范畴的创造性延伸在罗布-格里耶的同时代人中很常见。在米歇尔·布托尔（1926—　）的与《嫉妒》同年出版的小说《变》（1957）中，主角（同时也是设想中的叙述者和读者）就是“你”（如果我们假设叙述者和主角是同一个人，形式代词的选择又扩大了与自身的陌生距离）。故事一开始，效果很强烈：“你把左脚放在铜槽上，用右肩，你徒劳地试图将拉门再推开一点。”而在娜塔莉·萨洛特（1900—1999）的《金果》（1963）中，有关一部名为《金果》的小说（又一个类似于纪德的《伪币制造者》的嵌套形式）的大量对话的主题保证了通常由主人公赋予小说的连续性。

与此同时，抒情诗往往处于拓展人物和声音概念的前沿，在将文本的这些组成部分更加复杂化方面推进得更远。在伊夫·博纳富瓦的《论杜弗的动与静》（1953）中，一个“我”有时指的是一个名为“杜弗”（语法上是阴性的）的实体，似乎具有人

113 类特征，但有时也会变成景观、动物和各种其他物体。抒情诗常常表现出它所处的环境的特征，并被环境特殊化，但博纳富瓦却走得更远。杜弗似乎被她所处的地方侵犯（而代词“她”的选择赋予其在这首诗中完全不确定的人性化）。通过创造专有名词“杜弗”，博纳富瓦让读者疑惑法语名词douve的哪一个含义最贴切：城堡的护城河、一种植物（长矛草）、寄生蠕虫，还是藤蔓植物。人物与地点的强烈联系将这一时期的抒情诗与其他体裁，如电影，结合在一起。

## 人物与地点



常常与新小说联系在一起，玛格丽特·杜拉斯（原名玛格丽特·陶拉迪欧，1914年生于印度支那，1996年在巴黎去世）为电影《广岛之恋》（阿仑·雷乃导演，1959）创作了剧本，并于1960年单独出版。这一时期的作家经常从小说到电影再回到小说——在与雷乃合作之后，杜拉斯自己后来执导了许多电影，就像罗布-格里耶在为雷乃的《去年在马里昂巴德》（1961）撰写剧本后也执导了许多电影。这些以书的形式出版的电影剧本，与当时许多没有拍摄甚至没有打算拍摄的小说，如《嫉妒》，几乎没有区别。作为印刷文本，这些剧本显然是法语文学的一部分，《广岛之恋》阐明一个主要人物形象的建构（或解构）与1945年被美国核弹摧毁的广岛之间的密切关系。

正如雨果的《巴黎圣母院》中的人物既是大教堂也是人类角色一样，敲钟人卡西莫多为教堂发声，因此在杜拉斯的剧本中，在一部关于广岛的电影中扮演护士角色的无名的法国女演
114 员，以及成为她的情人的日本建筑师，几乎完全是为了讲述广岛

阿仑·雷乃的电影《广岛之恋》(1959) 中的一幕



被摧毁和战时法国的内韦尔被占领的经历。她给日本男人讲了一个她以前从未告诉过任何人的故事，故事是有关她在少女时期对一个德国士兵的爱。她和士兵计划结婚，但他被法国抵抗军杀死，而她则受到家人的惩罚，她被剃了光头，关在一个冰冷的地窖里几个月。家人把她放出来后，她连夜骑自行车去到巴黎，她正是在巴黎看到报纸头条宣布轰炸广岛的。他告诉她，她在广岛什么也没看见：“你在广岛什么也不曾看见。一无所见。”[①]她坚持：“我都看见了。毫无遗漏。”这番陈述在剧本中附有闪回到医院、博物馆、轰炸后的城市照片的拍摄指南。语言或形象上的毁灭的不可再现性贯穿于两个恋人的对话中。尽管女 115

① 《广岛之恋》译文摘自谭立德译本，上海译文出版社，2012年3月。下同。——译注

人在内韦尔的经历更容易描述，但在那个时候也是一个禁忌的话题。法国与德国占领军的大量合作是法国媒体几乎从未提及的主题，直到十年后马塞尔·奥弗尔斯的《悲哀与怜悯》问世。

杜拉斯的角色可信，但晦涩。他们就是他们所说的，而他们所说的关乎爱与毁灭。剧本的力量在很大程度上来自咒语般的对话，它从表面上真实的对话滑向与普通讲话相去甚远的话语，比如女演员反复说的一句话："你害了我。你对我真好"，这是杜拉斯作品中普遍存在的对战争、殖民主义和文化关系的色情观点最明确的表达之一，实际上，也出现在20世纪50年代末的其他小说和剧本中，当时法国正逐渐痛苦地失去殖民地。在这部电影的结尾，杜拉斯明确指出了男人和女人的城市身份。法国女人看着她的爱人——舞台上的指示牌上写着"他们彼此看着对方，却又视而不见"——说"广——岛。这是你的名字"，他回答说，"这是我的名字。是的。[我们就到此为止，仅此而已。而且，永远停留于此。]你的名字是内韦尔。法——国——的——内——韦——尔"。杜拉斯在这里近乎使用了中世纪最突出的人物寓言，然后向博纳富瓦的诗歌投去一瞥。

第九章

# 说法语的主人公无国界?

在20世纪的最后二十年和21世纪的前十年，第二次世界大战那一代的伟人们将法语文学的舞台让给了拥有新的关注点的一批新作家。这些同时代人中的很多小说家普遍将新小说的形式实验抛诸脑后。其中的许多作家，如安东妮娜·马叶（1929—　）、玛丽斯·孔戴（1930—　）、埃莱娜·西克苏（1937—　）、阿西娅·杰巴尔（1936—　）、达尼埃尔·皮纳克（1944—　）、拉法埃尔·贡菲扬（1951—　）、帕特里克·夏穆瓦索（1953—　）、米歇尔·维勒贝克（1956年生于留尼汪）和卡里斯·贝亚拉（1961—　），就像他们的前辈玛格丽特·尤瑟纳尔（1903—1987）、阿尔贝·加缪（1913—1960）、圣-琼·佩斯（1887—1975）和克洛德·西蒙（1913—2005）一样，出生于法国大陆——法国本土，或者常用称呼“六边形”——之外。其他人出生在六边形中：安妮·埃诺（1940—　）、让-马里·古斯塔夫·勒·克莱齐奥（1940—　）、迪迪埃·戴南科（1949—　）、玛丽·恩·迪亚耶（1967—　）和玛丽·达里厄塞克（1969—　）。

## 法语国家作家，或在法国的作家？

这些作家中的绝大多数都有一个共同点：他们表现出法
117 语文学矛盾的收缩与扩张。21世纪之交的法国失去了大量的殖民地（阿尔及利亚、印度支那、摩洛哥），但它的文化领域，即“软实力”，仍在增长，因为法国人身处最直言不讳地声称抵制美国文化影响的阵营。在过去的几十年里，人们常常将这些作家中的一些人——例如马叶、孔戴和夏穆瓦索——形容为“法语国家”作家，而其他作家——如西克苏、维勒贝克和加缪——从来没有被归为此类，尽管他们都出生在法国本土以外。谁是或什么是“法语国家”作家？是否存在“法语国家文学”？根据权威法语词典《法语宝库》的解释，这个词可以追溯到1932年，它的意思是“会说法语的人”，但在英语国家的大学里，这个词几乎只被用来指代来自非洲、加勒比和北美的作家。不可否认的是，今天法语文学的生命力很大程度上来自诸多重要作家的认可，例如塞内加尔的莱奥波尔德·塞达尔·桑戈尔、奥斯曼·塞姆贝内、谢赫·哈米杜·凯恩、比拉戈·迪奥普等；科特迪瓦的阿玛杜·库忽玛；摩洛哥的德里斯·克莱伊比和塔哈尔·本·杰伦；海地的罗杰·多尔辛维尔和勒内·德佩斯特；以及其他许多既使用法语语言又有法国殖民文化经历或文化记忆的作家。但这些作家所处的概念框架仍然存在疑问。



2007年3月16日，巴黎《世界报》发表了一份题为“为了法语的‘文学世界’”的宣言，由四十四位具有影响力的作家签署。在其中，他们宣称那一年标志着“法语国家（文学）”的终

结暨法语文学—世界的诞生。可以从很多角度来看待这样一批
杰出的“法语国家”作家是如何走到宣布文学终结的地步的，曾
经是文学让他们广为人知。可以说，“法语国家文学”的学术概 118
念——由其倡导者构想，主要是为了在法语文学研究中创造更
大的包容性——取得了如此巨大的成功，以至于超出了它的可
用性。也可以说，“法语文学”这一概念被其自身的不一致和不
连贯压垮了。最后，可以说，这个词似乎带有种族主义色彩，对
许多被如此指称的作者而言是种侮辱。正如常驻巴黎的摩洛哥
作家塔哈尔·本·杰伦所说：

> 法语国家的人被认为是外星人，从别处来的人，他被要求待在一个指定的地方，脱离“真正的”的法国作家。
>
> ——《我记忆的地下室，我房子的屋顶是法语词汇》，收入《为了文学—世界》，米歇尔·勒·布里、让·鲁奥编，巴黎：伽利玛出版社，2007，第117页。

这些不同的解释并非不相容。

总有理由将文学分门别类，包括一篇文章写就的地区、时期、作者的性别、阶级、种族、宗教、性向或政治派别；文本本身的形式或一般特征；传播或出版的方式等。在世纪之交，法语作家的一个主要的主题共识是，个人、国家和其他群体的明显稳定的身份类别不再被视为理所当然，包括法语国家——边界和归属本身并不过时，但是它们已经指数级爆炸，并于现在成为作者和叙述者的声音以及主人公无尽变化的源泉。

## 自历史而来的小说的新声

让我们考虑一下，比如，来自瓜德罗普岛的法语作家玛丽
119 斯·孔戴的一部非常成功的小说《黑人女巫蒂图芭》(1987)，其中的主人公和叙述者是一名非洲奴隶，从巴巴多斯被带到新英格兰殖民地，于1692年尝试当一名女巫。她在婴儿时期就成了孤儿，被赶出种植园，好让她死在森林里，她被一位非洲女巫医抚养长大，学习草药和通灵术。她不是奴隶，因为她是被赶走而不是被卖掉的，她看待生活的方式与非洲同胞不同，但她甘愿为爱变成奴隶。当丈夫被卖掉并从巴巴多斯被送到波士顿时，她一路跟随。蒂图芭这个人物是在真人原型的基础上创作的，孔戴从17世纪晚期马萨诸塞州的女巫审判档案中收集所有她能找到的相关资料(孔戴赋予了蒂图芭非洲血统，尽管这不是历史学家的主流观点)。但在试图为蒂图芭写一本从未写过的传记，或者更确切地说，是她从未写过或没有幸存下来的自传时，孔戴显然是为一位20世纪晚期的读者而写的，她必然会用现代的方式思考。蒂图芭用“种族主义”和“女权主义”这两个术语来描述观点和实践，第一个用来描述世界的真实面貌，第二个用来唤起孔戴认为当时的女性一定感受过的渴望。人物—叙述者蒂图芭不是单一意义上的想象出的人。蒂图芭不仅仅是孔戴想象中的历史人物的一个版本，也是一个具有想象力或远见的人物，某种程度上是逆向的玛丽斯·孔戴。作为一个聪明的女人，或者说“女巫”，蒂图芭可以看到死者并与之交流，也可以在死后与活着的人交流。



《黑人女巫蒂图芭》显然超越了“法语国家”小说的任何界限——因此，无怪乎玛丽斯·孔戴签署了2007年宣言。这是一

部用法语写成但并未展示法语语言文化的作品，而是展示了17世纪说英语的殖民地世界。蒂图芭，一个说英语的人，毫无歉意地用法语讲述自己的故事。这部作品经常提到其他文学传统，120
例如，纳撒尼尔·霍桑的《红字》(1850)中的女主人公海丝特出人意料地以一个朋友，也可能是蒂图芭的情人的身份出现。其他角色，好的和坏的，有英国人、美国殖民者、非洲奴隶或加勒比出生的非洲人和欧洲—非洲混血后裔的奴隶(比如蒂图芭自己，一个因母亲被“基督国王号”船上的英国水手强奸而出生的孩子)，以及葡萄牙犹太人。

蒂图芭的价值观和人格的一个一以贯之和非常明确的方面是，她抵制复仇的呼吁，甚至在面对反复和极端的暴力时也是如此，例如她母亲因反抗企图强奸她的种植园主而被处决(谋杀)。同样重要的是，她拒绝接受分裂为平静的“快乐奴隶”的外在自我和愤世嫉俗但“自由”的内在自我——这是她丈夫约翰·印第安采取的立场。蒂图芭含蓄地传达了这样一种观点：这种对内在“自由”的主张本身就是一种缺陷，它贬低了人的价值，阻碍了一切真正的幸福。



## 女主人公的蜕变

“女巫”是一个通常用来侮辱或威胁女性的术语，但孔戴却通过把蒂图芭塑造成一个真正的女英雄而实现了颠覆，这显然意味着读者对蒂图芭的认可。玛丽·达里厄塞克的《母猪女郎》[1996——法语书名*Truismes*玩了个关于truism(意为不言自明的道理)这个词和truie(母猪)一词的文字游戏]，其中叙述者—女主角发现自己被变成了一头母猪。达里厄塞克的创作类似于伏尔泰的《哲学辞典》以及卡夫卡的《变形记》，但是以一种独特的充满天真自嘲的声音。虽然女权主义的前提似乎相当明显（即男人看待和对待女人如同她是“母猪”——这是对女性的无数侮辱性的词汇之一，尤其是在她们的性取向方面），但
121 将这种自负展现出来是一种壮举。在一个非常现实的现代世界里，将隐喻的真理化为一个幻想场景，这在第一人称叙事中尤其困难。卡夫卡笔下的格里高尔·萨姆沙，在故事一开始就已经彻底变成了一只蟑螂，达里厄塞克笔下的无名年轻女子与之不同的是，她逐渐地变化和脱离她的小猪形态，与男性角色互动的界限也在变化和模糊。



当她变得越来越像猪时，她发现自己的性欲越来越高涨，在她做按摩师（事实上是做妓女）的“美容院”里，她新的性方面的主动性吸引了更多兽性的顾客，尽管她越来越像猪的皮肤、鼻子和鬃毛最终结束了她的家庭和职业生涯。当主人公以一种天真的方式讲述自己的经历时——事实上，甚至比老实人更不具有评判性——达里厄塞克探讨了男性对性的态度的矛盾性以及政治制度的腐败。作者巧妙地将文化背景和幽默交织在一起，当主人公爱上了一个名叫伊凡（名字似乎是故意选择的，以回忆中世纪的布列塔尼剧目）的狼人时，她甚至回顾了八个世纪前玛丽·德·弗朗斯在《狼人之诗》中聚焦的狼人传说。

## 对西方社会的批判

《母猪女郎》的圆满结尾——女主角决定当一头猪，因为“对在森林里生活而言这更实用”，她在森林里找到了伴侣，“非常漂亮，很有男子气概的”一头野猪——与八年前出版的一个无

情且悲观的轰动性丑闻形成了鲜明对比，“猪似的”这个形容词大概很适合后者：米歇尔·维勒贝克的《碎裂》（1998，在美国以《基本粒子》为书名出版）。事实上，两位主人公中的一个梦见 122
自己“外形是一头皮肤紧致、光滑的小猪”。这部作品的第三人称叙事是多调性的，包括一个学术传记，传记是有关两位主角之一的，他们是同父异母的兄弟，被分开抚养长大。其中一个，生物学家米歇尔，过着一种近乎禁欲的生活，致力于基因研究；另一个，布鲁诺，教授法语文学的中学老师，认为性是他生活的唯一理由。他们不同的人生道路给他们带来了不幸，也毁了所有接近他们的女人的生活。叙事本身设法使它所触及的一切都似乎令人厌恶：科学、宗教、食物、性、友谊。整个叙述贯穿着预言性的“科学”陈述，关于基督教信仰的终结和一个不可抗拒的唯物主义世界观的到来。米歇尔儿时的女朋友很爱他，青春期时被他断然拒绝，她被描述为绽放出毁灭她的美丽：

> 从13岁开始，受到她的卵巢分泌的黄体酮和雌二醇的影响，脂肪层在女孩的胸部和臀部形成。这些部位，在最好的情况下，会得到一个丰满、和谐、浑圆的外观。

叙述者和每一位男性主人公都有关于科学、决定论、宗教、人类学和社会价值观的长篇独白，他们的声音都提出了这样一种观点，即西方社会由于性自由和个人主义的兴起以及基督教和家庭的衰落而处于一种衰败晚期的状态——在所有这些中，1974年被认定为灾难年。就其穿插在漫长的哲学论述中的性描写（例如，布鲁诺以相当具有破坏性的方式手淫）的篇幅而言，维勒贝克的作品与萨德的很相似。另一方面，尽管这本书不停地说教，但从中可以获得什么样的要旨却十分不清楚。然而，就广泛的文化氛围而言，维勒贝克恰逢其时。《基本粒子》在“千禧年”到来之前两年出版，那时到处弥漫着不祥的预感。媒体曾警告说，计算机代码故障“千年虫”将使机场、银行，甚至家用电器
123 瘫痪。与此同时，各种起源的许多原教旨主义宗教运动正在各自的势力范围内，正为基督教和伊斯兰教右翼的候选人选举积极积蓄能量。

## 以及对东方的批判

维勒贝克持续的痛苦，暗含着对社会价值观的权威性重新组合的诉求，希望以此消除个人选择和集体异化，与之形成对比的是，与此同时，阿梅丽·诺冬（1967—　）出版了一部小说，欢乐地颂扬了家长式制度的背景下欧洲的个人主义和自我责任感，而《基本粒子》有时似乎是称颂家长制度的。在《诚惶诚恐》（1999）中，她以第一人称讲述了阿梅丽的故事，她是出生在日本的比利时人，精通日语，为一家日本大公司工作。阿梅丽小说的意境与杜拉斯在《广岛之恋》中的阴暗的、有棱角的、令人不快的精神完全不同，但它与这部电影剧本有着共同之处，都描绘了在个人以及他们对彼此的情欲（我们想起杜拉斯的文本中的一句话：“你害了我。你对我真好。”）方面，不同文明之间的关系。在诺冬的小说中，阿梅丽痴迷于监督她的日本女人的美貌，后者分配给她越来越贬损人格的任务，直至比利时女主人公除了打扫御本公司总部四十四层的男女厕所外，别无他职。阿梅丽对自己作为翻译和商务策划师的才华被完全滥用而感到讽刺的快

乐，其中对主管森吹雪的个人的情欲爱慕，与范围更广的文化魅力——西方文化对神秘东方的迷恋——是分不开的。因此，描写性段落既揭示了叙述者的教育和欲望，也揭示了它们的对象，在这部作品中，寓意的转向通过致敬帕斯卡尔《思想录》中最著名的段落之一[①]来表达： 124

> 在我面前两米，她脸上的景象令人着迷。她眼睑低垂着看数字，这使她看不到我在研究她。她有世界上最美丽的鼻子，日本鼻子，这只无与伦比的鼻子，有着精致的鼻孔，千里挑一。不是所有日本人都有这种鼻子，但有这种鼻子的一定是日本人。如果克利奥巴特拉有这样的鼻子，这个星球的格局将会彻底改变。

## 挥之不去的主题：第二次世界大战

“法语国家”的局限性以及可接受的主角的边界在《复仇女神》（2006）中遭到激烈的挑战，这部作品不仅荣获著名的龚古尔奖，而且还赢得了法兰西学院小说类大奖。作者是乔纳森·利特尔，1967年出生于纽约，小说出版时是美国公民（他后来也获得了法国国籍，尽管他并未定居法国）。一个美国人赢得这些奖项的怪现象本身无疑会引起争议，但对于一个有犹太血统的作家来说，以纳粹党卫军军官的视角写一部小说，而军官本人也曾参与杀害犹太人，这被许多人认为是相当骇人听闻的，特

① 指《思想录》中对克利奥巴特拉鼻子的描写：“克利奥巴特拉的鼻子：如果那只鼻子再短一些，世界的整个面貌都有可能改观。”《思想录》，钱培鑫译，译林出版社，2012年8月。——译注

别是因为与更狂热的刽子手相比，作者做了一些努力使叙述者“具有同情心”。主人公马克西米利恩·奥伊在讲述他如何写回忆录时，不经意地提到长期以来饭后呕吐的倾向，并说他更喜欢工作而非休闲，因为工作让他不去想战争（也许利特尔在法国中学时对帕斯卡尔的学习使得《思想录》里的评论在此产生回响，即保持忙碌以不去想重要的事情[1]）。奥伊经营着一家蕾丝厂，已婚，是一对双胞胎的父亲，他的目标是做外表体面的中产，以此掩
125 饰他的同性恋性向，并且使他来自战争的耻辱感消失。

利特尔的小说在形式上非常传统，尤其是与几十年前的新小说实验相比。似乎近些年法语小说主要的创作努力之一是构思不同寻常的主人公，他们的第一人称叙述延伸至不同的身份界限，强调民族、性别以及种族身份。

法语“文学世界”运动没有比法国作家让-马里·古斯塔夫·勒·克莱齐奥更好的代表了，他的小说《饥饿间奏曲》在2008年10月出版，此前他刚成为最新获得诺贝尔文学奖的法语语言作家。瑞典文学院甄选委员会的一名成员的颁奖词以下面这个问题开头：

> 人物对文学作品有什么作用？罗兰·巴特坚持认为所有文学惯例中最过时的是专有名词——彼得、保罗和安娜，他们从未存在过，但当我们阅读小说时，我们被期待认真对待他们并感同身受。

① “一个人无论怎样幸福，但假如没有某种阻碍无聊蔓延开来的热情或娱乐让他消遣或忙碌，他马上就会忧伤和可悲的。”摘自《思想录》，钱培鑫译，译林出版社，2012年8月。——译注

勒·克莱齐奥在这种观点盛行时开始了他的写作生涯，然而从第一部小说《诉讼笔录》（1963）开始，他就通过主人公的眼睛展示世界，他的主人公，例如《诉讼笔录》中的亚当·波洛，往往是他们敏锐观察的世界的局外人。勒·克莱齐奥的叙述涉及很多地方：《沙漠》（1980）和《奥尼查》（1991）中的非洲，《寻金者》（1985）和《检疫》（1995）中的毛里求斯（他祖先的故乡），《流浪的星星》（1996）中的巴勒斯坦，《乌拉尼亚》（2006）中的拉丁美洲。他展现了从他众多人物的角度来想象世界的极大能力，但勒·克莱齐奥顺应了过去几十年的法国小说潮流，从高度实验性的、往往难以追循的叙事转向了更直截了当的故事。 126

在《审讯》中，主角，有时也是叙述者，是疯子，而《饥饿间奏曲》跟随艾黛尔，一个相当普通的主人公，从1931年她十岁时，直到第二次世界大战结束。但在这两部相隔四十五年的小说中，人物都与海外世界有着千丝万缕的联系。亚当·波洛似乎刚从阿尔及利亚革命期间的法国军队服役归来，而艾黛尔的父母来自毛里求斯，她的故事以她最喜爱的记忆为开端：1931年她与亲爱的叔祖父参观了殖民地博览会。正如诺贝尔奖颁奖词所说，勒·克莱齐奥的作品“属于文明批判的传统，在法国本土可以追溯到夏多布里昂、贝尔纳丹·德·圣皮埃尔、狄德罗和[……]蒙田”。在这个方面，勒·克莱齐奥高度代表了他自己的时代，一个关于民族和语言认同的后殖民批评和辩论的时代。因此，他的作品无论就其起源还是就其持续变化而言，都是很好的法语文学入口。

## 无休止的邂逅

正如我们已经看到的，法语文学传统既将文本植根于其最初的历史时刻，又允许它们穿越几个世纪的时间相遇。文本，换句话说，有点像克劳德·莫奈著名的系列画作《睡莲》（1906—1927）中的睡莲。睡莲各自扎根在池塘底部的土壤中，但它们的茎向上漂浮，这样叶子和花朵就会在水面上移动接触。正如勒·克莱齐奥的作品穿越几百年的时间遇见贝尔纳丹和蒙田的作品，达里厄塞克对动物性和人性之间交替界限的描述也与玛丽·德·弗朗西的《短歌集》产生互动，而普鲁斯特的小说则经常提到17世纪的作家。维勒贝克作品的道德主义传统与帕斯卡尔和拉布吕耶尔的有相似之处，伊夫·博纳富瓦将波德莱尔的
127 回声融入他的诗歌中。这样的邂逅肯定会继续下去，而且多亏了图书贸易的往来，魁北克的读者很容易买到塞内加尔或阿尔及利亚作家的书，以前相隔甚远的作家今后一定会吃惊地发现彼此近在咫尺。法国在互联网文化资源开发方面也一直走在前列。法国国家图书馆在网上提供数以万计的书籍，而电台，如法国文化和法国国际广播电台，则提供文学文本阅读和文学讨论的下载服务。

与法语文学文化的日益增长的传播同样重要的是普及这样的观念，即至少在西方国家中，对英语世界而言，只有法语知识文化是最重要的替代品。对一些人来说，"备选"的概念很容易滑向"反对"的概念，从而意味着敌意和斗争。对其他许多人，包括这本书的读者来说，法语文学传统提供了一个受欢迎的看待世界的新视角，无论过去还是未来的世界。在一个受到相同
128 威胁的世界里，我们从来没有像现在这样需要法语的**差异**。

# 索　引

（条目后的数字为原文页码，见本书边码）

## A



## B



## C

## D

## E



## F



## G



## H

## I



## J



## K



## L



## M

## N



## P

## R



## S

## T



## U



## V



## W

John D. Lyons

# FRENCH LITERATURE

## A Very Short Introduction

OXFORD
UNIVERSITY PRESS

# Contents

# List of illustrations

# Introduction: meeting French literature

The heritage of literature in the French language is rich, varied, extensive in time and space, and appealing both to its immediate public, readers of French, and also to a global audience reached through translations and film adaptations. The first great works of this repertory were written in the 11th century in northern France, and now, at the beginning of the 21st century, French literatures include authors writing in many parts of the world, ranging from the Caribbean to Western Africa, whose works are available in bookshops and libraries in France and in other French-speaking countries. For many centuries, French was also a language of aristocratic and intellectual elites throughout Europe.

## What is 'French literature'?

Both 'French' and 'literature' are problematic terms. What are the boundaries of 'French'? Historically, the effective domination of the 'French' language among the population living within the boundaries of today's 'France' was realized only at the end of the 19th century, when universal schooling brought the language of Paris and the elites to the speakers of such tongues as Breton (*Brezhoneg*) spoken on the Brittany peninsula, Basque (*Euskara*) on the southwest coast, varieties of Occitanian (*Lenga d'òc*) such as Gascon and Provençal in the south, and Alsatian

(*Elsässerditsch*) in the northeast. Moreover, there are many important authors who have written and now write in French who do not live within the borders of the European territory known as 'France', though in many cases they are citizens of France (the residents of Martinique, Guadeloupe, New Caledonia, and so forth) or of former colonies of France such as Quebec and Senegal. Some authors whose first language is not French have chosen to write a significant portion of their work in French, for instance Samuel Beckett. Other authors, born in France and French citizens, have chosen not to write in 'French': Frédéric Mistral, like Beckett a winner of the Nobel Prize in Literature, wrote in Provençal. As for 'literature', the current use of the term dates from the 19th century, when what had long been called 'poetry' or *belles lettres* was amalgamated with other writings such as memoirs and essays as the basis for literary studies in universities. It is a bit flippant, but useful, to think of literature as what we read when we do not have to – what we read without immediate, circumstantial purpose.



## The protagonist as starting point

To get one's bearings in French literature means, in part, to have some idea of the major texts of the evolving tradition and a sense of how they relate and respond to one another. Coming into that tradition can be, at first, disorienting. Fortunately, perhaps, the situation of having to relate to an unfamiliar society and of having to determine one's own place while observing other people is a central topic of some of the principal texts of the French tradition. Whether by their choice or by circumstance, the protagonists of many French texts find themselves in situations of opposition to, or isolation from, most other members of their society. This is often a literary device for authors to make critical, polemical, or didactic points (and French literature can be called justly a literature of ideas), but it may also be a source of emotional turmoil that offers the reader an *experience* of empathy, rather than a purely intellectual insight.

It makes sense to look at literary works in terms of their central characters, or protagonists, since throughout history, epics, tragedies, short stories, and poems have very often taken the name of the protagonist as their title, whether it be *Beowulf* or *Hamlet* in English, or, in French, *Lancelot, Gargantua, The Misanthrope, Chatterton, Consuelo, Madame Bovary*, 'Le Mauvais vitrier' (The Bad Glazier), *Cyrano de Bergerac, Nadja, The Story of O*. But even in works that do not feature the central character's name in the title, the focus on his or her characteristics, thoughts, and actions makes the protagonist an obvious place to start an exploration of the literature. And it should be noted that the term 'protagonist' also applies to works, like many poems and autobiographical texts, in which the main figure is some version of the author ('some version' in the sense that we often assume a creative reworking of the first-person speaker, as when Ronsard embellishes or mythifies 'Ronsard' in his love poetry, or when Rousseau writes of himself in his *Confessions*). And since most works that make up the literary tradition have central characters, their study offers a convenient way to compare works to one another, within a single period or from one epoch to another.

Protagonists necessarily have problems. If they did not, there would be no story, no quest, no obstacle to overcome, no mysteries to solve, no desire to satisfy, no enemy to defeat. In the French literary tradition, moreover, the central figures often have problems of such a unique type as to warrant being called 'problematic heroes' – heroes and heroines whose very status and place in society is at stake – or even 'anti-heroes' (defined by the OED as chief characters who are 'totally unlike a conventional hero'). What kind of person is chosen as focal point of the plot and that person's relation to her or his society can tell us a good deal about a literary text and its time, whether that character is portrayed as very good within prevailing social norms or very unusual in an undesirable way. For instance, Rousseau's character 'Émile' in *Émile, or, On Education* (1762) is neither the most complex nor most believable character of the time, but he presented a revolutionary model of human nature and of the consequences for childrearing.

In the pages that follow, we will meet a number of protagonists who were often controversial at the time when their stories were first told or published, but who now are central to the French literary tradition and to our vision of the epochs from which they come. We will also see, for the sake of comparison, some of the other figures against whom they define themselves by their difference. In each of the following chapters, which largely correspond to conventional historical periods of French literature, three or four representative texts will be taken up in some detail, while others will be mentioned for brief comparison and suggested for future reading.

# Chapter 1

# Saints, werewolves, knights, and a *poète maudit*: allegiance and character in the Middle Ages

The protagonists of medieval texts tell us about the worldview of the period that chose to focus on them. When a literature arose in the vernacular, Old French, as distinct from Latin, in the 11th century, the territory we call France had different boundaries and nothing like the national identity or organization we know today. We would describe it as highly decentralized geographically and politically (the concept of 'de-centralization' is itself our way of projecting backwards the presumption that France should have a 'centre') and personalized in its social organization. In the feudal system, power, identity, land ownership or use, and even the sense of the passage of time from one epoch to another, depended on the person in power in a given place at a given time. Allegiances shifted, power and wealth within the leading families varied from generation to generation depending on the skill and luck of individuals. Threaded throughout this society was an international institutional framework, the Church, that provided a kind of meta-identity delineating the southern and eastern boundaries of Europe. In this context, it is not surprising that the protagonists of literary works, almost invariably in verse form, should be represented primarily in terms of their loyalty, the principal value of a feudal society.

## Lives of saints

The text that is usually identified as the very first substantial work of French literature concerns its hero's decision about the lord to whom he will be loyal. *The Life of Saint Alexis* (c. 1050) is the story of the only son of a wealthy nobleman in 5th-century Rome, who was married in his adolescence and fled on the night of his marriage, telling his bride that 'In this life there is no perfect love' (*En icest siecle nen at parfite amour*). He travelled across the sea to Syria, where he lived for seventeen years in anonymous, ascetic spirituality. But because he began to be honoured, he fled from where he was living, and setting sail, he was involuntarily carried back to Rome. He returned, unrecognizable, to live for seventeen more years as a holy beggar under the staircase in his father's house. His identity was discovered only at his death, from an account of his life that he wrote on his deathbed, but *The Life of Saint Alexis* that we read must be significantly different from Alexis's own account, which was written from his point of view. The narrative *Life* continues after this death to include the lamentations of his mother, father, and virgin widow and points towards the complexity of the project of holy heroism, saintliness, itself. His mother cries out, speaking to her dead son, 'Oh son, how you hated me!' (*E filz… cum m'ous enhadithe !*). There remains an ambiguity about whether she supposes that Alexis resented her for not recognizing him upon his return from abroad – he did not: the narrative of the *Life* makes it clear to the reader, but not to the family, that Alexis was determined not to be recognized during his life – or whether she supposes that this hatred drove him to his initial departure and animated his whole withdrawal from his family.

The poem makes it clear, in any event, that this type of heroism exacts a cost. The emotional cost is greater for those who love the saint than for the saint himself, since he, after all, has chosen his priorities. Yet while the family suffers, the community as a whole is shown to benefit from the presence of a saint, whose soul has gone directly to live with God in heaven: 'The soul separated from the body of Saint Alexis; / it went straight to paradise' (*Deseivret l'aneme del cors sainz Alexis; / Tut dreitement en vait en paradis*). The people of Rome, the Emperor, and the Pope all celebrate that they have the body of a saint, who will henceforth serve as their advocate with God. *The Life of Saint Alexis*, like many texts from other periods, is open to varying interpretations, to varying arguments for and against the values represented by the hero. Yet this does not imply that the writer of the *Life* was himself ambivalent. It appears clear that for the writer, and for most 11th-century readers, Alexis represented a triumph of Christian, transcendent values. Family ambition and sexual love are less important than large social units, such as the Church, the city, and the empire. On the other hand, this edifying reading does not prevent us from seeing similar conflicts of values in later works in which protagonists sacrifice their families, like the hero of Corneille's *Horace* (1640) or the heroine of Flaubert's *Madame Bovary* (1856), for what appears to them a higher calling.



## Werewolf – a nameless hero from Celtic sources

Werewolves, like saints, make difficult bedfellows, and yet loyalty to a werewolf is the crux of a story (perhaps meant to be sung) that appeared in a collection of verse narratives a little over a century after the *Life of Saint Alexis*. The *Lais* of Marie de France (c. 1160–80) draw on two literary traditions from within what is today France: the troubadour poetry of Provence and the Celtic oral narratives of Brittany. They were probably composed at the English royal court for a French-speaking Norman audience. Many of the *Lais* concern unhappily married women (discussions about love were pursued with great sophistication in the milieu of Eleanor of Aquitaine, who had been successively Queen of

France and of England), but one of them stands out both for the peculiarity of its title character, Bisclavret, and for showing sympathy to a husband married to a disloyal wife.

Marie points specifically to the Celtic origin of the story of Bisclavret while recognizing that her audience is French: 'I do not want to forget Bisclavret: / Bisclavret is his name in Breton / But the Normans call him Werewolf' (*Ne voil ublïer Bisclavret / Bisclavret ad nun en bretan, / Garwaf l'apelent li Norman*). The hero – simply known as 'a lord' (*un ber*), he is thus really nameless – is just like other people except for a need to shed his human identity several days each week. This metamorphosis no doubt represents the fondness of Celtic literature for magic and for permeable boundaries between humans and other living or imagined creatures. But it has often been noted that Marie minimized the supernatural elements in traditional stories that she retold, and in the case of *Bisclavret*, the hero's transformation into non-human form may simply be a way of representing ordinary outbursts of violence or times when one is not 'oneself'. Simply put, the husband's eccentricity consists of taking off his clothes and running around naked in the woods. The narrator tells us at the outset that 'in the old days, many men used to become werewolves', so that this characteristic is not in itself presented as being evil or necessarily alarming. The real problem, one that appears as a theme in texts of many other periods (such as Jean de La Fontaine's 'The Loves of Psyche and Cupid', *Les Amours de Psyché et de Cupidon*, 1669) is the absence of trust in the person one loves. He never showed her anything but gentleness, and he trusted her enough to reveal the deep secret that he is a werewolf. Yet the husband gets in return only fear and disgust. His wife steals the clothes that he needs to return to his human form, so that he is trapped in that of the animal, until the happy ending of the *lai* when justice is done. Tellingly, the husband's behaviour while in canine form, exhibiting great loyalty to the prince, is the value that assures his triumph and return to human identity.

### *Langue d'Oïl* and *Langue d'Oc*

The Old French language appeared in writing in 842 in the 'Strasbourg Oaths'. What we call Old French was the language of the north of what is now France and is sometimes called the *Langue d'Oïl* – that is, the 'language of *oui*', after the word for 'yes' – to distinguish it from the language spoken and written in the south (*Langue d'Oc*, or Occitanian, of which Provençal is the best-known dialect), where 'yes' was said as *oc*. Provençal was the language of the troubadours (*trobador* in Provençal: poets who recited or sang their own compositions) and of the *trobairitz* (women troubadours). Old French differs much from Modern French, which has remained largely consistent in written form since the 17th century. Today many French readers rely on the increasing numbers of bilingual editions of medieval poetry which present the Old French original and a Modern French translation side by side.



## Epic: the *chanson de geste*

Although the gentleman wolf of *Bisclavret* was a knight, the *lai* does not concentrate on what he did while in human form. Yet the conduct of the knight is the core of the characterization of protagonists in two other major genres of the period, the *chanson de geste* and the *roman*. In a highly personalized system such as feudalism, the protagonist's usefulness as well as loyalty was repeatedly scrutinized. Heroes sought occasions to demonstrate their cleverness and valour. In the *chanson de geste*, of which the earliest and greatest is the anonymous 12th-century *Song of Roland* (*La chanson de Roland*), military prowess and loyalty to the sovereign come to the fore. In the contemporaneous *roman* (or romance), the knight is challenged to find an equilibrium between military glory and success in a relationship with a beloved woman, as we see in Chrétien de Troyes's *Erec and Enide* (*Erec et Enide*, about 1170).

The *Song of Roland*, like the approximately 120 other surviving *chansons de geste* – literally, 'songs about the things done' from the Latin *res gestae* – concerns events during the reign of Charlemagne (King of the Franks from 768 to 814, and crowned Emperor in 800), but it was composed three hundred years after the events concerned. The *Song of Roland* recounts a battle that occurred as the Frankish army withdrew from northern Spain leaving a rearguard commanded by the hero, Roland, who is described as Charlemagne's nephew. The details, including this kinship, vary markedly from current historical representations of this rather minor battle in the Pyrenees against what are described as 'pagan' and polytheistic Saracens (in the historical encounter

**1. The Emperor Charlemagne finds Roland's corpse after the battle of Roncevaux, from *Les Grandes Chroniques de France*, c. 1460**

that was the basis for the *Song of Roland*, the adversaries were, in all probability, not Muslim).

All is magnified in *Roland*, through huge numbers, intensely gory description of combat and injuries, repetition of incidents and formulaic descriptive phrases. In an exclusively male society, the characters demonstrate their valour in fights that dismember and kill a large number of combatants at the battle at Roncevaux, but the core dilemma for the hero is actually a moral one: whether or not to send an alarm to the main body of the army, the only reasonable course in view of the disproportion of the opposed troops (twenty to one). Yet Roland refuses to call to Charlemagne for help by sounding his horn, the Olifant, as his companion Olivier urges. Roland replies, 'God forbid that my kinsmen through me be blamed / Nor that sweet France fall into dishonour' (*Ne placet Damnedeu / Que mi parent pur mei seient blasmét / Ne France dulce ja chëet en viltét*).

This heroic, almost superhuman, unreasonableness is what elevates Roland as a subject to be celebrated in song and worthy, within the epic itself, to be the object of vast mourning on the part of the Emperor and his army. And yet this pride is also a terrible flaw that leads to the death of the twenty thousand members of his detachment. The paradoxical nature of this dilemma is emphasized by Olivier's change of attitude in the course of the battle. Having at first urged Roland to sound the Olifant when there was still the possibility of assistance, by the time Roland realizes that defeat is imminent, Olivier veers to the opposite position and argues that he should not call for Charlemagne but recognize his own culpability: 'The French have died because of your irresponsibility' (*Franceis sunt morz par vostre legerie*). Through the character of Roland, the anonymous writer presents the burden of delegated authority in a feudal system, where physical strength, skill, and courage are important, but where the requirements of loyalty and individual and collective honour create contradictory demands.

## Romance

The protagonists of the romances have other problems and quite different virtues – or, rather, loyalty and honour are tested in different ways in a world in which the knight's relation to a woman is at least as important as his relation to his lord and his companions in arms. Originally, *roman* was simply a way of designating the Old French vernacular language as opposed to Latin, but by the late 12th century, it designated a type of story, in which an individual hero, through a quest, grows in virtue and self-understanding, and in which the love of a woman plays a large role. Indeed, the status of women in the romance tradition, where they are portrayed with respect and accorded great deference, is one of its striking innovations with respect to most classical models. The romances are traditionally divided into three groups by subject matter: 'The matter of Rome' (from antiquity, though more often concerning Greek legend and history), 'The matter of Britain' (from Celtic and English sources), and 'The matter of France' (about Charlemagne and his knights).

*Erec and Enide* is one of the five surviving romances by Chrétien de Troyes, whose name indicates his connection to the city of Troyes, site of the court of the counts of Champagne. While Chrétien was at that court, it was essentially ruled by the regent Marie de Champagne, daughter of Eleanor of Aquitaine. Like his four other romances – *Yvain, the Knight of the Lion*; *Lancelot, the Knight of the Cart*; *Cligès*; and *Perceval, or the Story of the Grail* – *Erec and Enide* belongs to the Celtic repertory of tales of the court of King Arthur, materials that had been translated into Latin and French from Breton. Erec, a young knight at the court, is escorting Queen Guinevere and her maidservant in the woods during a hunt when they come upon an unknown knight accompanied by a lady and a dwarf. The dwarf strikes Guinevere's maid with a whip and subsequently also wounds Erec on the face and neck. Erec is obliged to remedy this insult to the Queen, but he is not armed for battle. There is an odd echo of Roland's situation in

Erec's, since the two women and he are behind and out of touch of the company of hunters with the King. In fact, they are so far behind that they cannot hear the hunting horns, but unlike Roland, Erec resigns himself to deferring revenge until he is better armed, because rash courage is not real nobility (*Folie n'est pas vasalages*).

Subsequently tracking down the knight with the dwarf and defeating him, Erec falls in love with Enide, the daughter of an impoverished nobleman who loaned the hero the necessary arms and armour. Erec, blissfully married to Enide and living at Arthur's court, would seem to have everything and to be at the end of his story, but this is only the first third of the romance, and now the real challenge arises. Overcome by amorous pleasure with his wife, Erec begins losing his reputation as intrepid warrior. It falls to Enide to give him the bad news, 'Your reputation is diminished' (*Vostre pris en est abaisiez*). In a certain sense, Enide has lost her husband through his surrender to her. She had married a respected knight and finds herself with a besotted lover. Erec's solution is to set out, with Enide, looking for challenges in order to prove himself once again. The series of dangerous encounters that follows looks in many respects like the sort of initiatory ordeal through which a young man would pass in order to reach adulthood and marriage, but in this case Erec is accompanied by his wife, on whom he has imposed the requirement that she not speak. It seems like a regression on Erec's part: he wants to have adventures as if he were still alone and not part of a couple. However, at the crucial moment in each of Erec's dangerous encounters, Enide violates the condition of silence to give her husband important information or advice. Thus Erec and Enide prove that they can function as a couple and reconcile erotic love and knightly valour. Their last adventure leads them to encounter a couple that has failed to find this balance and have ended up cut off from the society around them, failing both in love and in service to the outside world.

## The lyric 'I'

In the texts about Alexis, Roland, and Erec and Enide, there is no doubt who is the protagonist, even though there is another figure in the text, the 'I' who tells the story. The writer, or the writer's self-representation as narrator, appears very early in French literature. Marie de France frequently reminds her audience that she has composed the story of *Bisclavret* and the stories of the protagonists of her other *Lais*, as in the opening verse of 'The Nightingale' (*Laüstic*): 'I will tell you of an adventure' (*Une aventure vus dirai*). But this use of the first person puts the poet in the position of presenting someone else's story.

Later in the Middle Ages, the poet moves to the central position as protagonist and tells her own story or his own story. In a certain sense, we could say that the poet, the person who tells the story and says 'I', is at the centre of one of the most important texts of medieval Europe, the *Romance of the Rose* (*Roman de la Rose*), a long verse narrative written in two parts: the first by Jean de Lorris towards 1230 and the much longer second part by Jean de Meung towards 1275. But in the *Rose*, the poet as concrete individual quickly explodes into his thoughts and the various psychic forces that either drive him towards the woman he loves (the 'rose') or hinder his pursuit. These forces become allegorical characters – Idleness, Love, Fear, Shame, Nature, Reason, and so forth – whose speeches and acts fill the romance, as they do the thoughts of the lover, in the literary tradition of the *psychomachia*, or 'battle in the soul', so that the writer does not appear in his everyday, concrete existence but as a kind of everyman experiencing the suffering and perplexities of love.

At the time the *Rose* was being written, the poet Rutebeuf (c. 1245–85) offered a much more concrete poetic persona when he made himself and his everyday misfortunes the subject in such narratives as 'Rutebeuf's Lament about his Eye' (*Ci Encoumence la plainte Rutebeuf de son œul*). Willing to write about the non-heroic events of his own life (such as his own unfortunate marriage – 'I recently took a wife / A woman neither charming nor beautiful'), he also creates a poetic voice that tells of the concrete happenings of his time in a world that was falling into decay. Rutebeuf had two major successors, poets who, like him, made themselves and the events of their lifetime the focus of their work. The first is Christine de Pizan (c. 1364–c. 1434) and the second François Villon (c. 1431–63). Christine de Pizan, born in Venice, came to Paris as an infant when her father became advisor to King Charles V. Much of her work takes an autobiographical form, such as 'Christine's Vision' (*L'Advision Christine*, 1405) and particularly 'The Mutation of Fortune' (*Le livre de la mutacion de Fortune*, 1403). For Christine (the use of the first or given name for this author, and many other woman writers of the early period such as Marguerite de Navarre, in preference to the surname, is a feature of the literary-critical tradition), the use of the first person singular, the 'I', in writing is itself an important gesture, or rather a construct, the creation of an authoritative voice for a woman. This is vividly conveyed in a passage of 'The Mutation of Fortune', in which Christine, become a widow, is symbolically transformed into a man, her voice deepening so that she can pursue the career of a professional writer.



François Villon, though his life was brief and his writings few, has commanded a place of choice in French letters since the 15th century, reprinted continuously since the Renaissance, when he was popularized by the poet Clément Marot (1496–1544), who recognized in Villon a precursor both in lyricism and misfortune. Villon is the quintessential *poète maudit* ('the accursed poet', or poet with endless bad luck). His mythic life, very much embellished, has been the subject of a half-dozen films, and his poems have often been put to music – in 1953, Georges Brassens recorded a musical setting of Villon's 'Ballad of Ladies of Olden Days' (*Ballade des dames du temps jadis*). A student, poet, thief, and convicted murderer, Villon may be called the first of a long series of criminal protagonists (whom we see later in the

In the poem known as the '*Balade des pendus*', Villon takes his typically elegiac stance. Here is the first stanza.

Frères humains qui après nous vivez

N'ayez les cuers contre nous endurciz,

Car, se pitié de nous pauvres avez,

Dieu en aura plus tost de vous merciz.

Vous nous voyez cy attachez cinq, six:

Quant de la chair, que trop avons nourrie,

Elle est pieça devoree et pourrie,

Et nous les os, devenons cendre et pouldre.

De nostre mal personne ne s'en rie:

Mais priez Dieu que tous nous veuille absouldre!

[Brother humans who live after us / Do not harden your hearts against us, / For if you take pity on us wretches, / God will more quickly have mercy on you. / You see us here, strung up, five or six / As for the flesh, which we have too much fattened / It is long ago devoured and rotted, / And we the bones are becoming ash and dust. / At our misfortune let no one laugh: / But pray to God that He forgive us all!]

picaresque novel). Although many, if not most, French poets have been middle or upper class, there is a persistent attraction in the lyric tradition to the marginal (perhaps precisely to compensate for the rigid social stratification of society).

Villon sets the pattern for much subsequent French poetry in which the passing of time and the coming of death are the overwhelming themes, linked to concrete details of life in Paris.

The main character, the poet, defines himself as a creature whose ephemeral existence is measured by the fragility of the world around him, as in 'The Ballad of Ladies', which gave the world the ubiquitous refrain, 'Where are the snows of yesteryear?' (*Mais ou sont les neiges d'antan?*). Despite the anti-heroic nature of Villon's self-description as literate singer living on the fringes of society (a persona very welcome to such 19th-century successors as Nerval and Baudelaire), there is much in this description that parallels the life of a saint, for the saint also lives in the constant presence of death, in abjection, and in disillusion.

# Chapter 2
# The last Roman, 'cannibals', giants, and heroines of modern life: antiquity and renewal

The Renaissance, renewing contact with antiquity, challenged French cultural identity and the identity of each individual in France. For France and Frenchness, the cultural vitality of Italy was a source of emulation and of anxiety. The odd reversal that constituted Renaissance culture meant that the recent achievement of French writers, painters, architects, and musicians was increasingly seen as out of date, while the much older literary, philosophical, and artistic legacy of Greece and Rome, being rediscovered, had an aura of freshness. In Italy, this shift had occurred much earlier, beginning in the mid-15th century with the fall of Constantinople and the influx of Greek scholars and manuscripts to the peninsula.

The French had been at war in Italy since 1494. These campaigns, continuing under François I, King of France (ruled 1515–47), intensified the importation of cultural influences from Italy. We can say that François quite literally brought Italian Renaissance culture to France when he invited Leonardo da Vinci to reside at his chateau of Amboise in the Loire valley, where the artist and polymath died in 1519. Leonardo was followed by such other Italian artists as Cellini, Primaticcio, and Serlio. The Italian influence in France was intensified by the 1531 marriage of François's son, the future Henri II, to Caterina de' Medici, who brought with her a large entourage from Florence. François also established the *Collège des lecteurs royaux* (now called the Collège de France) as an alternative to the medieval Sorbonne and appointed, often from abroad, the most distinguished scholars of Greek, Hebrew, and classical Latin to provide the means for French people to have direct textual contact with the ancient world. Towards the end of the 15th century, printing arrived in France from Germany, and the rapid spread of printing shops made books, including the Bible, available to a growing public of readers.

Two major issues of identity soon arose. The first was the nature of the French language and French culture themselves – could French rival the languages of antiquity and contemporary Italian as a vehicle of poetic and intellectual expression? And the second was the volatile matter of religion. Evangelical movements, urging direct knowledge of the Biblical text, offered the responsibility or the burden of choice to individual consciences. Jacques Lefèvre d'Étaples published the first French translation of the Bible in 1529.



## A French Boccaccio

Close to François I, there was a heady sense of opportunity and renewal. His sister, Marguerite de Navarre, encouraged and patronized the evangelical movement. She also wrote (or collaborated in the writing of) one of the most fascinating collections of short stories in the French tradition, *L'Heptaméron* (first printed in 1558, nine years after her death). The title is not the author's but was given to the collection because it has seventy stories; Marguerite de Navarre seems to have intended the finished book to have one hundred. Each of the stories centres on a person, often a woman, said to have been a contemporary of Marguerite herself. There are kings, queens, duchesses, and knights, but also mule-keepers, monks, ferry-tenders, nuns, and notaries. Rapes, murders, imprisonment, and adulterous liaisons are common, but so are scatological jokes. Often the villains are members of Catholic religious orders or servants of the King, and the characters who are cast in a good light are, frequently (it is difficult to generalize about this apparently simple but deeply complex book), those who follow their conscience and struggle against institutional abuses. Although the term 'realism' was not used to describe literature until several centuries later, the prologue to Marguerite's book makes a claim to accurate representation of the contemporary world.

Marguerite relates this claim directly and forcefully to France's attempt to define its national culture in the wake of Italian Renaissance influence. The prologue establishes a frame-narrative for the tales that follow: a group of five ladies and five gentlemen agree to tell stories that they know from personal experience to be true. In this way, the book asserts simultaneously a form of literary 'nationalism' in that it acknowledges Boccaccio's *Decameron* as its model but declares that in this, French, collection, the stories will all be true and will not be altered by rhetoric. Whether this rule is strictly followed is a matter of debate, but its statement, and other subsequent details of timing and localization in the stories, show an attempt to create a domestic literary model of realism that is closely connected with a critical attention to themes of confession, truth-telling, and willingness to assert individual righteousness against traditional Church, familial, and other social structures. In short, Marguerite's work, though it includes stories that are reminiscent of earlier storytelling traditions (the medieval *fabliaux*), emphasizes a new sense of the nation as literary milieu while it also grounds the 'truth' in the consciousness of individuals. While kings remain kings and innkeepers remain innkeepers, all of the characters of the *Heptaméron* have an equal claim to our attention.

## A new genre: the essay

The central character of Michel de Montaigne's writing is himself, and this first-person character, this *moi*, appears in greater detail than what we found in Rutebeuf, Christine de Pizan, or Villon. The *Essais* (literally, 'attempts') cover everything from digestion, sexual dysfunction, and fantasy to man's place in the universe, the existence of God, friendship, and eloquence. Coming a generation later than Marguerite de Navarre (1492–1549), Michel de Montaigne experienced the fervour of the newly established humanism (that is, the study of ancient letters) from his very infancy. His father had been a soldier in the French armies in Italy, and apparently brought back great enthusiasm for an uncorrupted classical Latin (as opposed to the Church Latin of the medieval French universities). Montaigne may very well be the last person whose first spoken language was Latin. He gives an account of this seemingly impossible situation in his chapter 'On the Education of Children', where he explains that his father hired a scholar of classical Latin not only to speak Latin to the baby but to provide all family members and servants with enough Latin to interact with the child from day to day. Montaigne knew the language of Cicero before learning that of Chrétien de Troyes. Montaigne was, then, in a sense, the last Roman and an emblematic figure of the French Renaissance, holding together in one person an active social, economic, and civic life (he was mayor of Bordeaux and a *politique* – a political moderate – during the wars of religion) and both an intellectual and imaginative commitment to the texts of Greek and Latin antiquity. In 'Of Vanity', Montaigne recalls that he was familiar with accounts of the Roman capital before he saw the Louvre and that he knew about Lucullus, Metellus, and Scipio before he knew anything about famous Frenchmen. His attachment to the language of Rome was so deep that when, as an adult, years after he had ceased speaking the language of his infancy, he saw his father fall, the first spontaneous expressions of alarm that came to his lips were in Latin. And to complete this life-long identification with Rome, in March 1581 he received the title of 'citizen of Rome' in the form of a *bulla* (certificate with seal), or, as he wrote in French in 'Of Vanity', a *bulle*, which means both 'bull' in the sense of certificate but also 'bubble' – the quintessential representation of vanity itself.

Montaigne's detailed self-description in his *Essays* (1580, with multiple revisions in the 1582 and especially the 1588 and posthumous 1595 edition) had an immediate international resonance. Not only did Montaigne give the world a new genre, the 'essay' (his book was translated into English in 1603 by John Florio as *The essays or Morall, politike and militarie discourses*), but he helped set in motion two trends that became hugely important in the following century: the introspective study of the self, the *moi*, on the one hand, and the dispassionate and often demystifying description of society, on the other. These two trends, most visible in the 17th-century writings known as 'moralist' literature, were not the individual creation of Montaigne nor were they exclusively French. We can see a demystified view of society in Machiavelli earlier and soon after Montaigne in the Spanish writer Gracián, for instance, but more than the analysis of an individual person and of social interaction, the *Essays* show a mind at work, thus drawing the reader in and providing one model for an early-modern personality.

Montaigne's style of writing provided an ideal of naturalness, the kind of book where, as Blaise Pascal wrote later, you expect to find an author but you are surprised and charmed to find a man. Pascal points here to the newness of the essay as a genre. When he says that one does not find an 'author', he means an authoritative figure whose words are received with reverence. Although the *Essays* draw upon many classical sources which, in retrospect, we can call 'essays' (Plutarch's *Moralia* and many texts by Seneca, for instance), Montaigne's decision to say that his book was a collection of 'attempts' signalled this shift in the relation of writer and reader. The author's declared tentativeness about his writing invited readers to be more engaged, perhaps to disagree, and perhaps to find similarities between their own experiences and those of Montaigne. In Montaigne's wake, over the centuries a large number of French writers excelled in this form. Most recently these include Charles Péguy, Paul Valéry, Albert Camus, Paul Nizan, Maurice Blanchot, Roland Barthes, Marguerite Yourcenar, and Pascal Quignard.

Montaigne represents himself as a multi-faceted character. It is, of course, essential to remember that what we have in the *Essays* is not an historical figure pieced together from multiple documents, but rather the first-person character that Montaigne has created through his writing. He insists on the facets of his personality, presenting them often as the opposition between inside and outside, between a Roman and a Frenchman, between 'Montaigne and the mayor of Bordeaux', and between the solitary reader in the tower of his château and the household scene outside his windows. Such awareness of his own complexity permits an ironic detachment leading to surprising juxtapositions: comments on his digestion or his kidney stones appear alongside soaring philosophical speculations, and the activities of simple country people teach as much as the deeds of princes and popes. One of the most memorable examples of this ironic levelling occurs at the end of the chapter 'Of Cannibals', where Montaigne reflected in memorable terms on the valuation of cultural difference and the term 'barbarism'. In a typically sinuous text that starts with a quotation from Plutarch's 'Life of Pyrrhus', turns to the recently discovered American continent and its inhabitants, Atlantis, divination, Stoic philosophy, and many other matters, Montaigne concludes that the 'savages' or 'cannibals' of the New World were not inferior to the French. Montaigne met such an American in Rouen in 1562, and finding his conversation quite intelligent, exclaims, with delicious irony, 'All of that is pretty good. But, of all things, they don't wear breeches!'



For Montaigne, and for many of his contemporaries, the newly discovered peoples of the Americas seemed a possible parallel to the rediscovered ancients. So for his first readers it was probably not so strange to see the *Essays* pass back and forth, as they often did, between Greco-Roman life and that of contemporary Brazil. These new-found peoples offered a glimpse of noble and simple life like that of Homeric heroes or, indeed, a possible pre-Adamite race of humans. The parallel between the distant European past and the American present appears in Montaigne's chapter 'On

Coaches', where he describes the Mexican conception of the major epochs of the world. Like us, he writes, they believe that the world is drawing to its end and is degenerating. In the past there were giants, both figuratively and literally.

## Rabelais's mysterious giants

Two of the world's most memorable giants appear in the books of the physician François Rabelais (c. 1490–1553), who also gave the world two important adjectives: *Gargantuan* and *Pantagruelian*. Rabelais did not invent the two giants Gargantua and Pantagruel – they existed already, as witnessed by an anonymous chapbook of tales that appeared in 1532 under the title *Gargantua: Les grandes et inestimables cronicques du grand et énorme géant Gargantua* – but he turned them into important characters in the literary pantheon, in a series of books published from 1532 to 1552, the first under the anagrammatic pseudonym Alcofrybas Nasier. Successively a Franciscan and then a Benedictine monk, before becoming a physician and making at least three trips to Italy, Rabelais was associated with reformist movements within the Catholic Church and was keenly interested in the new humanist learning and its implications for education and for religion.



The prologue to *Gargantua* sets forth the idea that the book contains secret wisdom and urges readers to suck out the 'substance in the marrow' (*la sustantificque mouelle*). This metaphor of a hidden core is preceded by such sayings as 'the habit does not make the monk' for 'one may be dressed in monastic garb who, inside, is quite other than a monk'. Are Rabelais's books coded messages addressed to Evangelical Christian sympathizers who were deeply sceptical of the Catholic theologians of the universities and of the monastic orders? Are they, on the contrary, the opinions of a rationalistic atheist? Or is the claim to convey a hidden message simply an additional joke accompanying the openly comic material? The debate still rages, but it is clear that for all the carnivalesque goings-on (for instance,

**2. Illustration by Gustave Doré (1854) for Rabelais's *Gargantua* (1534)**

Garguantua, arriving in Paris, relieves himself and drowns several hundred thousand Parisians) there are major questions about social institutions raised in the midst of the drinking, urinating, and brawling. The discontinuous, episodic nature of each book in the series thrusts the main characters to the foreground as the major structural elements. Pantagruel is the hero of the first book, and then his father Gargantua becomes the hero in the second book (a flashback, or 'prequel', to the first), while Pantagruel's companion Panurge is the focus of the third book – Panurge wishes to marry but fears being cuckolded and tries a variety of ways to predict his fate in marriage.

As we look backwards from our modern vantage point towards Rabelais's heroes, it is striking to note the quite relaxed integration of popular and learned cultures, of grossly physical with highly erudite and spiritual questions – the eating and drinking in *Gargantua* is explicitly connected with Plato's *Symposium*. Although some works of the following century strive to maintain this mix of character, subject, and tone (for example, Charles Sorel's *Histoire comique de Francion*, 1623–33, quite clearly inspired by Rabelais), for the most part the enormous physicality and appetite of Gargantua and Pantagruel and their humour are absent from the high-culture novels, comedies, and tragedies of the 17th century. In terms of the century-long effort to assimilate the humanistic culture of antiquity into a French, as opposed to an Italian or Italianate, model, Rabelais clearly succeeded in giving the French hugely learned and subtle protagonists deeply rooted in French geography, customs, and language.



## The French sonnet

The lure of Italian sophistication and the countervailing pull backwards towards French simplicity appear as themes in Renaissance lyric, particularly in such works as Joachim du Bellay's *The Regrets* (1558), in which the first-person poet-character compares life in Rome to his memories of home. Du Bellay's importance for shaping modern French literature goes beyond his many successes in lyric, for he was also the author of the manifesto of his innovative poetic group, the Pléiade, a group of seven poets formed in the late 1540s that included Pierre de Ronsard. This manifesto, the *Defense and Illustration of the French Language* (*la Défense et Illustration de la Langue*

*Française*, 1649) argued for enriching the vocabulary of French and building its cultural repertory to make it equal to Italian and the languages of antiquity. The *Defense* appeared ten years after the royal ordinance of Villers-Cotterêts by which François I made the vernacular the language of official documents (replacing Latin). Thus the *Defense* furthers the promotion of French linguistic nationalism that the King had begun, and it also assigns to the professional poet a role that is not limited to singing the praises of kings and military heroes. Not only does the *Defense* make it clear that poetry – in the broad sense, not only lyric, but also epic, comedy, and tragedy – is a discipline, rather than a sudden inspiration or simply the result of a certain temperament, but also that the poet's work as word-maker and language-builder assigns to him a broad and varied cultural mandate. Du Bellay proposed various ways of creating and importing words into French, but he particularly promoted the idea – the doctrine of imitation – that French writers should make literary equivalents of ancient works rather than simple translations. In other words, that France should have French epics, French lyrics, and so forth, rather than simply import the works of others. Du Bellay's polemical work serves as a document of the serious ambitions of poets in the period, but today we may also see it as an early expression of France's struggle to maintain its own identity in the face of whatever other culture is the dominant global model, whether it be that of Renaissance Rome or of today's Hollywood.



Following such models as Ovid, Horace, and Catullus, each of the major writers in verse shaped for himself or herself a distinct character or persona in the ballads, rondeaux, poetic epistles, elegies, epitaphs, blazons (verse descriptions, particularly of parts of the female body), complaints, epigrams, and odes that appeared abundantly in the 16th century. Many of the most important works took the form of long sequences of ten-verse (the *dizain*) or fourteen-verse (the sonnet) units. The *dizain* is the unit that Maurice Scève, one of the poets of Lyon (who include also Pernette du Guillet and 'Louise Labé' – the latter may in fact be simply a fictitious identity under which a collective of male poets published their works), used for his long hermetic love poem, *Délie, object de plus haulte vertu* (*Délie, object of the highest virtue*, 1544), a sequence of 449 *dizains*. The sonnet, on the other hand, has had more durable success, and the form itself testifies to the impact of Italian literature. Clément Marot, the first great poet of the 16th century, like Rabelais a protégé of Marguerite de Navarre, brought the Petrarchan sonnet to France in the 1530s.

It was in the 1550s, though, that the sonnet triumphed in the works of the Pléiade poets, each of whom gives a different tonality to the form in connection with the different persona the poet wished to create. Pierre Ronsard, for instance, variously portrays the character 'Ronsard' as suffering horribly from love or as the triumphant poet whose transcendent verbal gifts will be able to confer immortality upon the woman who grants her favours. Take, for instance, the well-known sonnet from the *Second Book of Sonnets for Hélène* that begins:

> *Quand vous serez bien vieille, au soir à la chandelle,*
> *Assise auprès du feu, dévidant et filant,*
> *Direz chantant mes vers, en vous émerveillant:*
> *'Ronsard me célébrait du temps que j'étais belle'.*
>
> [When you will be very old, during candle-lit evenings, / Sitting next to the fire, carding and spinning, / You will say, singing my verses with amazement, / 'Ronsard sang my praises when I was beautiful'.]

The poet cleverly inserts himself into the text, not by presenting himself here in the first person but rather by having a character speak about him as if he were a prodigy. 'Ronsard' becomes a character for retrospective admiration in this text which is a variation on the ancient *carpe diem*. As the 'Prince of Poets', Ronsard was not shy about celebrating his own talent, and, implicitly, the supreme position of the poet in society. In his 'Response to Insults and Calumnies', he wrote of his success in reviving ancient poetry and asserts to his detractors, 'You cannot deny it, since from my plenitude / You are all filled, I am the centre of your study, / You have all come from the grandeur of me' (*Tu ne le peux nier, car de ma plenitude / Vous estes tous remplis, je suis seul vostre estude, / Vous estes tous yssus de la grandeur de moy*).

## An exemplary sonnet-sequence: du Bellay's *The Regrets*

Let us return to Ronsard's companion du Bellay, whose *The Regrets*, often considered his greatest work, is particularly useful for capturing the emulation, enthusiasm, and anxiety that French writers felt when facing the more advanced culture of Italy. The poet, as first-person character of his own disillusioning adventures in the capital of Roman antiquity, highlights national and linguistic identity, promoting the idea of a humble, frank-speaking native son of the Loire valley adrift in the pomp and decadence of the papal court. But *The Regrets* is also a book that advances the idea of a poetry based on accidental encounter – 'Following the various incidents of this place, / Whether they are good or bad, I write at random' (*Mais, suivant de ce lieu les accidents divers, / Soit de bien, soit de mal, j'escris à l'adventure*). While this claim is literally unsustainable in the context of a sequence written in the dauntingly artful and constraining form of the sonnet, it situates the poetic 'I' as a humble observer of the contemporary world. This is a poetic persona that, even if it is somewhat rooted in Villon and Rutebeuf, gains momentum much later in the French tradition, with Baudelaire and the Surrealists, and even appears to prefigure James Joyce, insofar as du Bellay, while exploring the city, tries on a comparison to ancient poets and epic heroes, most strikingly Ulysses.

*The Regrets* are an open-ended, varied work with multiple tones – satiric, elegiac, conversational, descriptive, and at times stirringly celebratory ('France, mother of arts, of arms, and of laws', *France, mère des arts, des armes et des lois* – a striking reversal of his

Heureux qui, comme Ulysse, a fait un beau voyage,

Ou comme cestuy-là qui conquit la toison,

Et puis est retourné, plein d'usage et raison,

Vivre entre ses parents le reste de son aage!

Quand revoiray-je, helas, de mon petit village

Fumer la cheminee: et en quelle saison

Revoiray-je le clos de ma pauvre maison,

Qui m'est une province, et beaucoup davantage?

Plus me plaist le séjour qu'ont basty mes ayeux,

Que des palais Romains le front audacieux:

Plus que le marbre dur me plaist l'ardoise fine,

Plus mon Loyre Gaulois, que le Tybre Latin,

Plus mon petit Lyré, que le mont Palatin,

Et plus que l'air marin la doulceur Angevine.

Joachim du Bellay, from *Les Regrets*

Happy the man who, like Ulysses, has travelled well, or like that man who conquered the fleece, and has then returned, full of experience and wisdom, to live among his kinsfolk the rest of his life.

When, alas, will I again see smoke rising from the chimney of my little village and in what season will I see the enclosed field of my poor house, which to me is a province and much more still?

The home my ancestors built pleases me more than the grandiose facades of Roman palaces, fine slate pleases me more than hard marble,

My Gallic Loire more than the Latin Tiber, my little Liré more than the Palatine hill, and more than sea air, the sweetness of Anjou.

Translated by Richard Helgerson

nation's relation to Rome). Its most direct successor in modern French literature may be Baudelaire's post-Romantic *Fleurs du mal*. It was only a few years after *The Regrets* that the wars of religion between varying factions of Protestants and Catholics (1562–98) profoundly changed French culture and set the stage for the more highly structured and often less personal literature of the 17th century.

# Chapter 3
# Society and its demands

## A precarious peace and the new civility

Politeness, moderation, discretion, self-censorship, irony, and a great attention to the formal rituals of civil and religious life are the hallmarks of 17th-century France. Looking back from today, it is tempting to speak of a very repressed and repressive society. Seen from the point of view of those who had lived through the ferocious civil and religious wars of the late 16th century, the peace and stability, and a modicum of religious tolerance, were no doubt welcome. The 1594 coronation of the first Bourbon monarch, Henri IV, brought peace to France through compromise. Henri, son of the intransigent Protestant Jeanne d'Albret, converted to Catholicism, while the militant Catholic League, bane of the late Valois monarchs (accused of being too willing to coexist with the Huguenots), put down their arms.

In 1598, Henri proclaimed the Edict of Nantes, granting Protestants the right to worship. Under Henri IV and his son and successor Louis XIII, Paris grew rapidly in size and became the habitual home of the royal court. Both the nobility and a prosperous middle class flocked to the new neighbourhoods – especially to the Marais (named from the reclaimed swamp on which it was built) on the right bank of the Seine slightly upriver from the Louvre. The upper classes of

French society became more urban and more urbane, though not without effort. Many books, plays, and letters attest to the earnest discussions of how to achieve the proper skill in witty conversation, letter-writing, and dress. This effort to fit in and to avoid giving offence, or at least to channel violence into inventive verbal forms, hints that physical aggression was lurking just under the surface. Henri IV was assassinated in 1610, as his predecessor Henri III had been in 1589. Repeated edicts failed to prevent duels – there were as many as four hundred a year under Henri IV.

Everyone was aware of the precarious peace, and throughout France there was an effort to promote ways of interacting politely and to avoid setting off a new round of hostility. In this climate flourished a literature that promoted an ideal of moderation, discretion, and even concealment, yet was fascinated by excess, by the exceptional, and by the superlative. It is as if the polite and decorous 17th-century French still dreamed of the martyrdom and the transgressive heroism of the preceding century and also reflected on the difficulty of determining a set of norms. There was great emphasis on avoiding highly visible partisanship and zealotry, and on being a reasonable person, an amusing, sensitive, and accommodating companion – in short, an *honnête homme*. This term is not easily translated, and it is important to note right away that it does not mean 'honest man' in the sense of someone who speaks with sincerity and complete frankness. The *honnête homme* is someone who 'fits in', who is not notably eccentric. On the other hand, 17th-century readers and authors were captivated by the stories of protagonists who go far beyond the norm, who do not 'fit in' at all and who are excessive in word and deed.



## Molière's comedy of character

As the ideal of the polite society reached its peak, theatre showed that politeness and heroism were an uneasy fit. Take Molière's

**3. Chateau of Vaux-le-Vicomte, designed by Louis Le Vau, in an engraving by Perelle (1660)**



comic hero Alceste in *The Misanthrope* (1666, called in French *Le Misanthrope, ou l'Atrabilaire amoureux*). The full title refers to the medical doctrine that character was based on substances in the blood, the 'humours'. Hence, Alceste is a man with too much black bile who is in love. The role of Alceste, performed by the playwright himself in the first production, was certainly played for laughs. Molière was known for his comic stagecraft, and there is much to laugh about. The hero, who insists that one should speak one's mind fearlessly in all matters, falls in love with a woman who is his complete opposite, a flirtatious young widow. Célimène carefully cultivates a number of suitors by making each think that he is the exclusive object of her affection. Alceste also refuses to conform to many ordinary social norms. He will not condescend to flatter the judge in an important legal matter involving his entire fortune, and he even refuses to utter the usual formulas of polite approval when an amateur poet shows him a sonnet. He recognizes that he is a misfit in the court where an important quality is the gift to 'hide what is in one's heart' (as Alceste's friend Philinte says). For his sincerity, Alceste faces three risks: losing Célimène's love, losing his fortune, and losing his life or his reputation in a duel. These risks seem to be of quite unequal importance, and it is probably Molière's comic intent to show the bizarre disproportion between various gestures of frankness and their results. The possible duel, a serious matter and reflective of the brittle civility that could pass in minutes from witty repartee to drawn swords, leads to the intervention of the *Maréchaux de France*, a high tribunal charged with settling conflicts of honour and thus avoiding bloodshed. Despite Alceste's repeated proclamations that he will not conform to society and that he will eventually run away to live in solitude, he seems to need society – if for no other reason than for the pleasure of his own indignation. In this respect, he differs from such other contemporary outsiders as the wolf in Jean de La Fontaine's fable, 'The Wolf and the Dog' (*Le Loup et le chien*, in *Fables*, 1668). The wolf, despite the many material advantages that the dog enjoys in captivity, really prefers to remain entirely outside society. The misanthrope, on the other hand, seems only to be able to exist within proximity to those he distains.



It is tempting to think that Alceste is entirely ridiculous, an unstable individual with too much bile, no social skills, and no sense of proportion. Yet the play dispels that view by having the other characters in *Le Misanthrope* admire Alceste and vie for his friendship, love, and approval. Some of these characters may themselves be lacking in judgement, like Oronte, author of the sonnet, but others, like Alceste's friend Philinte and Célimène's cousin Éliante appear to be good judges of character. Philinte is a fine example of the 17th-century *honnête homme*: he never advances any particular achievement of his own (La Rochefoucauld said just this in his 1664 *Maxims*: 'The true *honnête homme* is the one who does not attach his pride to anything in particular'), he views human imperfections with tolerance and detachment, saying that 'there is no greater madness than to try to set the world straight'. Alceste describes Philinte as phlegmatic (another imbalance of the humours),

**4. Engraving by François Chauveau (1668) for La Fontaine's fable *Le Loup et le chien***

meaning that he is too placid. And this may be a key to Alceste's attractiveness for those around him, men and women alike: they are spellbound by his vigorous, unbending candour, reflected in his physical agitation: he seems to be constantly in motion, with the others running after him. They may well find it refreshing to see someone free of the self-consciousness and dissimulation that is their daily lot.

## Corneille's outsized heroes

This ambivalence about heroism in the *Misanthrope* may be a comic example, but it is not isolated. The pattern we see there, of a society that is spellbound, yet appalled, by the energetic, dissenting hero, appears in other, more serious forms. We can see that the 17th-century insistence on politeness – the expectation of conformity to what fits the situation (in French, *convenance* or *bienséance*) – is based on the fear that people who stand out and who say heroically what they think could so easily cross over into the explosive violence of the still-recent civil wars. In *Horace* (1640), based on Livy's account of the ancient combat between the three Roman champions, the Horatii, and the three champions of the nearby city of Alba Longa, the Curiatii, Corneille presents the moral dilemma of one of the three Romans, who must fight his best friend and brother-in-law, Curiace. The fight will be limited to three warriors from each city, in the interest of a quick and relatively bloodless decision about political dominance. Unlike the reluctant Curiace, Horace claims to be so completely focused on his duty that from the moment when he learns the identity of his adversary he no longer 'knows' Curiace: 'Alba named you, I know you no more'. So far, this may be no more than a case of doing what it takes in the line of duty – a bit cold-hearted, perhaps, and not very polite, but the way to victory. Indeed, Horace does win for the Roman side, for he is the last man standing of the six.



However, it is at this point, the moment of the hero's return from the battlefield, that Horace's attitude towards his own heroism crosses the line into civil violence. Horace's sister Camille was Curiace's lover, and she does not greet him with the respect that he demands, saying to her 'render [the honour] that you owe to the fortune of my victory'. He is, to say the least, unfeeling, focused entirely on his brilliant achievement and, as he said earlier, unwilling to recognize any personal attachment or identity in this state of war. But this extremism, or even fanaticism, is matched by his sister's – it runs in the family, apparently – for instead of yielding and keeping silent, she insults him and escalates the verbal combat to the point of cursing the Rome that Horace claims to incarnate. She calls down the fire of heaven on the city. The altercation between Camille and her brother is the most violent part of the play as it appears on stage, for the sword fight between Albans and Romans takes place off stage, as does almost all physical violence in French drama after the 1630s.

And this second encounter ends badly for Horace. He becomes so enraged that he kills his sister. For what he then calls 'an act of justice', he is put on trial. The play culminates, then, in a full act devoted to the incompatibility between unflinching, unfeeling, Horatian-style heroism and the requirements of a society of laws, individual identities and duties, and political hierarchy. In the civil society that is depicted in Corneille's version of Rome, the purely masculine virtues required in war cannot be allowed to run unchecked. As Horace's chief accuser, Valère, points out, by shedding his sister's blood, Horace has not only killed an unarmed woman but a Roman citizen. The violence that was tolerable when it took place outside the city and aimed itself against non-Romans has now entered the city itself to threaten all. The most general paradox that Corneille displays here is that while the peaceful civil order is based on fratricide (Rome's war against its kindred city Alba, like Horace's murder of his sister, is set in the perspective of Rome's legendary founding by Romulus, killer of his brother Remus), such violence should never be rekindled.



Though important for any consideration of heroism, the general paradox of the warrior's return to the city is less original than the insight into Horace's own experience of this status that Corneille subtly conveys. Generations of audiences and readers have generally found Horace to be much less appealing a character than his opponent Curiace, but the play suggests a terrible suffering within the hero. The price of his victory has been the sacrifice of all feeling, all perception that is not directly oriented towards slaying the designated enemy. And that sacrifice is directed at a single moment, after which, inevitably, the hero begins to decline into an ordinary life that is forever closed to him. Horace asks to be executed, claiming that 'Death alone today can preserve my glory / And it should have come at the moment of my triumph'. At the end of *Horace*, just as at the end of *The Misanthrope*, the audience is left to puzzle over how such an outsized, unyielding protagonist can fit back into the ordinary social world.

## The decline of the hero

Heroes, in other words, are useful to have around at certain moments, but fit awkwardly into the social framework over the long haul. They are not necessarily even 'good' by prevailing moral standards. La Rochefoucauld wrote memorably that 'There are heroes of evil as well as of good'; we need only think of two of Corneille's other protagonists, both heroic and monstrous – Medea in his first tragedy *Médée* (1635) and Cleopatra in *Rodogune, princesse des Parthes* (1644) – or of Racine's later depiction of the Emperor Nero in *Britannicus* (1669). As literary theorists tried to square the heritage of ancient tragedy with Christian, modern values, there was considerable unease at placing characters capable of extreme acts, good and bad, in the position of 'hero'. Corneille's younger rival Jean Racine paraphrased Aristotle's dictum in the *Poetics* on tragic heroes, saying that they should have 'a middling goodness, that is, a virtue susceptible to weakness'. Racine worked to create characters with this middling goodness, or *bonté médiocre*. Avoiding the spectacular qualities and acts of such Corneille protagonists as Horace, Chimène in *Le Cid*, and Auguste in *Cinna*, Racine in most of his tragedies depicted protagonists who are quite middling, even 'mediocre' in the modern sense. They are people like ourselves, or like the version of ourselves we see on day-time television, but in magnificent verse. Such are the protagonists of *Phèdre*, in which the eponymous protagonist is an unfortunate woman who has fallen in love with her adolescent stepson – she considers herself a monster, but this is the 'monster' next door, who, once rebuffed, acquiesces to a plan to accuse Hippolyte of raping her.

We can see why it has been said that Racine turned tragedy into bourgeois melodrama. In his *Andromaque* (1668), a tragedy which takes its title from Andromache, the widow of the Trojan hero Hector, now become the slave of Achilles' son Pyrrhus, Racine illustrates this concept of the protagonist of middling goodness with such thoroughness that one might even be tempted to say with Karl Marx that 'history repeats itself, the first time as tragedy, the second as farce'. The main characters of this play belong – with the possible exception of Andromaque herself – to a post-heroic generation. Their parents were the great Homeric heroes and heroines of the *Iliad*, Agamemnon, Helen, Menelaus, Achilles, and yet the new generation of Hermione, Orestes, and even (though to a less marked extent) Pyrrhus is obsessed with a desire to live up to and compete with its forebears. Hermione recalls that her mother was so beautiful that the Trojan war was fought to bring her back to Greece, yet she cannot even get Pyrrhus to honour his promise of marriage to her. Orestes dithers irresolutely over his unrequited love for Hermione, failing to carry out his ambassadorial mission, which is to find and slay Hector's son Astyanax to eliminate all trace of the royal family of Troy. Pyrrhus himself is described as the 'son and rival of Achilles'. But while their parents shook the world with epic battles, this group ends up with a sordid palace intrigue of murder and suicide.



Yet despite the clear difference between the larger-than-life protagonists of Corneille and even Molière and Racine's self-consciously mediocre characters, there is a remarkable similarity with regard to the ambivalent theme of heroism. The reason that the protagonists of *Andromaque* arrive at their dreadful end is that they tried to stage heroic feats for which they did not have the ability and which, in any event (and this is the most striking parallel with the historical situation of 17th-century France) belonged to the past and should have been left in the past. In *Andromaque*, just as in *Horace*, the moment in which it was useful to act as violent military heroes has gone by, and the protagonists would have been well advised to adopt the skills of peacetime. A certain amount of heroism is admirable, as Molière's *honnête homme* Philinte might have said, but there is a time and place for everything.

These major dramatic works give us some sense of the continuity in the way civility, conformity to circumstance, and politeness were proposed as ideals, even when they were projected back into the French version of Greco-Roman antiquity. But we should now recall the social circumstances that gave these ideals such weight, and even urgency. The transition from the religious wars of the 16th century to the more stable, and even more bureaucratic, regime of the Bourbon monarchs was not at all easy. The assassination of Henri IV was a great blow; the subsequent regency of Marie de Médicis ended with a *coup d'état* staged by her son, King Louis XIII, whose long-serving prime minister, Cardinal Richelieu, executed, imprisoned, or exiled members of the 'devout party' which derived in large part from the Catholic League that had been such a challenge to the last Valois and to Henri IV before his conversion. But outright civil war returned at mid-century during the tumultuous and complicated time known as the 'Fronde' ('slingshot' in French), which lasted from 1648 to 1653, and set troops loyal to the regent Queen Anne of Austria against a fluctuating alliance of nobility and *parlementaires* (members of the Paris legislative court).

This confrontation ended, after devastating large parts of the country, by reaffirming the monarchy. The ambivalence towards aristocratic, independent heroism – newly illustrated by the rebellion or treason of the Prince de Condé and of the King's uncle Gaston d'Orléans who allied themselves with Spain against the Queen – could only be reinforced by this catastrophic and wasteful adventure, which left a deep impression on the young Louis XIV, only ten years old when the Fronde began. In the decisive steps taken to further centralize power and to remove any remaining independence from the upper aristocracy, Louis made conformity – outward conformity, at least – a central value of French culture of the second half of the century. This certainly is one of the reasons why the status of the hero as it appears in the three major dramatists shows a significant downward trajectory from Corneille to Racine, even though all three show heroism as leading to conflict.

Another reason for the change in the status of the hero may be the rise in influence, towards mid-century, of a disenchanted worldview associated with the religious movement known as Jansenism, centred on the convent of Port-Royal, and influential with many leading writers of the 'moralist' tendency, such as Blaise Pascal and François de La Rochefoucauld. This movement was not simply about advocating austere morality (though some, like Pascal, were quite ascetic), but rather in large part it consisted of giving a pessimistic view of human society and its motives, and aimed at a dispassionate analysis of relationships. It saw mankind as anything but heroic.

In the second half of the century, a different type of protagonist emerged, in keeping with the intensification of court and

### Salons and the rise of literary women

The term 'salon' is now used somewhat anachronistically (the term itself became prominent only in the 18th century) to describe the private meeting places where women received guests in the 17th century – major contemporary terms for such places were *ruelle*, *alcôve*, or *réduit*, meaning the narrow space between a bed and the nearby wall in which guests might stand or sit to converse with the hostess, who remained recumbent. Two such *salons* stand out: the *Chambre bleue* of the Marquise de Rambouillet and the *samedis* (Saturdays) of Madeleine de Scudéry. These cultivated women controlled the space into which they invited distinguished male as well as female guests, making the *salons* women-centred conversational places in sharp distinction to the taverns in which male writers might meet on their own. The values promoted in this environment included freedom from arranged marriages and friendship between women and men. Detractors of women such as Boileau called them *précieuses*, a term Molière popularized in his *Précieuses ridicules* (1659) and *L'École des femmes* (*The School for Wives*, 1662).

urban life in proximity to the court, with the domestication of the aristocracy, and with moralist disenchantment. This new protagonist is typical of a trend – or of a number of converging trends – in which there is an 'inward turn' of literature, a turn towards 'literature of psychological analysis', a social and cultural movement called *préciosité*, and the rise of social spaces, the *salons*, organized by women.

## The novel of courtly manners

In this context, emphasis shifts to a new conception of the hero, or rather of the protagonist (since the term 'hero' was generally not used for non-military distinction): the person who exemplified exquisite refinement in friendship and love and was capable of exceptional fidelity to ideals. No one exemplifies this type of protagonist better than the central figure of Marie-Madeleine de Lafayette's brief novel, *La Princesse de Clèves* (published anonymously, 1678). This work, often praised as one of the first 'psychological novels' or 'novels of analysis', is set in the Valois court of the previous century. Arriving at Paris with her widowed mother at age 16, the protagonist, an innocent young woman, receives from her mother three basic instructions about the world she is about to enter. The first is to distrust appearances: what seems to be is almost never the case. The second, somewhat contradictory, lesson is to learn from listening to stories about the wretched experiences of other men and women at the court. And the third lesson is that for a woman, the only way to happiness consists of loving her husband and being loved by him in return – in short, to be completely different from other women, typified by those whose tales she hears and who are engaged in multiple, unhappy, adulterous love affairs. From the very start of her story, then, the heroine aims both to understand and to be different from other women, and to find that elusive happiness that is said to be available only to the happily married woman.

As the wife of the perfectly honourable Prince de Clèves, the young woman soon meets the highly desirable Duc de Nemours, whose reputation as a lover is universal. The love affair that follows is one in which the Princess and the Duke are alone on only two occasions, never touch, and are never publicly known to have feelings for one another. Despite the constant surveillance, intense curiosity, and gossip of the court, the story of the Princess's discovery of love and of her own nature is known to no one except, in part, to the Princess, her husband, her mother, and the Duke himself. It is tempting to say that it is a story in which nothing happens, yet, adjusting the scale of perception, we can see how Lafayette has moved events inward, into the minds and feelings of her characters, where life-and-death struggles occur and virtue is pitted against betrayal. Tiny, almost imperceptible, signals allow the characters to communicate with one another. For instance, the Duke, wishing to show his affection for the Princess in a way that could never be understood by anyone except herself, identifies himself at a tournament by wearing yellow and black. Everyone wonders why, since these colours had no apparent connection to him. The Princess, however, immediately understands that it is a favour to her, for one day at a conversation at which the Duke was present, she had said that she liked yellow but could not wear it because she was blonde. On another occasion, the Princess did not go to a ball, claiming to be ill (though she appeared to be in radiant good health). This is another of those secret signals, since the Princess has heard it reported that the Duke said that there was no greater suffering for a lover than to know that his mistress was at a ball that he himself was not able to attend.

The heroism of the battlefield, the exotic locations, the very visible hostilities that pit the protagonists against one another in tragedy, epic, and the huge romance novels of earlier in the century, have here been replaced by the subtle decoding of glances, details of dress, and presence or absence at balls and other social gatherings. But what gives the Princess a status equivalent to the protagonists of these other texts is her problematic uniqueness. With her mother's initial guidance, the Princess formed and then executed a heroic project: to be different from all other women. Some of this distinction is visible to a few of the members of the court. One of the queens says that the Princess is the only woman who tells her husband everything. In fact, the Princess confesses privately to her husband that she loves someone else, while keeping that man's name secret and promising never to be unfaithful – this avowal was one of the most shocking and controversial aspects of the novel when it appeared. But the Duke himself is the only person in the novel who knows the full extent of her heroic resolve. After her husband's death (of a broken heart, because he has improperly decoded a set of appearances and wrongly believes his wife to be unfaithful – this is a novel in which misinterpretation is lethal), in a brief conversation, the Princess admits to her lover that their passion is mutual, but that she will never marry him. She intends, as she tells him, to act according to a duty that 'only exists in my imagination' not to marry the man who was, indirectly and unwittingly, the cause of her husband's death. Throughout the novel, and particularly in its conclusion, the Princess is described as being unparalleled, unique, and exceptional. The last sentence of the novel ends: 'her life, which was rather short, left examples of inimitable virtue'.



With *The Princess of Clèves*, Lafayette showed the cost of being exceptional and not following the prevailing model of conduct – in this, the story fits the model we saw earlier in tragedy and comedy – but she also shows how changes in French culture and in the status of women modified the standard for what is worthy of attention and for what constitutes exceptional achievement. For 17th-century feminists, a woman's decision to be independent, not to remarry, and to form her own ideal of conduct constituted a story at least as interesting as that of a male military hero. Starting with her mother's lesson that a happy marriage was the only worthy goal for a woman, the Princess ended with a very different achievement.

# Chapter 4
# Nature and its possibilities

## The problem of 'nature'

Given the intense focus on society and its norms that characterized the 17th century, it is perhaps not surprising that the 18th century should react in part against this exclusive focus and shift the discussion to the question of nature. The opposition between nature and culture (or between *physis* and *nomos*) is very ancient, but it took on a new vitality in the 18th century. 17th-century French thought, particularly in literary circles, was not kind to nature. It seemed clear that the world was defective and that religion and art had the mission of correcting things or, at the very least, of filtering out the naturally occurring errors. Left to himself – to his temperament, since that was determined by the imbalance in his humours – Molière's Alceste would be miserable and unfit for society. His friends try to counterbalance that tendency by teaching him manners. In a more serious vein, Pascal taught that mankind's nature had been fundamentally altered by Original Sin, so that what we call 'natural' is only a perverse illusion – Pascal is here very close to Thomas Hobbes, a long-time resident of Paris, who had nothing good to say about the 'state of nature'. Finally, by the literary doctrine of *vraisemblance*, the French Academy and others taught that dramatists should not portray what happens in the ordinary course of things but rather what should happen, if the world were not imperfect. In short, any 17th-century writer who used the term 'nature' in a positive way meant something that was far removed from the world of experience. Writers often praised the 'natural' manner of speaking, only to point out that such a style could only be achieved by careful imitation of the best models; in other words, *le naturel* was the best form of artifice. As for the relatively modern notion that one could go 'into nature' (*dans la nature*) by leaving the city, such a sense of a privileged unspoiled space would have appeared complete nonsense to the subjects of Louis XIV.

This uniformly dismissive view of nature began to change in the 18th century. Society was still at the forefront of intellectual and literary discussions, but now nature became a component of that discussion in a much more varied and less predictable way. Indeed, for the Enlightenment, Nature – both human nature and the wild forces of the earth – was, broadly speaking, at the core of most important questions. Was nature good but somehow concealed and distorted by social institutions and habits? Or was nature indifferent, or even hostile, to mankind, and should people therefore cease to appeal to nature as the source of concepts of 'good' and 'rights'? Was nature composed of spirit and matter, or was nature purely material and fully available to us through sensations? Nature no longer seemed inaccessible to experience. The earlier, more optimistic views of Montaigne and Rabelais now returned in a very much amplified and better documented way. While Montaigne found much to praise (and many things that shocked him) in what he learned of the indigenous Americans, exploration, commerce, and colonialism brought much more information about life outside of Europe. It was not simply that the peoples of Brazil or of the South Pacific islands were closer to 'nature' (in the sense that their settlements were smaller and seemed less urban and technologically advanced), but also that the multitude of customs and fundamental laws, things that seem entirely self-evident, was found to be so different from one culture to another that what French people took for granted as 'nature' no longer seemed secure. The quest to discover, or rediscover, nature and to refound society on the basis of this surer knowledge was perhaps the major theme of the Enlightenment, *l'âge des Lumières*.

These issues are not always raised with the intention to challenge tradition, since, after all, many French writers argued in favour of the established order. At first glance, the plays and novels of Pierre de Marivaux (1688–1763) appear to have little to do with 'nature'. His comedies of manners are known for their highly artful banter, so characteristic of his style that it gave us the word *marivaudage* for witty, flirtatious dialogue. Yet when we consider the enthusiastic audience for his plays, for instance *The Game of Love and Chance* (*Le Jeu de l'amour et du hasard*, 1730), we can see that Marivaux and his contemporaries were keenly aware of the possible divergence between nature and culture within a social system based on what we would call 'class' and what was then called 'condition'. A young woman, wishing to learn the true personality of the young man to whom her father has arranged to marry her, disguises herself as her maid. Little does she know that the young man has made the same exchange of identity with his valet and for the same purpose. Two couples form, in both cases assembling a man and a woman of the same real, but not apparent, condition – the disguised upper-class characters fall in love with each other.

This was a reassuringly conservative conclusion for Marivaux and his public, and conveyed the message that rank in society is not a superficial convention (as some of the more daring passages of Pascal's *Pensées* a hundred years earlier seemed to suggest) but rather has deeper roots, whether purely inherited or based on long cultivation. But the very fact that the subject of an entire play could be made out of this experiment – and in fact, not only one play, for similar issues appear throughout Marivaux's work – implies that the fear of a misalignment between one's natural characteristics and one's condition was quite present in the first half of the 18th century. Plays highlighting such possible social misalignment continued to have great success in the following years, as Beaumarchais's *The Barber of Seville* (*Le Barbier de Séville*, 1775) shows. It is at least partly in order to accommodate the more serious and less conservative development of these social thematics that French theatre created new genres in the course of the century, including 'tearful comedy' (*la comédie larmoyante*) and the 'drama' (*le drame*).

## Enlightenment and the *philosophes*

While Marivaux was entertaining spectators by showing that, in the end, the social system was secure, a group that he particularly scorned, the *philosophes*, was raising serious questions about birth, rank, and the 'natural' basis of civilization. Jean-Jacques Rousseau (1712–78) published his *Discourse on the Origins of Inequality* (*Discours sur l'origine et les fondements de l'inégalité parmi les hommes*, 1755), arguing that humankind had been happy in the original state of nature prior to the institution of private property, laws, and the social superstructure that maintains inequality. Denis Diderot (1713–84) and Jean le Rond d'Alembert (1717–83) organized the *Encyclopédie* (1751–72, most of it published clandestinely), to which they and approximately 150 other writers contributed anonymous articles. The *philosophes*, a heterogeneous group rent by quarrels, were less 'philosophers' in the modern sense, or even in the sense that Descartes was a philosopher, than they were public intellectuals committed to undoing superstition and ignorance and advocating pragmatic or technocratic solutions to problems of human life in society. Much of their work consisted of promoting a deeper and demystified understanding of the material world as it can be perceived through the senses. This aspect can be seen in Diderot's *On the Interpretation of Nature* (1753–4) concerning sense perceptions, but the encyclopedists also promoted contractual monarchy based on natural law and free enterprise. Their theory of knowledge is empiricist and rationalist and, accordingly, their treatment of knowledge about God is squarely within philosophy rather than within a revealed religion.

One of the best examples of the efforts of the *philosophes* to reach a wide audience through entertaining yet didactic works is Voltaire's *Candide*, a *conte philosophique* (*philosophical tale*) published anonymously in 1759. The immediate target of this satirical tale is Gottfried Leibniz's *Essais de théodicée* (1710), in which the philsopher argued that God has created the best of all possible worlds, the 'optimal' world. In such a system, there is no objective evil. It was to describe Leibniz's position that the term '*optimisme*' entered the French language in 1737. The full title of Voltaire's tale is *Candide ou l'optimisme, traduit de l'allemand de M. le Docteur Ralph* [...]. The well-known story (the basis of the 1956 operetta *Candide* with score by Leonard Bernstein) follows the adventures of Candide, a German from Westphalia who was educated in his youth by Dr Pangloss (the Greek roots suggesting that he can speak about anything, probably a dig at Leibniz's prolific polymathic output) who teaches a teleological optimism: everything was created providentially for the best and could not be otherwise. Pangloss's assertions immediately appear absurd to the reader but not to Candide:

> everything being made for an end, all is necessarily for the best end. Consider that noses were made to wear spectacles: therefore we have spectacles. Legs were clearly made to be in hose, and we have hose.

As a literary creation, Candide is a highly successful character in both common meanings of the term: as a narrative 'person' and as the possessor of a certain 'character' (or personality trait) taken to its extreme. Voltaire describes him at the outset by saying 'He had reasonably good judgment along with complete simplicity; that's why, I think, they called him Candide' (*Il avait le jugement assez droit, avec l'esprit le plus simple; c'est, je crois, pour cette raison qu'on le nommait Candide*). For Voltaire's satire of Leibnizian optimism and of all those who cling to ideologies in order to avoid facing unpleasant realities, it is important that the personage we follow around the globe be a mixture of perceptiveness and exceptional persistence within the rigid doctrine that Pangloss taught. Thus Voltaire was able to continue accumulating examples of natural horror (the Lisbon earthquake of 1755), Roman Catholic hypocrisy and intolerance (the *autodafé* in which the Portuguese priests burned three men to prevent further earthquakes; the grand inquisitor's sexual activities; the Jesuit kingdom in Paraguay), the murderous cruelty of European kingdoms and the empire, the mutilations of African slaves in Surinam, and various examples of venality and corruption, while Candide only very slowly gives up his reassuring Panglossian certitude that there must be a good reason for all this. By the time he sees the slave whose leg has been amputated as punishment for attempting to escape and whose hand has been cut off to get it out of the way of the sugar grinder, Candide does, however, exclaim 'Oh Pangloss! ... you did not know of this abomination. That's it – I will have to renounce your optimism.' When asked at this point what 'optimism' is, Candide replies, 'It's the mania of claiming that everything is all right when you are suffering' (*c'est la rage de soutenir que tout est bien quand on est mal*). If Leibniz had been Voltaire's only target, and if he had not so perfectly matched his hero to the road show of horrors to produce such comic dissonance, *Candide* would not have survived in the popular imagination. But what Voltaire does here provides a microcosm of the work of the *philosophes* in setting reason against deep-seated cultural habit, against all the institutions that extinguish both the capacity for judgement, the responsibility for clear perception of the world, and a natural empathy.



## The tension between social façade and inner nature

One of the most enduring literary successes of the century, an immediate best-seller with continued broad appeal (and the basis of at least four films), was Pierre Choderlos de Laclos's epistolary novel *Les Liaisons dangereuses* (1782). One of the characteristics of the epistolary form makes it particularly hard to locate a message or intention in any simple way, since there is no overall narrative voice. The book has variously been seen as anti-aristocratic (this is how the book was perceived by many of Laclos's contemporaries), feminist, anti-feminist, moralistic, and immoral. As a collection of letters set mostly in chronological order, the work at first seems to offer neutrality in point of view, but the letters written by the two highly self-conscious dominant characters, the Vicomte de Valmont and the Marquise de Merteuil (dominant both in the number of letters they write – though there are twice as many from Valmont – and in their clever manipulation of the other letter writers), essentially take up the functions of the narrator in a conventional single-narrator novel. They not only tell what happens, but analyse motivations and predict outcomes. We can consider the novel as having, therefore, two non-omniscient narrators who are competing with each other not only to present a certain view of what happens but to make things happen. Both are cynical rationalists with a keen understanding of human nature (that is, patterns of behaviour) but with blindspots that lead them both to ruin. We can see echoes of La Rochefoucauld in this psychology; Merteuil explicitly states that she learned about life by reading the works of 'the most severe moralists', and La Rochefoucauld was especially acute in noting that people are blind to their own susceptibilities and motivations. Although Valmont and Merteuil consider themselves completely emancipated from religion and morality, they need to adjust appearances in order to function within the codes of their society, codes that are different for men and for women. For Valmont, as a male libertine, a public reputation as a successful seducer of women is a source of pride and has little negative impact on him. For Merteuil, it is quite different. She needs to seduce imperceptibly and always in circumstances that maintain for her a public reputation as a pious young widow. Even the men she seduces must not know that she has seduced them but must believe that they have seduced her. The unequal status accorded to men and women by society is thus an important theme and one that, along with the portrayal of a corrupt and idle aristocracy, is representative of the contemporary questioning of social convention and education.

By the end of the novel, Valmont's and Merteuil's rivalry (the smouldering remains of an earlier love affair between them) leads them to take vengeance on each other. Merteuil does this in the more subtle fashion by exploiting the gap between Valmont's gendered self-perception as publicly successful libertine seducer, on the one hand, and his real and passionate love for Madame de Tourvel, his most difficult conquest to date. Valmont, as Merteuil saw, is blind to his own nature. Confident in his rationalist stance, he believes that physical pleasure and virtuosity in seduction are his only motives. By exploiting the vanity that is indissociable from this form of male self-image, Merteuil provokes Valmont to destroy his only chance at emotional fulfilment. Valmont's subsequent revenge upon Merteuil is much cruder and easier and is also based on the gender disequilibrium created artificially by society. He simply leaves the packet of letters to be published, thus making her a pariah. The discrepancy between Valmont's deepest emotion and his socially determined vanity marks *Les Liaisons dangereuses* as valorizing nature over the social norms that alienate people from their deeper, hidden selves.



## Flora, fauna, and 'nature'

Laclos's novel is concerned with human nature in the form of what we would call psychology. What counts is the social world, and the changes of place from Paris to a country manor are only described as they inflect the interactions among groups of people – in this respect, Laclos's work is closer to novels of the preceding century. But many writers of the 18th century reflect an explosively growing interest in non-urban spaces and contextualize human behaviour and perception along a city/country divide. By mid-century, the work of the Swedish botanist Carl Linnaeus had reached France, and it became increasingly fashionable to *herboriser*, that is, to look for plant specimens. Buffon (Georges-Louis Leclerc, comte de Buffon) published the first volume of his *Histoire naturelle, générale et particulière* in 1749. Flora and fauna from a wide variety of climates became of interest to the general public, and alongside the new importance accorded to plants and animals were the people who lived among them. Country dwellers were no longer seen exclusively as persons deprived of the advantages of the city, for the life of the fields and the forests now seemed to offer protection from the artifice and corrupting influences of the city. This is a significant extension of the image that Jean de La Bruyère, in his *Caractères, ou les moeurs de ce siècle* (1688), drew of the pitiless and soul-less artificiality of Parisian and court life. La Bruyère portrayed the culture of his time as corrupting and created caustic images of the artificiality of the upper classes, but did not go so far as to suggest that things are really better outside the court and the city. Rousseau extended his critique of urban civilization, already set forth in the *Discourse on the Origins of Inequality*, in his *Letter to d'Alembert on Spectacles* (*J.J. Rousseau Citoyen de Genève, à Mr. d'Alembert sur les spectacles*, 1758), in which he denounced the corrupting Parisian theatre in favour of the honest festivities of the 'happy peasants' in the small cities of the provinces. Childhood took on a new importance with Rousseau – it continues to be a significant interest for the Romantics, starting with Chateaubriand. Rousseau devotes a great deal of attention to his own childhood in his autobiographical *Confessions* (finished in 1769, but published in 1782). And in *Émile ou De l'éducation* (1762), an exemplary narrative of a radically new form of upbringing, Rousseau, in the role of tutor, permits his young pupil only one book, Defoe's *Robinson Crusoe*, in the hope that Émile will model himself on the self-reliant Crusoe living in a state of 'nature'.

In 1788, the year before the meeting of the *États Généraux* at Versailles, which is customarily seen as the beginning of the Revolution, Rousseau's younger friend Bernardin de Saint-Pierre (1737–1814), an engineer, published one of the best-selling novels of the 18th century, *Paul et Virginie*. It is the quintessence of the nature versus culture theme of its time

**5. A scene from Bernardin de Saint-Pierre's novel *Paul et Virginie* (1787), in a 1805 engraving after François Gérard**



and created, in Virginie, a heroine whose abandonment of the simpler ways of her childhood upbringing in the wilderness leads directly to her death. The action of the novel takes place in Mauritius, then known as the Île de France, where as children, Paul and Virginie grow up as best friends and almost siblings. At adolescence, their feelings change to romantic love, but Virginie is sent away to live in France with a wealthy and elderly aunt. When the aunt tries to force Virginie into a marriage, she refuses and is sent back to the island. As the ship nears land, a hurricane strikes and grounds the boat. The last sailor on the vessel tries to convince the heroine to take off her encumbering dress and swim to the land, but she refuses and accepts her fate. The author is emphatic on this matter of clothing and the quite dysfunctional modesty that Virginie brought from her European education. Modern readers may be tempted to laugh at the pathetic description of her corpse: 'Her eyes were closed; but the pale violets of death intermingled on her cheeks with the roses of modesty. One of her hands was on her dress, and the other, clutched to her heart, was tightly closed...'. She grasps, of course, Paul's portrait.

Bernardin brought together, as did Rousseau, the concepts of human nature and of nature in the sense of flora and fauna, setting up the romantic idea that nature exists in a special way in certain places, that by leaving the city one comes closer to 'nature', and by leaving Europe altogether one might find nature unspoiled – or one might, at the very least, come to a new understanding of oneself and of society by having a different vantage point. Paul and Virginie develop as upright, generous, frank, and somewhat austere young people not only because they are spared the corrupting social influences of their contemporaries in Europe but also, more mysteriously, because they are close to the earth of their tropical island. The contention that the basic trope of the novel as a genre is metonymic rather than metaphoric (that is, that it conveys significance by associating things in terms of spatial proximity rather than similarity) is useful for an understanding of the use of description in *Paul et Virginie* (and as it will be subsequently for the novels of Sand, Flaubert, and Balzac). Not only do the descriptions of plants and landscapes give an idea of the heroine's and hero's temperaments, but the interaction with these places shapes these temperaments. In the spirit of Rousseau's *Émile*, Paul is fully capable of felling a tree without an axe, making a fire without a flint, and making a warm meal from a palm bud. Paul, in short, seems an avatar of Robinson Crusoe. His greatness depends on what he can do, not on his birth.

# Chapter 5
# Around the Revolution

> 'Because you are a great lord, you think you are a genius!... Nobility, wealth, rank, estates, all that makes you so proud! What did you do for so many riches? You simply took the trouble to be born, and nothing more: otherwise, a fairly ordinary man!'
>
> (*Parce que vous êtes un grand seigneur, vous vous croyez un grand génie!... Noblesse, fortune, un rang, des places, tout cela rend si fier! Qu'avez-vous fait pour tant de biens? Vous vous êtes donné la peine de naître, et rien de plus: du reste, homme assez ordinaire!*)

With these words in a soliloquy, Figaro, the valet to Count Almaviva, describes his master, in Pierre Caron de Beaumarchais's masterpiece *The Crazy Day, or The Marriage of Figaro* (*La Folle journée, ou Le Mariage de Figaro*), which was finally performed at the Comédie Française on 27 April 1784 after six years of censorship and intrigue. Less than five years later, in January 1789, the *États Généraux* were called into session for the first time since 1614 and, with hindsight, we perceive this as the beginning of the French Revolution.

Beaumarchais's comedy has become symbolic of the cultural ferment that led to the Revolution, though, like all historical events, there is a certain arbitrariness in choosing one single moment as the 'beginning'. The 18th century as a whole was full of signals of a growing disaffection for an absolute monarchy, a growing conviction that social institutions were based on an implicit contract rather than on divine authority or on an unquestioned nature of things. In the multi-talented Figaro, Beaumarchais created an internationally recognized personage who incarnates the wit, talent, and resentment of those who are not noble in title but who form the enterprising and successful *tiers état* (the 'third estate', as distinct from the aristocracy and the Church). Figaro has at one point the audacity actually to call himself a *gentilhomme*, explaining 'If Heaven had wanted, I would be the son of a prince' – and his references elsewhere in the play to chance (*le hasard*) make it clear that it is precisely a matter of pure chance that he and his master the count occupy their actual positions.

Figaro is also the amusing barber of *The Barber of Seville* (*Le Barbier de Séville*, 1775), in which work it is debatable whether he is the central figure or in a supporting role, and the very fact that he is the eponymous character and yet working for the benefit of another points to tensions in both the literary and the more broadly social context. In that earlier play, he helps the count defeat the machinations of the ageing Dr Bartholo and marry Bartholo's beautiful and wealthy young ward. The intricate and extremely amusing goings-on in these two comedies are at least in part responsible for the many works based on them, ranging from Mozart's *Le nozze di Figaro* only two years after the play to one of the early French films of Georges Méliès, *Le Barbier de Séville* (1904), as is the resourcefulness of the protagonist. It is worth noting that the titles of both comedies refer to Figaro.

Who is Figaro? The structure of *The Marriage of Figaro* places this question somewhat unexpectedly in the middle of the play, the third of the five acts, which consists of a judicial proceeding to enforce a contract. Figaro had borrowed a large sum of money from a much older woman and had promised to marry her if he failed to repay the loan. In centring his play on this moment, Beaumarchais emphasizes the themes of finance, contract, law, birth, and class power – all themes that were central to the Revolution. Figaro's employer, the count, who is also trying to seduce Figaro's fiancée, is also the presiding judicial authority, and this arrangement calls into question the foundation of any just law. The only reason that Figaro is able to avoid this marriage is the chance discovery that he is the long-lost son of the woman from whom he borrowed the money. Figaro turns out to be of 'higher' birth than he had seemed, yet there is still a disparity between rank and talent. Figaro's question 'What did you do for so many riches?' remains a valid one, for it is clear that the powerful count is neither smarter nor more energetic than his valet and considerably less moral. Where Marivaux played with the idea that a person's intelligence, sensitivity, and talent might be at odds with his or her class (birth) origins, only to conclude in each case that, when the true identity of each is established, inherited privilege is justified, for Beaumarchais this is no longer the case.



When Figaro reclaims his birth identity in *The Marriage of Figaro*, Beaumarchais does more than reflect the political and social controversies of the day. He also points to the parallel agitation in literature itself. As Victor Hugo was to show a few decades later in the preface to *Cromwell*, the division of dramatic genres into comedy and tragedy no longer seemed to keep pace with perceptions of human society. The 18th century had burst out of this binary structure, inherited from 17th-century neo-Aristotelianism, and had produced many plays called *drames*. Beaumarchais himself had written a *drame*, *Eugénie*, that was performed at the Comédie Française in 1767, and on that occasion he also published his *Essay on the Serious Dramatic Genre* (*Essai sur le genre dramatique sérieux*). He again brought up this question in a 'Moderate Letter' (*Lettre modérée*) that he published as a preface to the printed version of *Le Barbier de Séville*. In this often sarcastic letter, he notes the classical distinction between comedy and tragedy and the traditional exclusion of anything in between. Aristotle had defined comedy as the representation of men lower than ourselves and tragedy as that of men superior to ourselves. Beaumarchais exclaims:

> To attempt to present people of a middle condition, overwhelmed and in wretched situations, shame on you! One should only show them ridiculed. Ridiculous citizens and unfortuante kings – those are the only real and possible theatrical works.
>
> (*Présenter des hommes d'une condition moyenne, accablés et dans le malheur, fi donc! On ne doit jamais les montrer que bafoués. Les citoyens ridicules et les rois malheureux, voilà tout le théâtre existant et possible.*)

The shift in dramatic genres corresponds, then, to a change in the type of person who can be the central figure, the hero, like Figaro.

## One extreme of the 'nature' debate

The century-long questioning of the basis of the social order and growing scepticism about the claims that the social order was founded on nature, itself based on divine providence, led to far more radical expressions. The Marquis de Sade (1740–1814) published *Justine ou les Malheurs de la Vertu* (1791) anonymously, the year after the Revolution brought about his release from a long imprisonment. *Justine* was an instant success. Although this novel, like most of his copious writings, is known for its depiction of the kind of sexual activity that gave us the adjective 'sadistic', Sade's writing concerns much more than 'unnatural' sexual practices. Anyone reading Sade primarily for titillation is likely to be disappointed: much of the narrative is interrupted by philosophical reflections on the permanence of evil and the pleasure that it gives the perpetrators. Although Sade took the side of the Revolution and was, despite his aristocratic origins, elected to the National Convention in 1790, he differed from the *philosophes* of the Enlightenment by not believing that society could bring about improvements in man's lot.

**6. Napoleon Bonaparte throwing a book of the Marquis de Sade into the fire, in a drawing attributed to P. Cousturier (1885)**

The liberation from revealed religion that permitted the Revolution to found a state on human reason was taken by Sade as the opportunity for complete freedom in the service of pleasure in a world in which the strong use and destroy the weak. One of the heroine's persecutors calmly explains the process by which primitive men invented a transcendent being to explain natural phenomena that frightened them. In its structure, *Justine* combines the loose, open-ended picaresque plot with the atmosphere of the gothic novel. Justine as heroine is a female Candide, but where Candide represents common sense at last freeing itself from a doctrine that is obviously ridiculous, in *Justine*, more daringly, the central tenets of religion and the traditional state are presented as absurd, while Justine tries vainly to resist on behalf of religion and virtue. In a dedicatory letter, Sade presents the triumph of vice as a literary innovation, saying that novels almost always show good rewarded and evil punished, but:

> to show an unfortunate woman wandering from one calamity to another, a plaything of wickedness, target of every debauchery, exposed to the most barbarous and monstrous appetites [...] with the goal of drawing from all that one of the most sublime lessons of morality that mankind has every received – this is [...] to reach the goal by a road little travelled until now.

Sade's atheistic libertinism was always out of step with the Revolution as a whole, with its emphasis on civic virtue and equality (both in short supply in Sade's novels) and became more so as time passed. Arrested by Napoleon under the Consulate, Sade died in the Charenton mental hospital just before the Bourbon Restoration.

## From 'heroes' to great men (and women)

'Men are born and remain free and equal in rights. Social distinctions can be based solely on what is useful to all' (*Les hommes naissent et demeurent libres et égaux en droits. Les distinctions sociales ne peuvent être fondées que sur l'utilité commune*), proclaims the first article of the Declaration of the Rights of Man and of the Citizen (*La Déclaration des droits de l'Homme et du citoyen*, 26 August 1789). This brief and eloquent official document, adopted by the National Constituent Assembly, demonstrates that the central issue of the struggle that lasted from 1789 until the Bourbon Restoration in 1814 was the status of each individual man (two years later Olympe de Gouges pointed out the omission of women's rights in her proposal for a *Déclaration des droits de la femme et de la citoyenne* – her text was rejected and she died on the guillotine in 1793).

Figaro had prefigured this demand for equality, and Justine suffered as eternal victim of an aristocratic libertinism. Looking forward and backwards from these representative literary figures, we can see (with help from Beaumarchais's *Moderate Letter*) that all works reveal ideas, usually implicit and taken for granted, about which people are worth writing about, about whose stories are important. The choice of central figure can fall on a hero, as in the case of Roland, who represents the highest aspirations of society as perceived by the author; on an eccentric, like Molière's misanthropic Alceste; or on a villain or anti-hero, consummate example of some deep vice, like the hypocrite Tartuffe in another comedy of Molière, *Le Tartuffe*. The Revolution broadened the spectrum of those whose stories were considered worthy of attention – following the line advocated by Beaumarchais, but not far enough for de Gouges – and it would continue to broaden in the following centuries. Nonetheless, it would be a vast simplification to say that French literature had simply become more 'egalitarian' and shifted from Roland to Figaro, from Gargantua to Candide. There had always been central characters who represented those of modest condition, from the street-smart self-taught lawyer Master Pierre Pathelin (in *La Farce de Maistre Pathelin*, c. 1464) to the police officers of Lyon in François de Rosset's *Histoires tragiques de nostre temps* (1614). However, these people were generally presented as either comical or shocking in a society within which literature reflected the unchanging assignment of people to life-long places within class (or 'condition'). While they might be protagonists, they were not 'heroes' if we mean by this term those who are held in highest esteem.

**7. Voltaire's remains are transferred to the Pantheon, 1791, engraving after Lagrenée**



The Revolution, following developments throughout the Enlightenment, changed that. On 4 April 1791, the Constituent Assembly ordered the transformation of the just-built church of the abbey of Sainte Geneviève into a 'Pantheon of Great Men' (*Panthéon des Grands Hommes*). This was a decisive shift, from the older concept of the 'hero' to the new idea of 'great man'. Henceforth, not only exceptional military valour but also outstanding merit in non-military service would be recognized as earning a place at the pinnacle of society. Heretofore, the highest aristocracy, from whom the monarch came, had been fundamentally a military caste (the *noblesse d'épée*), and one of the highest functions of the poet had been to sing the glory of the military hero. The physical monument known as the Pantheon (where today the writers Rousseau, Voltaire, Victor Hugo, Émile Zola, and André Malraux are buried) marks the culmination of this shift in the conception of greatness, and it has been shown that the Enlightenment idea of the 'great man' and of a national Pantheon preceded the architectural site that we now associate with that name.

## Literature and its epoch

Literature concerning the Revolution continued to be written long after the Bourbon kings returned. On this point, two observations should be made, one obvious and the other less so. It is obvious that in the quarter-century between the *États Généraux* of 1789 and the installation of Louis XVIII as king in 1814, less could be written about the events of those years than in the centuries that have followed. France thus has many novels, plays, and poems about the Revolution from the following period. A less obvious observation is that whenever we write about literature within an historical framework, it is difficult to resist the (false) idea that the French people of the past had available to them the same range of texts that we do. Of course, for the most part, they had more; they had the many books that were printed once and never reprinted or that were best-sellers at the time and then disappeared into the depths of the Bibliothèque Nationale de France. It has been said that there were well over a thousand plays produced during the Revolution – but (as Villon might have asked): where are the plays of yesterday?



On the other hand, in some instances we have works that contemporaries did not have. De Gouges's *Déclaration des droits de la femme et de la citoyenne* was printed in 1791, but how many people actually saw this proposal, which now figures in many university courses about Revolutionary France? In the case of Sade, his manuscript *Les Cent Vingt Journées de Sodome*, which he wrote in the Bastille and lost on his release, was not widely available in print until the 1930s. Should this work by Sade be considered part of the history of the literature of the 18th century, or of the 20th? Such questions, of course, are not limited to this particular period, nor even to unpublished or little-circulated works. Montaigne's *Essais* (first edition 1580; revised editions in 1588 and 1595) are routinely viewed as part of the literary culture of the 16th century. Yet the third book of the *Essais*, containing some of the most important chapters, could only have been read during the last 11 years of the 16th century, whereas Montaigne was a hugely important author during the century after his death. And Irène Némirovsky's novellas, written before the author died in Auschwitz, were published more than sixty years later as *Suite Française* (2004). They belong in one sense to the culture of the Second World War and the Holocaust, and in another sense to the literary culture of the early 21st century.

## Looking back at the Revolution

So the Revolution continued to inspire literary works in various and sometimes paradoxical ways, and to focus on characters who could not have been imagined prior to this great upheaval. Claire de Duras's short story *Ourika* (1823) appears in many ways as a very modern text that has affinities both with the anti-slavery and pro-woman writings of Olympe de Gouges and with today's feminism and interest in non-European cultures. On the other hand, the narrative *Ourika* emerges out of a highly conservative point of view that ends by condemning both the progressive aristocracy of the Enlightenment and the Revolution for creating excessive hope for emancipation. In her own terms, the central figure of the story, Ourika, is a kind of monster created by the Enlightenment and by an incomplete Revolution. Her first-person narrative (which is presented as committed to paper by an attending physician) relates her arrival in France as an orphan from Senegal who was bought as a slave at the age of two by a kind-hearted colonial governor and given to his aunt, who raised her as a beloved child. Ourika lives happily in luxury and is given a 'perfect education', learning English, Italian, painting, and reading the finest authors. She knows that she is *une négresse* but is far from considering this a defect. Everyone finds her charming, elegant, and beautiful. She is an outstanding dancer. In short, everything seems wonderful to Ourika until the day when she overhears a conversation in which her generous patroness tells a friend about Ourika, 'I would do anything to make her happy, and yet, when I think about her position, I see it as hopeless. Poor Ourika! I see her as alone, forever alone in life!'

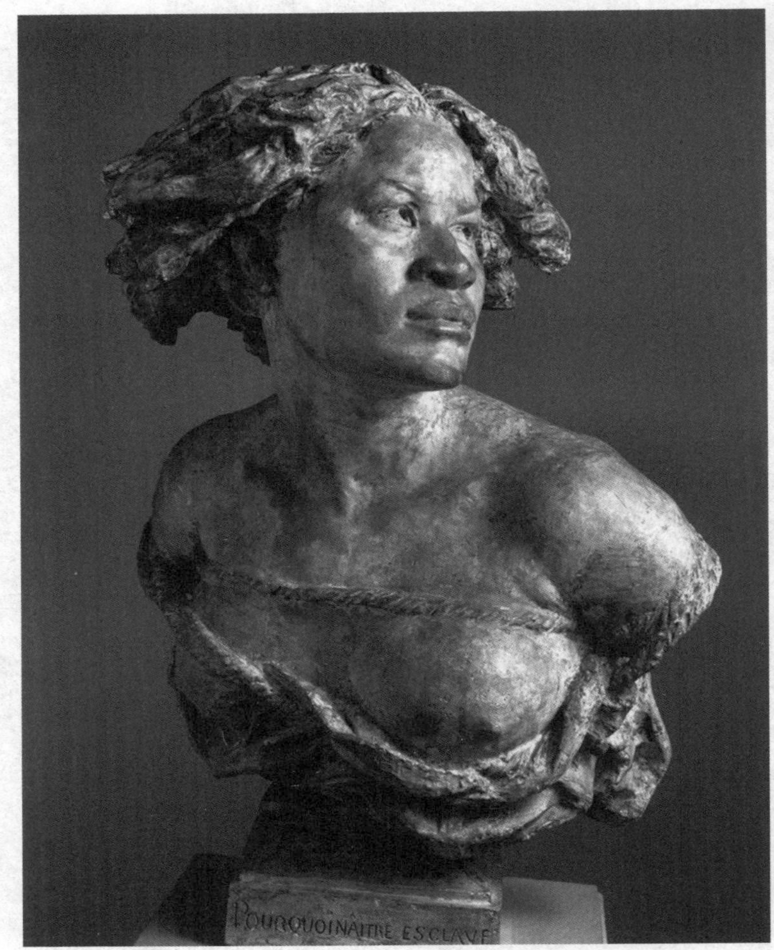


**8. Bust by Jean-Baptiste Carpeaux, entitled 'Why be born a slave?' (1868)**

From that point onward, Ourika realizes that her race makes her unmarriageable in a society in which only marriage can confer station, respectability, and an honourable relationship with a man. In the words of one of the characters in the story, Ourika's upbringing has 'violated the natural order' (*brisé l'ordre de la nature*). She could only marry an inferior, venal man who 'for the sake of money, would consent perhaps to have negro children'. Ourika ends up in a convent, ashamed both of the African slaves who revolted in Haiti and at the executions and confiscations of the Revolution in European France. She fits in nowhere except in the convent, neither in the old French, white aristocratic order in which she was raised, nor in her native Senegal, nor in the supposedly egalitarian democratic society. Claire de Duras, who hosted a very influential Paris salon during the Restoration, shows in *Ourika* the conservative or reactionary face of French Romanticism. This short narrative incorporates some of Rousseau's and Bernardin de Saint-Pierre's ideas of the harmful effects of society and the natural order – Ourika is like a Senegalese Virginie, lost when transported to Europe. But Duras's idea of the 'natural order' is an anti-Revolutionary one, belonging to the world of the Restoration aristocracy which returned to France from exile.



Many of these exiled aristocrats wrote with decided nostalgia for the old order, often going far back into the past for their settings or continuing the 18th-century exploration of exotic locations, but with an anti-Enlightenment, Christian emphasis like that presented by François-René de Chateaubriand, author of the very influential *The Genius of Christianity* (*Le Génie du Christianisme*, 1802). In his novella *René*, published originally as part of this longer work, he portrays the troubled hero René, a lonely, tormented, self-centred aristocrat, haunted by his incestuous love of his sister (here, again, the insistence on the tragic consequences of violations of the natural order), who finds truth among the North American Indians. René's flight to Louisiana may have been suggested by the earlier and extremely popular *Manon Lescaut*, by Antoine François Prévost (1731), in which the courtesan Manon – a prototype for many a subsequent 'femme fatale' – and her lover seek to live peacefully in the French colony, but where Manon dies of exposure and exhaustion in the inhospitable wilderness. Chateaubriand, a somewhat paradoxical follower of Rousseau, used the New World as the vantage point from which to criticize modern mankind: alienated, self-important, and without the humility to submit to tradition. With Chateaubriand, the ideas of the 'modern' and of progress take on meanings quite different from the ones they had before the Revolution. The Enlightenment had largely accepted from the 17th century the promotion of classical antiquity as far superior to the intervening Middle Ages. Chateaubriand accepted the idea of progress, but attributed it to Christianity, and thus shifted emphasis from antiquity to the centuries of Christian dominance. He engaged in a public controversy with the important theorist and critic Germaine de Staël, author, among many other works, of *On Literature Considered in its Relations with Social Institutions* (*De la littérature considérée dans ses rapports avec les institutions sociales*, 1800), in which he set out his strong opposition to any positive concept of modernity not based on Christianity. His revalorization of the medieval over the classical worldview had many followers in the 19th century.



On the other side of the political and cultural divide that issued from the Revolution is Stendhal (pen-name of Marie-Henri Beyle, 1783–1842), who served in the Napoleonic armies, and who created a kind of anti-René in Julien Sorel, hero of *The Red and the Black* (*Le Rouge et le noir, Chronique de 1830*, 1830), an ambitious young man of very modest class inspired by Napoleon, yet living under the oppressive Bourbon monarchy. As an adolescent, his favourite books are Rousseau's *Confessions* and *Le Mémorial de Sainte-Hélène*, an account of Napoleon's conversations during his last years as a prisoner, after his defeat at Waterloo. Stendhal, considered the forerunner of the 'realist' novel, both creates a fascinatingly complex character and evokes the long-lasting social tensions and turbulence that followed the Revolution up until the July Revolution (like Stendhal's novel, 1830). Although Julien's two dominant traits are hypocrisy and ambition, he is surrounded by women and men who love and help him during his social ascent and then his spectacular crime and execution. The contrast between his heroic aspirations – however anti-heroic the means he adopts to achieve them – and the philistinism, complacency, and greed of the society around him, is typical of the Romantic conception of the hero found soon after in Alfred de Vigny's play *Chatterton* (1835) and many works of the subsequent decades.

# Chapter 6
# The hunchback, the housewife, and the *flâneur*

As Stendhal's novel showed, the France of the early decades of the 19th century was divided politically and culturally between, on the one hand, the desire for reconnection to traditional institutions (such as the Roman Catholic Church, monarchy, the countryside and village) that imparted the sense that everyone had a relatively fixed place in the social order and, on the other hand, the aspiration to ideals of human potential, freedom, and universal rights. This dichotomy often took the concrete form of the opposition between Paris and *la province* (anywhere else in France; significantly, in French, this is expressed as a singular noun and conveys as much the sense of a condition as of a place).

## Nostalgia and history

The aftershocks of the French Revolution and the reactions against it continued to the very end of the 19th century – the Dreyfus Affair and Zola's resounding editorial 'J'Accuse!' in 1898 exposed the persistence of aristocratic privilege in France – but another revolution, the Industrial Revolution, was at work shaping French society and the perception of time, place, human relations, and human creations. Fascination with the Ancien Régime and the Christian cultural heritage, exemplified by Chateaubriand, became a trend, taking on greater historical weight through the work of historians like Jules Michelet, literary historians like Sainte-Beuve, and architects like Viollet-le-Duc. The latter is responsible for rebuilding (in ways that are now often seen as more fanciful than historically accurate) the cathedral of Notre Dame de Paris, the Mont Saint-Michel, and the fortified city of Carcassonne. Following upon the writings of Chateaubriand and de Staël, Victor Hugo vigorously asserted a theory of social and aesthetic progress in the preface to his drama *Cromwell* (1827), framed historically within the concept of three ages of human society – the primitive, the ancient or antique, and the modern – which correspond to the sequence of development of literary genres: lyric, epic, and dramatic.

The 'modern' period for Hugo is quite extensive, for he equates it with the dominance of Christianity in Europe. Drama was born on the day Christianity said to man:

> 'You are double, you are composed of two beings, one perishable, the other immortal; one carnal, the other ethereal; one chained to its appetites, needs, and passions, the other born up on the wings of enthusiasm and reverie; one always bent towards earth, its mother, the other always springing towards heaven, its homeland'. This is the day that drama was born.

From this concept of doubleness, Hugo derives an insistence on the mixed character of all modern art, which should depict the sordid as well as the sublime, the trivial as well as the important. In rejecting the drama of the 17th and 18th centuries, Hugo (like Stendhal in *Racine et Shakespeare*, 1823–4), saw the English dramatist as superior to the French tragedian because Shakespeare included the melancholic, the earthy, and the grotesque alongside the sublime. Accusing the French Academy and its neo-Aristotelian poetics of stifling Corneille's creativity, Hugo particularly praised the author of *Le Cid* as 'an entirely modern genius, imbued with the Middle Ages and Spain, forced to lie to himself and to throw himself into Antiquity'.

**9. Engraving by Luc-Olivier Merson (1881) inspired by Victor Hugo's novel *Notre Dame de Paris* (1831)**

## Heroes of the grotesque

The link between the grotesque and the medieval appears in Hugo's *Notre Dame de Paris* (1831, fourteen years before the restoration of the crumbling monument was undertaken, in part because of the impact of Hugo's work) – a novel best known in English as *The Hunchback of Notre Dame*. Although Hugo disapproved of the English title, because for him the cathedral itself was the central character, the association of a deformed body and a generous spirit in the fictive late 15th-century bell-ringer Quasimodo provides one example of the doubleness that the author so prized. The hunchback first appears in the novel when a festive crowd decides to elect its own 'pope of fools' on the basis of the ugliest grimace. The contestants in turn poke their faces through a broken circular window in a chapel wall – thus, in effect, uniting the grimacing face with the stone to suggest a gothic grotesque or gargoyle. Finally, a head appears that is universally acclaimed. It is perfect: 'But then surprise and admiration reached their pinnacle. The grimace was his face. Or rather, his whole body was a grimace' (*Mais c'est alors que la surpise et l'admiration furent à leur comble. La grimace était son visage. Ou plutôt toute sa personne était une grimace*). This is Quasimodo, who is both metonymically and metaphorically tied to the cathedral itself: he is constantly present in the church, and he is also similar to the building in its gothic aesthetic.

But the best-known dramatic example of this grotesque doubleness is *Lorenzaccio*, Alfred de Musset's drama published seven years after Hugo's preface to *Cromwell*. Neither *Cromwell* nor *Lorenzaccio* were ever performed during their authors' lifetimes, both were too incendiary by the standards of censorship of the time, and both were, in their published form, considered impossible to stage – Musset's play seems to require from sixty to a hundred actors and extras. Musset based *Lorenzaccio* in part on a text by his lover George Sand (Amandine Aurore Lucile Dupin, Baroness Dudevant), a *scène historique* entitled *Une conspiration en 1537*.

Musset's work concentrates on the main hero's moral character, which at first seems, both to the audience and to almost all of his contemporaries within the play, to be entirely vicious. Completely absorbed in the pleasures of drink and sex, Lorenzo serves as procurer for his master and cousin, Alexandre, Duke of Florence, for whom he quickly and skilfully acquires the sexual services of the women of the city, by threats, promises, and money. A coward, he never carries a sword and is called by the Duke himself a *femmelette* (a 'womanling') after Lorenzo faints when challenged to a duel. As the scenes unfold, Lorenzaccio (the contemptuous form of the name that the Florentines have given him) seems entirely to merit everyone's scorn as bully, spy, toady, and coward. But then it appears that Lorenzaccio's character has been deliberately assumed for the purpose of killing Alexandre – in this way, Lorenzo would simply be a highly successful actor, concealing a unified and noble self. What makes Lorenzaccio fascinating to Musset, however, is something much darker: Lorenzo, the originally pure, studious, idealistic scholar of ancient Rome, who modelled himself on Lucius Junius Brutus, the killer of Tarquin, is not merely feigning to be vicious but rather he has really become Lorenzaccio.



Hugo's concept of a double man, both hideous and sublime, is realized in Musset's hero, who has really become addicted to the brutally licentious life while still aspiring to a heroic gesture of political and personal purity. We are led to suppose that what we have seen of Lorenzaccio in the first scene is not simply a feint but a true expression of his own desires:

> What is more curious for the connoisseur than to debauch an infant? To see in a child of fifteen the future slut; to study, seed, insinuate the thread of vice under the guise of a fatherly friend...
>
> (*Quoi de plus curieux pour le connaisseur que la débauche à la mamelle? Voir dans une enfant de quinze ans la rouée à venir; étudier, ensemencer, infiltrer paternellement le filon mystérieux du vice dans le conseil d'un ami...*)

Disseminating corruption throughout the families of Florence as within himself, Lorenzaccio has become such a cynic, or such a realist, in regard to human nature that his intention to follow through on his solitary plot to kill Alexandre has no connection whatever with the anti-tyrannical agitation among certain groups of Florentine families. In representing the character of the Florentines – and through them, no doubt, his 19th-century contemporaries – Musset shows that those who are outwardly 'noble' and quick to defend their honour are ineffectual. Lorenzaccio, outwardly despicable, manages to achieve the death of Duke Alexandre, though this really changes nothing. At the end of the play, as at the beginning, the Florentines complain and conspire, and life goes on as always.

## The provincial life

The exasperated sense that heroic striving is vain, and that the coarse, materialistic, conservative common sense of the bourgeoisie will always triumph over those who seek something more out of life often was embodied in the contrast between fast-changing, fashionable Paris and the stodgy, rustic, and boring provincial life. Balzac's immense collection of novels, which, in the course of its evolution, he decided to call *The Human Comedy* (*La Comédie Humaine*) is divided into various series and subseries that reflect the importance of the Paris – *province* distinction, such as the 'Scenes of the life of the provinces' (*Scènes de la vie de province*), the 'Scenes of Parisian life', and 'Scenes of country life'. Yet the greatest hero to strive against the prison of the provincial life is Emma Bovary, the protagonist of Gustave Flaubert's novel *Madame Bovary*.

When it first appeared as a serial in 1856 in the *Revue de Paris*, the work had the highly significant original title, *Madame Bovary, moeurs de province*. For Emma, a woman more intelligent than any of those around her, though with only a convent education, the most powerful magic is contained in the words, 'They do it in Paris!' (*Cela se fait à Paris!*), five words that suffice to propel her into the arms of her second lover. Paris is for her the ultimate place of dreams, though the dimension of place is insufficient without the figure of an ideal role or persona. Flaubert's novel is full of representations of the effect of representation, fictions that propel actions. Emma delights in heroines who come to her from stories told by the nuns, novels, magazines, and even from plates! As a child in the convent, 'they had supper on painted plates that depicted the story of Mlle de La Vallière' (the young mistress of Louis XIV, who once fled from the court to a convent). In her remote Norman village, Emma receives magazines from Paris, and she reads the novels of George Sand and Balzac. At one point, her mother-in-law tries to keep her from reading novels – a hint that Emma is a latter-day Don Quixote, maddened by reading. Her life cycles through fits of intense energy and striving to make something of herself, followed by periods of lethargy and sickness. This alternation contrasts with provincial routine, so regular in its seasonal cycles that it seems to be unchanged since time immemorial. Though she stands out from her milieu – and thus permits Flaubert to create a multitude of picturesque characters with all the acuity of a Dickens – Emma is neither a person of great intelligence nor refinement. Her unhappiness illustrates something said in Hugo's *Notre Dame de Paris*, 'A one-eyed man is much more incomplete than a blind one. He knows what he is missing' (*Un borgne est bien plus incomplet qu'un aveugle. Il sait ce qui lui manque*).

The view of *la province* conveyed in Flaubert (as in the novels of Stendhal and Balzac) shows that the cult of nature and of village life, so dear to followers of Rousseau and Bernardin de Saint-Pierre, had by mid-century provoked a backlash. There is nothing uplifting and noble about herding cows in Flaubert's work, and vistas of fields with flowers do not bring Emma any consolation. In fact, through Emma's cliché-ridden imagination, Flaubert parodies the romantic notion of an idyllic escape to the countryside when Emma fantasizes eloping with Rodolphe to 'a village of fishermen, where brown nets were drying in the wind, along a cliff with little huts. That is where they would settle down to live: they would have a low house with a flat roof, in the shade of a palm tree, at the end of a gulf, on the seaside'. This is both particularly comic and also very sad, in that Emma, who lives in the country, has internalized the fantasies of the city dweller she aspires to be.

Since Emma is a reader of Flaubert's friend and fellow novelist George Sand, it is difficult to resist comparing the character of Emma to the heroine of Sand's earlier work *Consuelo* (1842), a vast historical novel, set in the 18th century, that is almost picaresque in its structure though not in its tone. *Consuelo* follows the life of Consuelo from her impoverished childhood in Venice to her eventual marriage to the half-mad Bohemian (Czech) aristocrat Albert of Rudolstadt. Point by point, the two novels are entirely opposite: Emma is trapped in a prosaic French village, while Consuelo's life is almost a travelogue of the Austro Hungarian empire; Emma yearns for the aristocratic life and for the sophistication of the city and the theatre, while Consuelo spends a good deal of time fleeing all of these things. The life around Emma seems intensely boring but she tries to infuse it with excitement, while Consuelo's life is fully Romantic in the atmosphere and adventures that take place in medieval castles with subterranean passageways and gloomy forests. But most of all, the temperament of each heroine is directly opposed. Consuelo is goodness itself, always patient, generous, resourceful, caring for others, indifferent to wealth and prestige, and with no need for exotic escape.

## Urban exiles

'Any where out of the world', was Charles Baudelaire's diagnosis of human aspirations, so well represented by Emma Bovary and so foreign to Consuelo. The expression, in English, was the title of one of the prose poems in the volume *Le Spleen de Paris* (1869). In 'Any where out of the world', he evokes the power of the eternal 'elsewhere': 'This life is a hospital where each patient is obsessed with the desire to change beds'. This interest in what is happening in the other parts of the world/hospital is a key to the fascinating paradox that Flaubert, like Balzac, Sand, Stendhal, and others, could entertain sophisticated readers with stories of the supposedly stifling provincials, who, in turn, are shown to spend their time longing for Paris (or longing for village life as if they were Parisians). What could Parisians like Baudelaire find to interest them in the life of an unhappy provincial housewife?

Baudelaire was one of the many admiring readers of Flaubert's novel. In his review essay on *Madame Bovary* – which appeared several months after the trial that acquitted Flaubert for outrage to public and religious morality – Baudelaire described the novel as the triumph of the power of writing, a power so great that it scarcely needed a subject. Baudelaire either knew or intuited a famous formulation that Flaubert used in a letter to his lover Louise Colet five years earlier, saying that his dream was someday to write 'a book about nothing... that would have almost no subject or at least where the subject would be almost invisible' (1852). Baudelaire found in *Madame Bovary* the triumph of this artistic challenge: to take the most banal subject, adultery, in the place where stupidity and intolerance reign, *la province*, and to create a heroine who faces this 'total absence of genius' in a masculine way. This heroine, Madame Bovary herself, 'is very sublime in her kind, in her small milieu and facing her small horizon'. Baudelaire, in praising both Flaubert's novel and its heroine, seems at times to identify with her, despite the radical difference in places.

The quintessential Parisian poet, Baudelaire is almost unimaginable elsewhere, but this is not to say that he sings the praises of Paris. Having absorbed Hugo's teaching about the grotesque and about human doubleness, Baudelaire was fascinated by the ugly and by the sublime, by all that was unpredictable and out of place. Perfectly Parisian, Baudelaire, as both poet and as subject of his poetry, cultivated his sense of being in the wrong place as much as Emma Bovary did hers. He wrote of Emma that in her convent school she made for herself a 'God of the future and of chance', and one of the great values of the capital for Baudelaire was its capacity to produce random encounters that generated lyrical fusions.

It is understandable that the metropolis in mid-century should offer freedom and opportunity on a quite different scale from any other city in France, for it was growing explosively. In 1801, Paris had had virtually the same population as at the end of the 17th century, roughly half a million inhabitants in an area of less than 14 square kilometres. By the end of the century, the population quintupled, and Paris had annexed nearby towns and villages so that the urban area was eight times larger. Such an environment favours the 'God of chance' Baudelaire attributed to Emma Bovary, and he seized for himself a poetic persona well adapted to this moment, that of the stroller (*le flâneur*), a role that he describes in an essay on the painter Constantin Guys, 'The Painter of Modern Life': 'For the perfect stroller, for the passionate observer, it is an immense pleasure to dwell in the multitude, in the undulating, in movement, in the fleeting, and the infinite'. The sonnet 'To a Woman Passing By' (*À une passante*, in *Les Fleurs du mal* [*Flowers of Evil*]) illustrates the intensity and the chance nature of the encounters that the poet-stroller prizes in the immense, fast-moving, modern city. The two quatrains, with no addressee, describe a crowded street scene and then the vision of a striking woman. The tercets start by evoking the woman's glance, and then the poet addresses the woman directly. The lightning-like strike of the glance turns the poet's thoughts forward from this encounter to the improbability of future encounters, and shifts the sonnet into a thematic well known to Emma Bovary and her readers: the longed-for elsewhere and another time, when love is fulfilled. The single italicized word, *jamais* (never) – Baudelaire almost never used italics – stresses the other-worldly character of this time, which may not come in this life. The woman, who is in mourning, may indeed be Death, but she may also be simply a woman in the crowd whose ephemeral image nourishes the poet's imagination and to whom the poet attributes an equal role in this mental exchange. The very title of the poem suggests extremes, the fullness of life in a city in which people move rapidly and pass one another (as they do not in a village) and also the eventual absence of movement of someone who has passed beyond life – life and death themselves telescoped into the antithesis of a lighting flash followed by darkness.

A variant of Hugo's double man, the stroller is exquisitely attuned to time, and especially to the vanished past and to the dissonance

### À une passante

La rue assourdissante autour de moi hurlait,
Longue, mince, en grand deuil, douleur majestueuse,
Une femme passa, d'une main fastueuse
Soulevant, balançant le feston et l'ourlet;

Agile et noble, avec sa jambe de statue,
Moi, je buvais, crispé comme un extravagant,
Dans son oeil, ciel livide où germe l'ouragan,
La douceur qui fascine et le plaisir qui tue.

Un éclair... puis la nuit! – Fugitive beauté
Dont le regard m'a fait soudainement renaître,
Ne te verrai-je plus que dans l'éternité?

Ailleurs, bien loin d'ici! trop tard! *jamais* peut-être!
Car j'ignore où tu fuis, tu ne sais où je vais,
O toi que j'eusse aimée, ô toi qui le savais!

### To a Woman Passing By

The deafening road around me roared.
Tall, slim, in deep mourning, making majestic grief,

A woman passed, lifting and swinging
With a pompous gesture the ornamental hem of her garment,

Swift and noble, with statuesque limb.
As for me, I drank, twitching like an old roué,
From her eye, livid sky where the hurricane is born,
The softness that fascinates and the pleasure that kills,

A gleam, then night! O fleeting beauty,
Your glance has given me sudden rebirth,
Shall I see you again only in eternity?

Somewhere else, very far from here! Too late! Perhaps *never*!
For I do not know where you flee, nor you where I am going,
O you whom I would have loved, O you who knew it!

Translated by Geoffrey Wagner, *Selected Poems of Charles Baudelaire* (New York: Grove Press, 1974)

of near misses. He lives vividly both in the Parisian present and in the past and the elsewhere. In 'The Swan' (*Le Cygne*, dedicated to Victor Hugo, 1860), Baudelaire builds his poem around another chance encounter in a Paris undergoing the colossal transformations that Haussmann carried out between 1853 and 1870 and that created the city of wide boulevards and standardized building heights that we know today. In the process, most of medieval Paris disappeared, thus endowing the vestiges of the Middle Ages with a new, nostalgic, value.

In 'The Swan', Baudelaire creates a deft mosaic of different moments, especially three: the present, in which he is crossing the newly constructed Place du Carrousel between the Tuileries and the Louvre; a past moment when there had been a menagerie in that place; and the imagined moment in Greek antiquity when the Trojan prince Hector's widow Andromache, become the slave of Pyrrhus, bends over the cenotaph of her heroic husband.

**10. Maxime Lalanne (1827–86), 'Demolition work for the construction of the Boulevard Saint-Germain', a scene from Haussmann's renovations of Paris**

Baudelaire assembles these moments along the thematic axis of absence: in crossing the Carrousel, he sees that the menagerie is no longer there. In that menagerie, a swan had escaped from its cage, and vainly sought water from the dry pavement. The poet imagines the swan remembering the lost lake of its youth and then imagines Andromache remembering Hector. The last three quatrains of the poem evoke a myriad of others who have lost something, and specifically those who have lost a place, like the 'emaciated and tubercular Negress...seeking...the missing palm trees of proud Africa'. The stroller is thus the guise in which the city poet can multiply his experience of narrative characters, for he identifies himself with each in turn: Andromache, the swan, the African woman, and perhaps even with the dying hero of the *Song of Roland*: 'An old memory blows a horn with full force'.

The endless change that seemed to Baudelaire to be the only constant of Paris accelerated a decade after *Le Cygne*. The Franco-Prussian War of 1870–1 ended the Second Empire and brought the insurrection known as the Paris Commune and its bloody suppression. Paris almost tripled its surface area in the second half of the century, and the continued development of the rail network centred on the capital brought more workers.

**11. Claude Monet, *La Gare Saint-Lazare* (1877)**

One side of this change is reflected in the naturalist novels of Émile Zola (1840–1902) with their attention to the gritty underside of this prosperous period, the heyday of the French colonial empire. These include *L'Assommoir* (1877) and *La Bête humaine* (1890), both about the ravages of alcoholism in working-class families. But in reaction to naturalism in the novel and theatre came Symbolism, which found in Baudelaire its harbinger and in Stéphane Mallarmé its greatest exponent. Much of his poetry, in appearance frivolous and occasional (for instance, a series on women's fans, on a coiffure, etc.), concerns death and memorialization, particularly monuments to poets. With Ronsard and Hugo, Mallarmé is probably the poet who most vigorously championed the power of language itself to challenge death. Mallarmé's protagonists are therefore most often poets, celebrated in a series of sonnet 'tombs' such as *Le Tombeau d'Edgar Poe* (1876), but in time Mallarmé reached the highest point of abstraction with a protagonist named, simply, Igitur (Latin, 'therefore') in a posthumous prose text dating from around 1870, *Igitur, ou la folie d'Elbehnon*. The hero finishes in the tomb after challenging Nothingness with a roll of the dice: 'The character, who, believing in the existence of the Absolute alone, imagines himself everywhere in a dream [...] finds action unnecessary' (*Le personnage qui, croyant à l'existence du seul Absolu, s'imagine être partout dans un rêve [...] trouve l'acte inutile*). This text may be the earliest form of the great hermetic poem that Mallarmé published almost thirty years later, in which we seem to encounter once again Igitur's roll of the dice: *A Roll of Dice Will Never Abolish Chance* (*Un coup de dés jamais n'abolira le hasard*, 1897). In its graphic disposition, apparently spattered across the page in different fonts and type sizes, this is one of the most inventive texts in all of French literature, and it was crucially important for the following century.

*LE NOMBRE*

EXISTÂT-IL
autrement qu'hallucination éparse d'agonie

COMMENÇÂT-IL ET CESSÂT-IL
sourdant que nié et clos quand apparu
enfin
par quelque profusion répandue en rareté
SE CHIFFRÂT-IL

évidence de la somme pour peu qu'une
ILLUMINÂT-IL

LE HASARD

*Choit*
*la plume*
*rythmique suspens du sinistre*
*s'ensevelir*
*aux écumes originelles*
*naguères d'où sursauta son délire jusqu'à une cime*
*flétrie*
*par la neutralité identique du gouffre*

**12. A page of Stéphane Mallarmé's poem, *Un coup de dés jamais n'abolira le hasard* (1897)**

# Chapter 7
# From Marcel to Rrose Selavy

## The world of Proust's novel

The heady metaphysical aspirations of Mallarmé's spare lyric, which seem at times ready to leave language and the printed page behind, appear at first to have little in common with the *roman-fleuve*, the immense, onward-streaming novel that marks the emphatic beginning of the 20th century, *In Search of Lost Time* (*À la recherche du temps perdu*, 1913–27) by Marcel Proust (1871–1922). Yet these two authors of the belle époque (a name given after the First World War to the preceding period of peace from the end of the Franco-Prussion War in 1870 until 1914) have in common an intellectual adventurousness nourished by the philosophical movements of the time. It is tempting to consider Proust's novel as a *Bildungsroman* (or as a variant thereof, the *Kunstlerroman* – the education of the artist), but one in which the usual linearity of that form has yielded to an extremely complex interplay of moments of experience and later moments of interpretation. This complexity is augmented by length, competing editions based on different opinions concerning the proper use of posthumous material, and different English translations with different titles. *À la recherche du temps perdu*, which in the current French Pléaide edition runs (with extensive notes) to more than 7,000 pages, is comprised of seven titled sub-novels. The first of these (published at the author's expense in

1913), *Swann's Way* (*Du côté de chez Swann*), contains the further subsections *Combray*, *Swann in Love* (*Un amour de Swann*), and *Noms de pays: le nom*. The last of the seven sub-novels, *Le temps retrouvé*, was published in 1927, five years after Proust's death. The novel – *À la recherche du temps perdu* – in terms of the chronological range covered stretches from these childhood memories of Combray, at the earliest, to the post-war Paris scenes of the last novel in the series, *The Past Recaptured* (*Le temps retrouvé*, literally 'time refound').

*Combray*, the very first section, opens with the narrator's account of going to sleep and waking – the startling first sentence is 'For a long time, I went to bed early' (*Longtemps, je me suis couché de bonne heure*). The reader has no way of knowing who is making this statement – and, in fact, the given name of the protagonist is mentioned only rarely throughout the seven narratives that make up the work as a whole – but it becomes clear very quickly that there is something very capacious and mysterious about this 'I'. Having fallen asleep while reading, he writes, he would sometimes wake a half-hour later still thinking about the book he was reading. But these thoughts often took a peculiar form: 'it seemed to me that I was the thing the book was about: a church, a quartet, the rivalry between François I and Charles V' (*il me semblait que j'étais moi-même ce dont parlait l'ouvrage: une église, un quatuor, la rivalité de François Ier et de Charles-Quint*). For several pages, the narrator pursues this investigation into the contents of the mind at its awakening, with comments on the identification of the thinking subject with a series of radically heterogeneous objects. The fact that the mind does not at first see them as objects but simply as part of itself is, for the reader, most striking. The narrator continues by tracing the phases of disengagement as the thinker rejoins the world of wakefulness and can no longer understand the dream thoughts that at first seemed so innocently obvious.

These opening pages of the novel, with the radical questioning of the boundaries of the self, have roots with a deep hold on the tradition of French literature. Montaigne, in a famous passage of the *Essais*, recounted his experience of returning to consciousness after a fall in the chapter 'On Practice' (*De l'exercitation*), as did Rousseau in one of his *Reveries of the Solitary Walker* (*Rêveries du promeneur solitaire*). Descartes, in his *Discourse on Method* (*Discours de la méthode*, 1637) had also tried stripping the consciousness of the self back to the simple awareness of being that precedes any actual knowledge of the qualities of that thinking self. In Proust's day, this Cartesian questioning had been given a new currency by the teachings of Franz Brentano and his two brilliant students, Edmund Husserl and Sigmund Freud. And Proust was certainly aware of the work of Henri Bergson, whose writings on the awareness of time have been frequently compared with Proust's work. Though Proust probably reached his interest in the phenomenology of the waking self independently, it is hard to deny that he brought a new vigour and concreteness to the exploration of consciousness, sensation, and memory.



He also gave a new prominence to childhood. The opening meditation on going to bed and waking leads into an account of the bedtime ritual during family summer vacations in Combray. To distract the child from the anguished separation from his mother that bedtime entailed, his family would let him project a magic lantern display onto the walls of his room, where Golo, the hero of the legendary tale represented by the images, exhibits the ability to morph himself according to the object on which he is projected – door knob, curtains, walls: 'Golo's body itself... dealt with any material obstacle, with any bothersome object that it encountered, by taking it as its skeleton, incorporating it, even the doorknob' (*Le corps de Golo lui-même... s'arrangeait de tout obstacle matériel, de tout objet gênant qu'il rencontrait en le prenant comme ossature et en se le rendant intérieur, fût-ce le bouton de la porte...*). Thus Marcel's ability, as the adult narrator, to imagine his waking self as a church or as the rivalry between the king and the emperor is prefigured in the child's experience of the hero's image in the lantern display as it transcends times and places in order to be himself. While Freud was, by another approach, teaching the long-term impact of childhood experience, Proust knit together childhood and adulthood in this persistence of narrative patterns and in the ability of people to identify – and to identify with – the protagonist's role.

This ability appears in the narrator's account of Swann, an adult friend of young Marcel's family, a Parisian who, like Marcel's parents, has a country house in Combray. As a child, Marcel dreads Swann's arrival for dinner parties because this means that his bedtime ritual will be perturbed, his mother will be occupied with her duties as hostess. In short, Swann appears as the cause of the terrible suffering due to the absence of the loved one. As an adult, however, Marcel sees that Swann would have known better than anyone what that suffering was like, for he suffered also from his love for Odette de Crécy. This treatment of Swann is simply an example of Marcel's characteristic plasticity as narrator – but also as protagonist – to focus on a wide range of people, of whom he discovers different aspects as he grows older. The fascination that appears in the early realization that 'Golo' could be himself but also a doorknob is the force that gives value to the subsequent realizations that people, attitudes, actions, and places that at first seemed entirely distinct and incompatible are, in fact, united. For instance, the paths in Combray that lead towards Swann's house (that is, that go *du côté de chez Swann*) seem at first to be entirely opposite those that go towards the château de Guermantes, and Swann and the aristocratic Guermantes family seem quite separate, but they are later shown to be connected. However, as even his perception of the spatial organization shows, the narrator's greatest talent is in creating unforgettable people. So that any reader of *À la recherche du temps perdu* is likely to carry around a mental repertory with characters such as Françoise the cook, Tante Léonie, Baron Charlus, Saint-Loup, Albertine, Elstir the painter, and so forth. These all flow out of the *moi* of the narrator himself, who becomes a super-character and the repository of the entire world that he recounts. Among the most moving pages of the novel are in the concluding section, *Le temps retrouvé*, where he realizes that the past is not gone because it still lives in him.

## The heritage of Mallarmé

Proust's contemporary Paul Valéry (1871–1945) was of a radically different aesthetic temperament. In contrast to the former's lengthy novel with its notoriously long and involved sentences (some spreading over several pages), Valéry's texts, both in prose and verse, are all very spare. Among the more unusual protagonists of French literature is his Monsieur Teste, the hero of a series of texts – one could call them prose poems or essays – in which Valéry explores his intellect in the form of an alter-ego, whose name evokes both 'head' (*tête*, or *teste* in older French) and 'text' (*texte*). Likewise in his verse poems, Valéry represents a self, a *moi*, that borders on the metaphysical. The closest heir of Mallarmé, and the last great Symbolist poet, Valéry's single greatest poetic achievement is *The Graveyard by the Sea* (*Le Cimetière marin*, 1920). Like much contemporary painting (one might think of Kandinsky), this verse poem in 24 stanzas evokes an event or scene that is then distilled to its essence, so much so that the physical incident is scarcely glimpsed. In *The Graveyard by the Sea*, the poet seems to describe an epiphany that he has during hours of thought while looking out at the Mediterranean from a cemetery. The question that he ponders is the relation between body, mind, and time (themes that run throughout the *Teste* texts also), with a concluding acceptance of the body and the demands and pleasures of physical life. More immediately accessible is the brief poem 'The Footsteps' (*Les Pas*), published a year after *The Graveyard*.

**Les Pas**

Tes pas, enfants de mon silence,
Saintement, lentement placés,
Vers le lit de ma vigilance
Procèdent muets et glacés.

Personne pure, ombre divine,
Qu'ils sont doux, tes pas retenus!
Dieux!... tous les dons que je divine
Viennent à moi sur ces pieds nus!

Si, de tes lèvres avancées,
Tu prépares pour l'apaiser,
À l'habitant de mes pensées
La nourriture d'un baiser,

Ne hâte pas cet acte tendre,
Douceur d'être et de n'être pas,
Car j'ai vécu de vous attendre,
Et mon coeur n'était que vos pas.

**The Footsteps**

Your footsteps, children of my silence,
With gradual and saintly pace
Towards the bed of my watchfulness,
Muted and frozen, approach.

Pure one, divine shadow,
How gentle are your cautious steps!
Gods!... all the gifts that I can guess
Come to me on those naked feet!

If, with your lips advancing,
You are preparing to appease
The inhabitant of my thoughts
With the sustenance of a kiss,

Do not hasten the tender act,
Bliss of being and not being,
For I have lived on waiting for you,
And my heart was only your footsteps.

Translated by David Paul

'The Footsteps' gives a very good idea of the way Valéry plays on the threshold of the physical and the metaphysical in much of his poetry. The poem is addressed to a 'pure person'. Is this a woman or a spirit? Is the 'divine shadow' literally divine, or is this hyperbole? Are the footsteps meant to be actual footsteps, or are they the metric feet of the poem itself? Or are the *pas* the poet's heartbeats (he says that his heart is nothing other than these *pas*), which he can hear because all is silent around him? And when those *pas* cease, it seems that the poet, as well as the poem, will come to an end. These are the kinds of questions that Valéry's poems provoke and that create opportunities for patient meditation, which for Valéry was a distinct superiority of poetry over the 19th-century novel.



## Surrealism

Valéry's acquaintance André Breton also reacted against the novel as genre, and *Nadja* (1928; revised edition 1962) is one alternative that he proposed. Breton's work is significant because of his role as leader of the Surrealists, a movement that reflected the continent-wide hunger for something new to replace both 19th-century literature and art and also the social order that had led to the butchery of the First World War. French Surrealism appears in the context of such other movements as Italian Futurism (already launched before the war but with its major impact in the decades thereafter), British Vorticism, Soviet Constructivism, the German Bauhaus, and Swiss and French Dadaism. André Breton was the author of the two *Surrealist Manifestos* (in 1924 and in 1929), thus becoming the public leader of the most significant of these movements (by 'movement' here is meant a group of writers who designate themselves as such and advocate a set of aesthetic and social doctrines). Breton advocated giving priority to the imaginative life and considered the 'real' life as most people know it to be only a pale reflection of the much more real (*surréel*, 'above real') life that was to be achieved upon the overthrow of narrowly rationalist forms of thought and the rejection of the limited options of adult life. In such a limited, ordinary person, dominated by practical concerns:

> All his gestures will be paltry, all his ideas narrow. He will only consider, in what happens to him and can happen to him, only the links to a mass of similar events, events in which he did not participate, *missed* events.
>
> (*Tous ses gestes manqueront d'ampleur; toutes ses idées, d'envergure. Il ne se représentera, de ce qui lui arrive et peut lui arriver, que ce qui relie cet événment à une foule d'événements semblables, événements auxquels il n'a pas pris part, événements* manqués.)



The life of the imagination, which most of us have lost, is cruelly rich in possibilities. In an apostrophe, Breton exclaims, 'Dear imagination, what I love above all about you is that you do not forgive' (*Chère imagination, ce que j'aime surtout en toi, c'est que tu ne pardonnes pas*). The world of imagination, for Breton, is not in the elaborate and carefully wrought creations of the novelists and poets of the tradition but, instead, in the everyday world that surrounds us without our noticing it. Breton was an early and enthusiastic reader of Sigmund Freud (as one can see from the term 'missed events' – coined on the model of the French term for what we call the lapsus or 'Freudian slip', an *acte manqué*), an admirer of Alfred Jarry's *Ubu Roi* (1896) and of Lautréamont's *Chants de Maldoror* (printed in 1868 but little known until the 1920s), and he promoted the concept of 'automatic writing' (*écriture automatique*), first practised in the collection of poetic

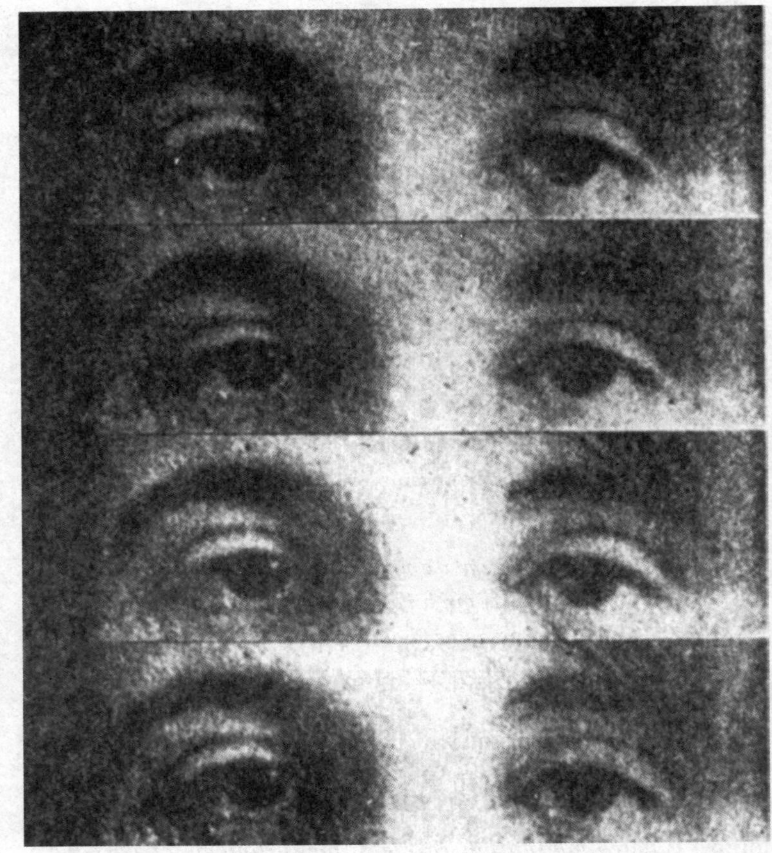

**13. 'Les yeux de fougère', photographic montage illustration for André Breton's *Nadja* (1928)**

prose *Magnetic Fields* (*Les Champs magnétiques*, 1919, with Philippe Soupault), as a way of breaking out of traditional forms and rationalist thinking.

Given Breton's preference for writing that eschewed any form of premeditation, moral censorship, and respect of traditional genres, it is not surprising that he assigned great weight to the creative role of chance in life. This is illustrated in his text *Nadja*, which is sometimes called a 'novel', though Breton fulminated against the tradition of the novel and stated that it was simply the record of real events, centred on his chance encounter with a young woman who called herself Nadja (though she made it clear that this was not her real name). He perceived in Nadja various parapsychological powers, and in answer to his question 'Who are you?', she answers, 'I am the wandering soul' (*Je suis l'âme errante*). He meets her several times, often by chance, and as they wander through Paris, each place becomes heavy with half-explained significance, suggesting that Nadja, at least, has had a previous existence in some of these locations. They dine in the Place Dauphine and later find themselves, by chance, in a café named 'Le Dauphin'; Breton explains that he had often been identified with the sea-mammal of the same name, the dolphin. Breton's respect for the reality of these Parisian places can be seen in the 48 photographs that are integrated into the text, some of them reproducing drawings made by Nadja, but most representing locations such as the Hôtel des Grands Hommes in the Place du Panthéon, Place Dauphine, the *Humanité* bookstore, the Saint-Ouen flea market, and so forth. These photographs ostensibly serve to avoid the lengthy descriptions that are so much a part of 19th-century realist and naturalist novels, but, since Breton does also describe things and people in words, they seem to have another purpose, or at least the effect, of preserving objects that have an almost talismanic importance for the author.



Breton's slim volume – *Nadja* is closer in size to a pamphlet than to most novels – does have at least one thing in common with Proust's sprawling work. Both authors consider the everyday world to be a source of great fascination and continue the progress of an ever greater inclusiveness in what can be deemed worthy of description and narration. For Proust, asparagus, diesel exhaust, and homosexual brothels figure alongside gothic churches and chamber music, while Breton found flea markets, film serials, and advertisements important to include in his text. Even more important is the role these authors give to involuntary mental processes in aesthetic creation. In a celebrated passage of *À la recherche du temps perdu,* Proust's narrator Marcel attributes the rediscovery of the events of childhood to the unpremeditated flash of memory that occurs upon tasting a madeleine dipped in a cup of linden tea. This aesthetic of *mémoire involontaire* is comparable to Breton's intention, as he stated it in *Nadja,* to tell of his life:

> to the extent that it is subject to chance events, from the smallest to the greatest, where reacting against my ordinary idea of existence, life leads me into an almost-forbidden world, the world of sudden connections, petrifying coincidences, reflexes heading off any other mental activity...

## An innovative novel from the right



Not all great shifts in writing come out of manifestos and self-proclaimed movements. In terms of prose style, *Journey to the End of Night* (*Voyage au bout de la nuit*) by Louis-Ferdinand Céline (1894–1961, born Louis-Ferdinand Destouches) had great impact on the diction of novels in the decades following its publication in 1932. And in addition to its influence on style, it contributed to the deflation of the protagonist's claim to the status of 'hero' in the noble sense. In this first-person novel, which begins with the First World War, the tough-talking, acerbic, working-class young narrator, Ferdinand Bardamu (the surname matches the author's and will be the name of the protagonist in Céline's subsequent novel, *Death on the Installment Plan* (*La mort à crédit,* 1936)), quickly decides that the war is a pointless butchery and gets himself hospitalized for mental illness, essentially for fear. He is, in short, anything but heroic, since the examples of heroism he sees around him seem to spring from lack of imagination or simple stupidity. Finding himself in a military hospital where the director's therapeutic idea is to infuse his patients with patriotic sentiments, Bardamu adapts by feigning compliance and even tells stories that become the basis for the recital of his 'heroic' adventures at the

Comédie Française. Wandering from Flanders to Paris, and then to West Africa, and from there to the United States, and finally back to Paris, where he becomes a medical doctor, Bardamu is a kind of Candide without the burden of an imposed philosophy. In fact, he is immune to almost every grand scheme of values, a precursor to the literature of the 'absurd' that became a recognized trend twenty years later. He serves, like Voltaire's character, as a critical lens through which to denounce American capitalism and the French military and colonial classes, and literature itself as vehicle of heroism. There is something Pangloss-like about the psychiatrist crowing about the recognition his method has received – 'I say that it is admirable that in this hospital that I direct has been formed under our very eyes, unforgettably, one of these sublime creative collaborations between the Poet and one of our heroes' (*Je déclare admirable que dans cet hôpital que je dirige, il vienne se former sous nos yeux, inoubliablement, une de ces sublimes collaborations créatrices entre le Poète et l'un de nos héros!*) – but Bardamu, who, after all, is narrator of this story, is the very first to see through all this hokum. Céline's narrator's corrosive, wordplay-filled descriptions achieve their goal of demystification by drowning the grandiose in the trivial or gross. Manhattan banks appear to him as hushed churches in which the tellers' windows are like the grills of confessionals, and only a few paragraphs later Bardamu describes the efforts of 'rectal workers' (*travailleurs rectaux*) in a public toilet.

Céline's use of slang and of the rhythms of popular, working-class speech are matched with a kind of narrow-focus narrative sequencing that keeps Bardamu's attention fixed on small details, while provoking the reader to extract from all of this the ideological significance of this additive critique. In various ways, Céline's innovations had a strong impact both on his younger contemporaries, like Albert Camus (in *L'Étranger*), and on much later writers such as Marie Darrieussecq (in *Truismes*). The huge and lasting fame of *Journey to the End of Night* has not been diminished by Céline's anti-Semitism and subsequent ties to the pro-Nazi Vichy regime (he was, after the war, declared a 'national disgrace'). However, the populist hero Bardamu, who had declared that 'the war was everything we didn't understand' (*la guerre en somme c'était tout ce qu'on ne comprenait pas*), has remained much more alive for the reading public than the contemporary anti-war heroes of another First World War novel, Roger Martin du Gard's *L'Été 1914* (1936, part of the longer work *Les Thibault*, 1922–40), for which Martin du Gard won the Nobel Prize for Literature in 1937. Perhaps, besides the inventiveness and the biting dark humour of Céline's work, this enduring success among anti-war novels is due to Bardamu's dead-pan cynicism, which seems closer to common perceptions of reality than the idealism of Martin du Gard's idealistic pacifist Jacques Thibault.

## The Second World War and the camps



Although Céline continued to write after the Second World War, his fame depends essentially on *Voyage au bout de la nuit* and *La mort à crédit*, because during and after the war, Albert Camus and Jean-Paul Sartre began to occupy some of the same terrain of populist critique and to provide coherent philosophical contextualization for the scepticism and anger that rolled so unpredictably through Céline's work. The war itself, and the German camps, ended the lives of many authors and changed the lives of others. It helped to form lasting institutions like the publishing house Minuit ('Midnight'), which had published works clandestinely during the war before becoming a major post-war press. The war ended much that was playful and experimental in the *entre-deux-guerres* period, and Robert Desnos (1900–45, died of typhus in Theresienstadt) is probably the best example. Editor of the review *La Révolution Surréaliste* from 1924 to 1929, Desnos published abundantly, drawing on the popular culture of Paris and on pulp crime serials such as *Fantômas*.

An illustration of the way ideas circulated as jokes within Surrealist circles is the character Rrose Selavy, who appears,

**14. Marcel Duchamp as Rrose Selavy, c. 1920–1, in a photograph by Man Ray**

among other places, in Desnos's 1939 book *Rrose Sélavy: oculisme de précision, poils et coups de pieds en tous genres* (*Precision Oculism, Complete Line of Whiskers and Kicks*). It was the multimedia artist Marcel Duchamp who created 'Rrose Selavy' in 1920 as an alter-ego. Duchamp was photographed in drag as 'Rrose' by Man Ray, and then Desnos made 'her' a character threaded through some of his poems, even as late as June 1944, just a year before his death. In 'Springtime' (*Printemps*, June 1944), we see the formerly playful figure now remembered as belonging to the imagination of a former time, or of a time that may come again later, after the poet's death in the theatre of war.

**Printemps**

Tu, Rrose Sélavy, hors de ces bornes erres
Dans un printemps en proie aux sueurs de l'amour
Aux parfums de la rose éclose aux murs des tours,
à la fermentation des eaux et de la terre.

Sanglant, la rose au flanc, le danseur, corps de pierre
Paraît sur le théâtre au milieu des labours.
Un peuple de muets d'aveugles et de sourds
applaudira sa danse et sa mort printanière.

C'est dit. Mais la parole inscrite dans la suie
S'efface au gré des vents sous les doigts de la pluie
Pourtant nous l'entendons et lui obéissons.

Au lavoir où l'eau coule un nuage simule
A la fois le savon, la tempête et recule
l'instant où le soleil fleurira les buissons.

**Springtime**

You, Rrose Sélavy, wander out of these bounds,
In a springtime haunted by the sweats of love,
By the scent of a rose that grows in the walls of the towers,
by the ferment of the waters and the earth.

Bleeding, the rose in his side, the rock-bodied dancer
Appears in the theatre, hard-ploughed.

A people of mutes, blind and deaf,
will applaud his dance and his vernal death.

Agreed. But the word traced in the soot
Fades at the whimsy of winds and rain-fingers
Yet we hear it and obey.

In the wash-house, where waters flow, double-dealing cloud
Feigns soap and timely tempest, adjourns
the instant of sun-blossomed bushes.

Chapter 8

# The self-centred consciousness

Published in the midst of the Second World War, *The Stranger* (*L'Etranger*, 1942) belongs to what the author, Albert Camus (1913–60), called his 'cycle of the absurd' along with his essay *The Myth of Sisyphus* (*Le Mythe de Sisyphe*) and his play *Caligula*. A simple glimpse of the titles of the three works shows an emphasis on central characters who do not fit into positive heroic positions within their society but are outsiders, failures, monsters – or all these at once. French literature, at mid-century, was certainly itself not marginalized. The generation of authors who lived as adults during the Second World War produced six winners of the Nobel Prize in Literature (François Mauriac, 1952; Albert Camus, 1957; Saint-John Perse, 1960; Jean-Paul Sartre, who refused the award, 1964; Samuel Beckett, 1969; Claude Simon, 1985). This was a time, clearly, when French writers had captured the attention of the world. In some ways, they were all either themselves outsiders (four of them born outside of European France) or wrote memorably about outsiders (Mauriac in *Thérèse Desqueyroux*, 1927; Sartre in *La Nausée*, 1938).

## An unlikely hero

The title of *L'Etranger* designates its protagonist Meursault, a young man of modest condition and education, who works in an office in Algiers, and who, for no particular reason, shoots and kills a young Arab. The story, told in simple language in the first person singular, shows Meursault gradually growing in awareness of his distance from the society around him. The text is not formally a diary, but seems to be written from time to time, sometimes to note what has just happened and at others to present what the protagonist plans to do. There is a rather affectless quality to Meursault, particularly at the outset, though perhaps it is not so much a lack of emotion *per se* as a lack of the conventional dramatization and expression of emotions in their usual social form. The first sentence offers a good example:

> Today, Mama died. Or maybe yesterday. I don't know. I got a telegram from the nursing home: 'Mother deceased. Burial tomorrow. Respects.' That doesn't mean anything. It might have been yesterday.
>
> (*Aujourd'hui, maman est morte. Ou peut-être hier, je ne sais pas. J'ai reçu un télégramme de l'asile: 'Mère décédée. Enterrement demain. Sentiments distingués.' Cela ne veut rien dire. C'était peut-être hier.*)



In the simple declarative sentences, there is much attention to detail and especially sensation, with little explanation. We see the world from Meursault's point of view, that of a kind of Candide, like Céline's Bardamu, without a philosophy to follow or to combat (Meursault's narrative does make one wonder what Voltaire's *conte* would have been like as a first-person narrative). Meursault enjoys swimming, smoking, sunbathing, and sex with his girlfriend Marie. At an outing at the beach, Meursault, playing the peacemaker, takes a revolver from a friend who is threatening to kill an Arab with whom he has had a run-in, but later Meursault uses the gun to shoot the Arab. His account gives no place to fear or hostility, but rather to the heat, the blazing brightness of the sun.

The most remarkable moment of the novel is Meursault's discovery of himself just before his execution. Throughout the narrative, the protagonist-narrator seems to record what happens without thinking about it. There is such neutrality and such a lack of affect in his view of the world that he himself seems sometimes to be a person who is not there, almost a recording device. But his imprisonment and trial – he is tried for who he is rather than for the death of the Arab – make him aware of his difference from others, and in his revolt he becomes somebody, a self: 'Even when you're in the dock, it is interesting to hear people talking about yourself' (*Même sur un banc d'accusé, il est toujours intéressant d'entendre parler de soi*). He discovers his existence within the 'tender indifference of the world' (*la tendre indifférence du monde*), and he concludes by hoping that there would be many spectators when he is guillotined and that they would greet him with shouts of hatred. A personage almost without characteristics finally conceives of himself in a heroic dimension.



## The drama of just waiting

If Meursault becomes heroic only by affirming his status as outsider, Samuel Beckett's protagonists clearly occupy the outsider position from the start. Beckett (a truly bi-national and bi-lingual author, both Irish and French) differed, however, from Camus in distancing his characters from the everyday social world. Often, the unsympathetic central characters and their consciousness constitute the entire text, like the voice of *The Unnameable*, a novel (1953). The most accessible and best-known of Beckett's works is no doubt his two-act play *Waiting for Godot* (1952), with its tragicomic tramps or clowns, a play that for some critics typifies the 'theatre of the absurd', a term that was applied also to the plays of Beckett's contemporary Eugène Ionesco (1909–94), author of *The Bald Soprano* (*La Cantatrice chauve*, 1950) and *The Chairs* (*Les chaises*, 1952). Beckett manages the feat of making riveting drama out of two men waiting, in a bare landscape next to a tree, for the arrival of a certain 'Godot' whom they have never met. Where does all this happen? Could these two characters simply be described as inhabiting the author's consciousness?

**15. Lucien Raimbourg and Pierre Latour in Samuel Beckett's *En attendant Godot*, a photograph from the 1956 Paris production by Roger Blin**

The whole work has about it an air of barrenness and desolation that is accentuated by the simplicity of the language. Beckett said that he wrote in a foreign tongue to 'impoverish' and to 'discipline' himself, so that there would be no style or poetry to the text. Whether or not this was Beckett's actual reason for writing in French rather than in English, the argument could be made that throughout history poetry distinguished itself from ordinary discourse precisely by the acceptance of linguistic constraints. For most of the millennium of French literature, lyric poetry has been written in fixed forms of verse length and rhyme scheme that 'disciplined' the writer. In a similar vein, significant works like the medieval *Roman de la Rose* stripped away concrete secondary characteristics from its personae to concentrate both on what is most central to their story and what is most universal. Although the actors of *Waiting for Godot* cannot easily be interpreted as allegorical abstractions – into terms like 'hope', 'despair', 'reason', and so forth – their dialogue conveys a darkly comical version of human existence reduced to its most schematic.

Vladimir and Estragon, called Didi and Gogo, were perhaps in the same place the day before, waiting for the same person, together or not, wondering whether or not to wait, looking for ways to pass the time, and trying to decide what they will do the next day. While waiting, to fill the time, they discuss hanging themselves from the tree – Vladimir suggests that this would give them sexual pleasure. After a ridiculous discussion about how they could do this, they do nothing – doing nothing is the overarching principle. At the end of each of the two acts, they decide to leave and the stage directions indicate 'They don't move' (*Ils ne bougent pas*). In the midst of each act, another pair of characters shows up: Pozzo and his servant or slave Lucky. The hint of the circus in the clownish aspects of Vladimir and Estragon is reinforced by this new pair, since the whip-wielding Pozzo seems to be a ringmaster who can make his creature Lucky, whom he leads around on a rope, perform stunts – at least in the first act. By the second act, Pozzo is blind and does not remember anything that happened on the previous encounter the day before. Lucky, who entertains with a long, breathless, nonsensical speech in act I (suggesting, perhaps, the uselessness of learning, or even of all human achievement, including sport), is mute by act II.

In a text so enigmatic, so stripped down, the task of finding some link between what happens on stage and the world of life and ideas falls to the audience. Readers and critics have not tired of seizing on the most minute aspects of the play as the basis for exegesis. The most obvious issue is the meaning of 'Godot' – is he 'God', and, if so, what is the significance of the suffix, '-ot'? Is it a diminutive? Does it indicate contempt? Towards the end of each act, a boy comes to deliver the message that 'Monsieur Godot' will not be coming on this day but the next day instead. In each instance, the boy insists that he has not come before. By following Godot's request that they wait for him to come, have Vladimir and Estragon lost their ability to act and locked themselves into a prison of waiting? Or does the thought that Godot might someday come provide the only solace that Vladimir and Estragon have? Otherwise what is there?

The play is full of little gems of dark humour in almost epigrammatic forms that are hard to forget – whatever meaning we might assign. Estragon says to Vladimir, 'We always find something, eh, Didi, to give us the impression that we exist?' (*On trouve toujours quelque chose, hein, Didi, pour nous donner l'impression d'exister?*). This is an extraordinary question, on the part of a fictive character in a play. After all, the question of the characters' existence is traditionally posed, if at all, by the audience, usually in terms of questions such as 'Is this character believable?', that is, 'Could such a character have existed?'. This is the sort of thing that was debated in the 17th century about Corneille's heroes and heroines. Later, in regard to Beaumarchais's Figaro, the character seems to be bursting out of his role, thrusting aside the hierarchy to take a place that he merits by sheer excess of invention, activity, and desire. In a way – and this was clearly on the minds of the royal censors in the late 1770s – the danger was that Figaro, or his like, would become excessively real and no longer simply be amusing figures on stage but rather appear in the streets of Paris to demand their rights. So to have a central character of a play, like Estragon, so far from 'heroic' in the evaluative sense, call attention to the tenuousness of his own sense of existence is quite striking.

## The collapse and reinvention of character

This is not atypical of the times. The notion of character, like so many other concepts or practices of the literary tradition, was called into question quite energetically in the thirty years after the Second World War. This happens in a myriad of ways and in many genres. For instance, in Ionesco's *The Bald Soprano* (*La Cantatrice chauve*), the characters' identities collapse into a small set of names. Monsieur Smith and Madame Smith discuss someone named 'Bobby Watson', or so it seems at first, since 'Bobby Watson' proliferates. Madame Smith says that she was not thinking of Bobby Watson but rather:

> I was thinking of his wife. She had the same name as he did, Bobby, Bobby Watson. Since they had the same name, you couldn't tell them apart when you saw them together. It was only after his death that you could really tell which one was which.
>
> (*C'est à sa femme que je pense. Elle s'appelait comme lui, Bobby, Bobby Watson. Comme ils avaient le même nom, on ne pouvait pas les distinguer l'un de l'autre quand on les voyait ensemble. Ce n'est qu'après sa mort à lui, qu'on a pu vraiment savoir qui était l'un et qui était l'autre.*)



Superficially, this is a play that makes fun of the British middle class and also of the French view of the British middle class. But it is also, at the peak influence of French existentialism (with which Ionesco is not usually associated), a glimpse of a wider anxiety about personal identity, and, in the passage quoted, of women's existence. If the woman Bobby Watson could not be distinguished from her husband Bobby Watson until after the latter's death, the reason may be given in a book published, with great success, only a year before: Simone de Beauvoir's *The Second Sex* (*Le Deuxième sexe*, 1949). De Beauvoir (1908–86) reached a huge audience in this book that analyses the cultural myths of womanhood in specific roles: the young girl, the lesbian, the married woman, the mother, and so forth.

At the same time, in literary theory and criticism as well as in political and social thought, the concept of persona or role or agent or central narrative character became an object of much discussion and experimentation in the novel. This genre, which had seemed to harden into a 'classic' form at the end of the 19th century, had for decades been under attack. Paul Valéry, the poet and philosopher of literature, had in 1923 taken the novel to task for its lack of rigour, for its loose and baggy structure. In a striking formula, he complained in regard to Proust that the novel as genre had in common with dreams that they refused to take any responsibility for their structure: 'all their digressions belong' (*tous leurs écarts leur appartiennent*).

## Novels about novels

Two years after Valéry's stinging remark about the novel, André Gide (1869–1951) wrote a novel about writing a novel, *The Counterfeiters* (*Les Faux-monnayeurs*, 1925). The character Edouard is writing a novel with the same title as Gide's novel, and this title itself announces the criticism of the realist novel. This structure of a text reflected within itself, as if a series of boxes within boxes, is now widely known in French by a term of heraldic origin, *mise en abyme* (literally, 'placed in the chasm'). This critical reflection of the text upon the text became common in the years before the war and into the 1960s. In *Nausea* (*La Nausée*, 1938) by Jean-Paul Sartre (1905–80), the first-person narrator, a historian, reflects at length on the relation between writing and being, and at the end of the narrative decides to stop writing history and to write a novel instead – perhaps a novel something like the novel we are holding.

These influential early examples of reflexivity in the novel are the background to the major movement of formal experimentation in what is called the *nouveau roman* ('new novel'), a term popularized by Alain Robbe-Grillet in his 1963 essay *For a New Novel* (*Pour un nouveau roman*). The term *nouveau roman* was apparently first used to describe this kind of writing by Émile Henriot in a negative review of Robbe-Grillet's novel *La Jalousie* (*Jealousy*, 1957; the term *jalousie* also means a window blind). *La*

*Jalousie* illustrates the ways in which the *nouveau roman* called into question the notion of central character, along with many other conventions attributed to the traditional novel.

*La Jalousie* is narrated by a nameless character. In fact, the verb 'narrate' may be misleading in this case, since the overall story is never really told but may be pieced together by the reader from what appear to be overlapping, sometimes repetitive, sometimes contradictory, fragments that are more like description (they are in the present tense) than storytelling. The persons named in *La Jalousie* are A…, Franck, and the latter's wife Christiane. Gradually it becomes clear that the narrator supposes a love affair between A… and Franck. We can infer – from notations telling us that four places have been set at the dinner table, but that Christiane will not be coming, etc. – that this narrator is a jealous husband. This text amply justifies the term *école du regard* ('school of the gaze') which was also used to designate the *nouveau roman*. Here is a typical passage:

> In the banana plantation behind them, a trapezoidal section stretches uphill where, because no clusters have yet been harvested since the suckers were planted, the quincunxes are still perfectly regular.
>
> (*Dans la bananeraie, derrière eux, une pièce en forme de trapèze s'étend vers l'amont, dans laquelle, aucun régime n'ayant encore été récolté depuis la plantation des souches, la régularité des quinconces est encore absolue.*)

The objects and events described are deliberately banal: table settings, the sound of a truck climbing an incline, the stain on the wall from a crushed millipede, the windows, hands on a table.

Although the source of these descriptions is never named, it – or rather, he, the husband – is not disembodied since there is heavy insistence on the point of view, in the literal sense that certain things are visible or not given the distance, angle, and lighting conditions specified in the text. The narrator's characteristics can also be inferred from what he notices, from the terms and precision of his description, from the obsessive return to certain moments and to certain traits that he notices in A.... Yet, other than through this effort at description of the physical world, we have no access to the thoughts of any of the characters, only a series of clues. The paradoxical situation of a central character who is both everywhere and yet, explicitly, nowhere, shows the extreme effort to renew the representation of the central persona, who is far from a 'hero', yet fundamental to the existence of the fiction itself.

Such inventive stretching of the category of the protagonist is common among Robbe-Grillet's contemporaries. In *Second Thoughts* (*La Modification*, 1957), a novel by Michel Butor (1926– ) that appeared the same year as *La Jalousie*, the protagonist (who is also the presumed narrator, as well as the presumed reader) is simply 'you' (*vous* – if we assume that the narrator and the protagonist are the same person, the choice of the formal pronoun adds another layer of strange distance from the self). At the outset of the story, the effect is quite strong: 'You've put your left foot on the copper groove, and with your right shoulder you vainly attempt to push the sliding door a bit more'. And in *The Golden Fruits* (*Les fruits d'or*, 1963) by Nathalie Sarraute (1900–99), the continuity usually given to a novel by the protagonists is instead assured by the topic of a multitude of conversations about a novel also called *Les fruits d'or* – another *mise en abyme* like Gide's *Les Faux-monnayeurs*.

At the same time, lyric poetry, which has often been in the forefront of attempts to expand the concepts of character and voice, pushed even further in complicating these components of the text. In Yves Bonnefoy's *On the Motion and Immobility of Douve* (*Du mouvement et de l'immobilité de Douve*, 1953), an 'I' sometimes addresses an entity named 'Douve' (grammatically feminine) who seems to have human features but also to become at times a landscape, an animal, and various other objects. Lyric poetry has often displayed its characters situated in, and particularized by, an environment, but Bonnefoy goes much further. Douve seems to be aggressed by the places in which she is located (and the choice of the pronoun 'she' confers a humanness that is not at all certain in this poem). By making up the proper noun 'Douve', Bonnefoy invites the reader to wonder which of the meanings of the French noun *douve* is most pertinent: the moat of a castle, a flowering plant (the Spearwort), a parasitic worm, or a stave. The strong association of character with place unites the lyric poetry of this period with other genres, such as the cinema.

## Character and place

Often associated with the *nouveau roman*, Marguerite Duras (born Marguerite Donnadieu in Indo-China, 1914; died in Paris in 1996) wrote the scenario for the film *Hiroshima mon amour* (directed by Alain Resnais, 1959) and published it separately as a book in 1960. Writers in this period moved often from novel to film and back – after her collaboration with Resnais, Duras herself later directed a score of films, as did Robbe-Grillet after writing the screenplay for Renais's *Last Year at Marienbad* (*L'Année dernière à Marienbad*, 1961). The screenplays, published in book form, are scarcely distinguishable from many other novels of the period that were not filmed nor even meant to be filmed, such as *Jealousy*. As printed texts, these screenplays are clearly part of French literature, and *Hiroshima mon amour* illustrates the close relationship between the construction (or deconstruction) of a main human character and the evocation of the destruction of Hiroshima by an American nuclear bomb in 1945.

Just as the character of Hugo's *Notre Dame de Paris* is as much the cathedral as the human character, Quasimodo, the bell-ringer, who gives the cathedral a voice, so in Duras's screenplay the nameless French actress who plays the role of a nurse in a film about Hiroshima and the Japanese architect who becomes her

**16. A scene from Alain Resnais's film *Hiroshima mon amour* (1959)**



lover exist almost exclusively to give voice to the experience of the destruction of Hiroshima and the wartime occupation of the city of Nevers in France. She tells the Japanese man a story that she had never told anyone before about her love, as an adolescent, for a German soldier. She and the soldier planned to marry, but he was killed by the French resistance and she was punished by her family, her head was shaved, and she was locked in a cold cellar for months. When her family released her, she bicycled to Paris during the night, and it was in Paris that she saw the newspaper headline announcing the bombing of Hiroshima. He tells her that she has seen nothing in Hiroshima: 'You have seen *nothing* in Hiroshima. Nothing' (*Tu n'as* rien *vu à Hiroshima. Rien*). She insists 'I have seen *everything*. Everything' (*J'ai* tout *vu. Tout.*). And this statement is accompanied in the screenplay by filming directions for flashbacks to the hospital, to the museum, to photographs of the city right after the bombing. The unrepresentability of the destruction in language or in images runs throughout the dialogue of the two lovers. Though the woman's experience in Nevers is easier to describe, it too is a taboo subject at this time. The massive French collaboration with the German occupying forces was a subject almost never mentioned in French media until Marcel Ophuls's *Le Chagrin et la pitié* ten years later.

Duras's characters are believable, yet opaque. They are what they say, and what they say is about love and destruction. The force of the screenplay is in large part the incantatory dialogue, which slides from apparently realistic conversation to something far from ordinary speech, like the actress's repeated utterance: 'You kill me. You do me good' (*Tu me tues. Tu me fais du bien*), one of the most explicit voicings of an erotic view of war, colonialism, and the relation of cultures that is ubiquitous in Duras's work, and appears, indeed, in other novels and screenplays of the late 1950s, when France was gradually and painfully losing its colonies. At the end of the filmplay, Duras makes explicit the identification of the man and the woman with their cities. The French woman looks at her lover – the stage directions note 'They look at each other without seeing' – and says 'You are Hi-ro-shi-ma', to which he replies, 'That is my name. Yes. [That is only as far as we have come still. And we will stay there forever.] And your name is Nevers. Ne-vers-in-Fran-ce' (*Hi-ro-shi-ma. C'est ton nom.—C'est mon nom. Oui. [On en est là seulement encore. Et on en restera là pour toujours.] Ton nom à toi est Nevers. Ne-vers-en-Fran-ce*). Duras here approaches the allegorical use of character most prominent in the Middle Ages and then glimpsed again in Bonnefoy's poetry.

# Chapter 9
# French-speaking heroes without borders?

In the last two decades of the 20th century and the first decade of the 21st, the grand old men of the Second World War generation left the stage of French literature to a new cast of writers, with new concerns. The many novelists among these contemporaries generally leave behind the formal experimentation of the *nouveau roman*. Many of these authors, such as Antonine Maillet (1929– ), Maryse Condé (born Beaucolon, 1930– ), Hélène Cixous (1937– ), Assia Djebar (Fatima-Zohra Imalayène, 1936– ), Daniel Pennac (1944– ), Raphaël Confiant (1951– ), Patrick Chamoiseau (1953– ), and Michel Houellebecq (Michel Houellebecq, born 1956, Michel Thomas, la Réunion), and Calixthe Beyala (1961– ), were, like their predecessors Marguerite Yourcenar (1903–87, born Marguerite Cleenewerck de Crayencour), Albert Camus (1913–60), Saint-John Perse (1887–1975), and Claude Simon (1913–2005), born outside of continental France – the French *Métropole*, or the 'Hexagon', as it is often called. Others were born within the Hexagon: Annie Ernaux (1940– ), J. M. G. Le Clézio (1940– ), Didier Daeninckx (1949– ), Marie NDiaye (1967– ), and Marie Darrieussecq (1969– ).

## Francophone writers, or writers in French?

Most of these authors have in common that they manifest a paradoxical shrinking and expansion of French literature. The France of the turn of the 21st century had lost a number of its colonies (Algeria, Indo-China, Morocco) but still sees its cultural sphere, its 'soft power', grow, as the French are among the most outspoken in claiming to resist the influence of United States culture. For the last several decades, it has been common to describe some of these authors – for instance, Maillet, Condé, and Chamoiseau – as 'francophone' writers, while others – such as Cixous, Houellebecq, and Camus – were never classified as such, though all of them were born outside European France. Who is, or what is, a 'francophone' writer? And is there a 'francophone literature'? According to the authoritative French dictionary, *Le Trésor de la langue française*, the term, which dates to 1932, simply means someone 'who speaks French' (*[Celui, celle] qui parle le français*), but in English-speaking universities the term has been used almost exclusively to designate writers from Africa, the Caribbean, and North America. It is undeniable that much of the vitality of today's literature in French comes from the recognition of such important writers as Léopold Sédar Senghor, Ousmane Sembène, Cheikh Hamidou Kane, and Birago Diop from Senegal; Ahmadou Kourouma from the Côte d'Ivoire; Driss Chraïbi and Tahar Ben Jelloun from Morocco; Roger Dorsinville and René Depestre from Haiti; and many others who have in common both the French language and the experience or cultural memory of French colonial culture. But questions remain as to the conceptual framework within which such writers are to be situated.



On 16 March 2007, the Parisian newspaper *Le Monde* published a manifesto entitled 'For a "world-literature" in French' (*Pour une 'littérature-monde' en français*), signed by a group of 44 influential writers. In it, they declare that that year marked the 'End of francophone [literature]. And [the] birth of a world-literature in French' (*Fin de la francophonie. Et naissance d'une littérature-monde en français*). There are different ways of looking at how such a distinguished group of 'francophone' authors came to the point of announcing the end of the literature that had brought them to the attention of a wide public. One could say that the academic concept of 'francophone literature' – conceived by its promoters primarily as a way of creating greater inclusiveness within the study of literature in French – had been such a great success that it outgrew its usefulness. One could also say that the concept of 'francophone literature' collapsed under the weight of its own inconsistencies and incoherence. And, finally, one could say that the term seemed racist and insulting to many of the authors to whom it was applied. As Tahar Ben Jelloun (1944– ), the Paris-based Moroccan writer, has said:

> To be considered francophone is to be an alien, someone who comes from elsewhere and who is told to stay in an assigned place somewhat off to the side of 'true' French writers [*écrivains français de souche*].
>
> '*La cave de ma mémoire, le toit de ma maison sont des mots français*', in *Pour une littérature-monde*, ed. Michel Le Bris and Jean Rouaud (Paris: Gallimard, 2007), p. 117.

And these various explanations are not incompatible.

There will always be reasons to sort literature into a multitude of categories, including the region in which a text is written; the period; the gender, class, race, religion, sexuality, or political affiliation of its author; the formal or generic characteristics of the text itself; the mode of diffusion or publication; and so forth. At the turn of the century, a major thematic consensus among writers in French is that the apparently stable categories of identity for individuals, nations, and other groups no longer can be taken for granted, including *francophonie* – not that boundaries and belonging are themselves outmoded, but that they have exploded exponentially and are now the source of endless variations of authorial and narratorial voices and of protagonists.

## A novel from history with a new voice

Let us consider, for example, a very successful historical novel by a French author from Guadeloupe, Maryse Condé (1930– )

*I, Tituba, Black Witch of Salem* (*Moi, Tituba, sorcière noire de Salem*, 1987), in which the protagonist and narrator is an African slave brought from Barbados to the colony of New England and tried as a witch in 1692. Orphaned as an infant and chased off the plantation to die in the forest, she is raised by an African woman healer to learn of herbal medicine and of communicating with the dead. Not a slave, for she was chased away rather than sold, she looks at life differently from her African compatriots, but she accepts to become a slave from love. She follows her husband when he is sold and sent from Barbados to Boston. The character Tituba is founded on a real person, about whom Condé gathered all she could from the archives of the witch trials of late 17th-century Massachusetts (Condé has given Tituba African ancestry, though this is not the prevailing view among historians). But in trying to give Tituba the biography that was never written – or rather, the autobiography that she never wrote or that did not survive – Condé clearly writes for a late-20th-century reader who will necessarily think in modern terms. Tituba uses the terms 'racism' and 'feminism' to describe outlooks and practices, the first to describe the world as it really was and the second to evoke an aspiration that Condé supposes women of the time must have felt. The character-narrator Tituba is a person of the imagination in more than one sense. She is not simply a version of an historical figure as Condé imagines her, but Tituba is also a character with the gift of imagination or vision to look forward to the future, a kind of Maryse Condé in reverse. As a wise woman, or 'sorcerer', Tituba can see and communicate with the dead but also with those who are alive after her own death.

*Moi, Tituba* clearly exceeds any bounds of the 'francophone' novel – it is not surprising, therefore, that Maryse Condé signed the 2007 manifesto. It is a work in French that does not represent a French-speaking culture but rather the English-speaking colonial world of the 17th century. Tituba, an English speaker, tells her story in French without any apology. The work often refers to other literary traditions; for instance, Hester, the heroine of Nathaniel Hawthorne's *The Scarlet Letter* (1850) makes a surprising appearance as a friend and perhaps lover of Tituba. The other characters, good and bad, are British, American colonials, African slaves or Caribbean-born slaves of African and mixed European-African descent (like Tituba herself, a child born of her mother's rape by an English sailor on board the ship *Christ the King*), and Portuguese Jews.

A consistent and very explicit aspect of Tituba's values and personality is her resistance to the appeal of vengeance, even in the face of repeated and extreme violence, such as the execution (the murder) of her mother for having resisted a plantation owner who attempted to rape her. Equally important is her refusal to accept the split into placative 'happy slave' exterior self and cynical but 'free' inner self – a stance adopted by her husband John Indian. Implicitly, Tituba conveys the view that this claim to inner 'freedom' is itself a deformity that debases the person and prevents any real happiness.

## The metamorphosis of the heroine

'Witch' is a term applied to women usually to insult or to threaten, but Condé has turned things around by making Tituba a real heroine, clearly implying approval of Tituba by the reader. A still more unlikely reframing of roles takes place in Marie Darieussecq's *Pig Tales* (1996 – the French title *Truismes* is a play on the word 'truism' and the word *truie*, 'sow'), where the narrator-heroine finds herself being transformed into a sow. Darieussecq (1969– ) has written something resembling Voltaire's *conte philosophique* and Kafka's 'Metamorphosis' but with a voice that is unique in its self-deprecating naïveté. While the feminist premise might seem rather obvious (i.e. that men both view and treat women like 'sows' – one of the infinite number of insulting terms for women, particularly in terms of their sexuality), making the conceit unfold is a *tour de force*. To take the metaphor of the *truie* and literalize it into a fantasy set in a very realistic modern world is particularly difficult to do within a first-person narrative. Unlike Kafka's Gregor Samsa, whose definitive transformation into a cockroach has already occurred at the start of the story, Darieussecq's nameless young woman morphs into and out of her piggish form gradually, and the boundary line of her interactions with the male characters is also fluctuating and indistinct.

As she becomes more of a pig, she finds her sexual appetite increasing, and in the 'beauty parlour' in which she works as a masseuse (in fact, as a prostitute), her new sexual aggressiveness attracts a more animalistic clientele, though her increasingly pig-like skin, nose, and bristles eventually put an end to her domestic and professional arrangements. As the protagonist recounts her experiences in a naive way – actually, even less judgemental than Candide – Darieussecq explores the ambivalences of male attitudes towards sex as well as the corruption of the political system. The author cleverly weaves together cultural references and humour, even recalling the legend of the werewolf that was Marie de France's focus in *Bisclavret* eight centuries before, when the protagonist falls in love with a werewolf named Yvan (the name seems deliberately chosen to recall the medieval Breton repertory).

## A critique of Western society

The final happy note of *Truismes* – the heroine has decided to remain a pig because 'it's more practical for living in the forest' where she has found a mate, a boar who is 'very beautiful and very virile' – contrasts with an unrelentingly downbeat *succès de scandale* that appeared eight years earlier and to which the adjective 'piggish' might well apply: *Atomised* (*Les particules élémentaires*, 1998, published in the US as *The Elementary Particles*) by Michel Houellebecq. One of the two protagonists in fact sees himself in a dream 'in the form of a young pig with plump, smooth skin'. This third-person narrative is multi-tonal, including an academic biographical account of one of its two protagonists, half-brothers, raised separately. One, the biologist Michel, leads a virtually asexual life dedicated to genetic research, while the other, Bruno, a *lycée* teacher of French literature, sees sex as his only reason for living. Their different paths bring them unhappiness and ruin the lives of any women who approach them. And the narrative itself manages to make everything it touches seem repulsive: science, religion, food, sex, friendship. The whole account is threaded with portentous 'scientific' statements about the end of Christian belief and the advent of a deterministic, materialist worldview. Michel's childhood girlfriend, who loves him and whom he rebuffs in adolescence, is described as she blossoms into the beauty that dooms her:

> From the age of thirteen years onward, under the influence of progesterone and estradiol secreted by her ovaries, fatty cushions are deposited at the level of a girl's breasts and buttocks. These organs, in the best of cases, acquire a full, harmonious, round aspect.

The voices of the narrator and of each of the male protagonists, who are given to long monologues on science, determinism, religion, anthropology, and social values, all advance the view that Western societies are in a state of advanced decay due to the rise of sexual freedom and of individualism and the decline of Christianity and of the family – in all of this 1974 is identified as the *annus horribilis*. To the extent that he intersperses long philosophical discourses with sexual details (Bruno, for instance, masturbates in quite disruptive ways), Houllebecq's work resembles Sade. On the other hand, it is very unclear what message might be taken from this book, despite its relentless didacticism. Yet Houellebecq is very much of his time in terms of the broad cultural mood. *Les particules élémentaires* appeared two years before the 'millennium', when a sense of foreboding was widespread. The media had warned that a glitch in computer code, the 'Y2K bug', would paralyse airports, banks, and even household appliances. Meanwhile, fundamentalist religious movements, of many origins, were building up the aggressive energy that led to elections of candidates from the Christian and Islamic right, in their respective spheres of influence.

## And a critique of the East

In contrast to Houellebecq's relentless misery with its implicit appeal for an authoritarian reimposition of social values in the hope of eliminating individual choice and collective alienation, Amélie Nothomb (1967– ) at the same moment published a novel with a joyous celebration of European individualism and self-responsibility in the context of precisely the type of paternalist system that, at times, *Les particules élémentaires* seems to value. In *Fear and Trembling* (*Stupeur et tremblements*, 1999), she tells the first-person story of Amélie, a Belgian born in Japan and fluent in Japanese, who comes to work for a large Japanese corporation. The mood of Nothomb's novel is entirely different from the dark, angular, jarring spirit of Duras's *Hiroshima mon amour*, but it has in common with that screenplay the portrayal of the relation between civilizations in terms of individuals and their erotic fascination for one another (we recall the refrain in Duras's text, 'You kill me. You do me good.'). In Nothomb's novel, Amélie is obsessed with the beauty of the Japanese woman who supervises her and who assigns increasingly demeaning tasks, until the Belgian protagonist has no other responsibility than to clean the male and female toilets of the forty-fourth floor of the Yumimoto corporate headquarters. In Amélie's ironic pleasure at the complete misuse of her talents as translator and business strategist, the individual erotic attachment to the supervisor, Fubuki Mori, and the broader cultural fascination – that is, the fascination of Western cultures with the mysterious East – cannot be separated. Therefore, descriptive passages reveal as much about the education and desires of the narrator as about their object, and in this one the allegorical turn is signalled by a reference to one of the best-known passages in Pascal's *Pensées*:

Two meters before me, the spectacle of her face was captivating. Her eyelids lowered on the numbers kept her from seeing that I was studying her. She had the most beautiful nose in the world, the Japanese nose, this inimitable nose, with the delicate nostrils, that one can recognize among thousands. Not all Japanese have this nose, but anyone who has this nose must be Japanese. If Cleopatra had had this nose, the geography of the planet would have been all shaken up.

## The theme that will not go away: the Second World War

The limits of the 'francophone' but also the boundaries of acceptable protagonists are challenged aggressively in *Les Bienveillantes* (2006), winner not only of the prestigious Prix Goncourt but also the Grand prix du roman from the Académie Française. The author is Jonathan Littel, born in New York in 1967 and a citizen of the United States at the time of the publication (he subsequently also obtained French citizenship, although he does not live in France). The oddity of an American winning these prizes would no doubt have provoked controversy in itself, but for an author of Jewish ancestry to write a novel from the point of view of a Nazi SS officer, who himself assists in killing Jews, was considered by many to be quite outrageous, particularly because there is some effort to make the narrator 'sympathetic' when contrasted with more enthusiastic killers. Maximilien Aue, the protagonist, in an account of how he wrote his memoirs, mentions off-handedly a long-standing tendency to vomit after meals and says that he prefers work to leisure because work keeps him from thinking about the war (perhaps Littel's study of Pascal in a French *lycée* brings this echo of comments in the *Pensées* about keeping busy to avoid thinking about the important things). Aue runs a lace-making factory, is a married father of twins, and aims at outward bourgeois respectability to cover his homosexuality and to make his shame from the war fade away.

Littel's novel is highly conventional in its form, especially when compared to the experimentation of the *nouveau roman* decades before. It seems that one of the major creative efforts in recent French novels is to conceive unusual protagonists whose first-person narratives stretch various boundaries of identity, with emphasis on national as well as sexual and racial identity.

There is no better representative of the movement for a 'world literature' in French than J. M. G. (Jean-Marie Gustave) Le Clézio, whose novel *Ritournelle de la faim* (*The refrain of hunger*) appeared in October 2008 just as the author became the latest French-language writer to win the Nobel Prize in Literature. The presentation speech given by a member of the selection committee before the Swedish Academy began with this question:

> Of what use are characters to a literary work? Roland Barthes maintained that the most antiquated of all literary conventions was the proper name – the Peter, Paul, and Anna who never existed but whom we are expected to take seriously and feel concerned about when we read novels.



Le Clézio began his writing career when this view prevailed, yet from his very first novel, *The Interrogation* (*Le Procès-verbal*, 1963), has shown the world through the eyes of his protagonists, who are often, like Adam Pollo of *The Interrogation*, outsiders to the world that they so sharply observe. Le Clézio's narratives concern a wide variety of places: Africa, in *Desert* (1980) and *Onitsha* (1991); Mauritius – home of his ancestors – in *The Prospector* (*Le Chercheur d'or*, 1985) and *The Quarantine* (*La Quarantaine*, 1995); Palestine in *Wandering Star* (*Étoile errante*, 1996); and Latin America, in *Ourania* (2006). He shows an immense ability to imagine the world from the point of view of his many characters, but Le Clézio, in keeping with the trend in French novels over the past decades, has moved from highly experimental, often difficult to follow narratives, to more straightforward stories.

Whereas in *The Interrogation* the main character, who is sometimes also the narrator, is insane, *Ritournelle de la faim* follows Ethel, a fairly ordinary protagonist, from 1931, when she is ten years old, until the end of the Second World War. But in both of these novels, separated by 45 years, the characters are connected in multiple ways to the world overseas. Adam Pollo seems to have just returned from serving in the French army during the Algerian Revolution, while Ethel's parents are from Mauritius and her story begins with her favourite memory, a visit with her beloved grand-uncle to the Colonial Exposition in 1931. As the Nobel presentation notes, Le Clézio's work 'belongs to the tradition of the critique of civilisation, which on French ground can be traced back to Chateaubriand, Bernardin de Saint-Pierre, Diderot, and [...] Montaigne'. In this respect, Le Clézio is highly representative both of his own time, a period of post-colonial criticism and debates about national and linguistic identity. His work is therefore a good place to enter into French literature, both in its origins and in its persistent variations.

## Endless encounters

As we have seen, the literary tradition in French both roots texts in their original historical moment and allows them to encounter one another across the centuries. Texts, in other words, are a bit like the water lilies of Claude Monet's famous series of paintings, the *Nympheas* (1906–27). The lilies are rooted separately in the soil at the bottom of the pond but drift on their stems so that the leaves and flowers shift and touch on the water surface. Just as Le Clézio's work encounters Bernardin's and Montaigne's across the space of hundreds of years, so also Darrieussecq's depiction of the shifting boundary between animality and humanity intersects with the *Lais* of Marie de France, while Proust's novel frequently refers to the writers of the 17th century. Houellebecq's work has resemblances to the moralist tradition of Pascal and La Bruyère, and Yves Bonnefoy weaves into his poetry echoes of Baudelaire.

Such encounters will certainly continue, and there will surely be surprises to come as writers formerly separated by vast distances find themselves in close proximity thanks to shifts in the book trade that make it easy for a reader in Québec to purchase a book by a writer from Senegal or Algeria. France has also been in the forefront of development of cultural resources on the internet. The Bibliothèque Nationale de France makes tens of thousands of books available online, while radio stations like France Culture and France Inter make readings of literary texts and discussions of literature available for download.

Just as important as the increased diffusion of French literary culture is the widespread perception that French intellectual culture is the single most significant alternative, at least among Western nations, to the English-speaking world. For some people, the notion of an 'alternative' easily slides into the idea of an 'opposition', and thus implies hostility and struggle. For many other people, including perhaps the readers of this book, the French literary tradition offers a welcome new vantage point from which to see the world, past and present. In a world threatened by sameness, we have never had a greater need for the French *différence*.

# Further reading

## General


Wendy Ayres-Bennett, *A History of the French Language Through Texts* (London: Routledge, 1996).

Peter France (ed.), *New Oxford Companion to Literature in French* (Oxford: Clarendon Press, 1995).

Denis Hollier (ed.), *A New History of French Literature* (Cambridge, MA: Harvard University Press, 1989).

Colin Jones, *The Cambridge Illustrated History of France* (Cambridge: Cambridge University Press, 1999).

Sarah Kay, Terence Cave, and Malcolm Bowie, *A Short History of French Literature* (Oxford: Oxford University Press, 2003).

Eva Martin Sartori (ed.), *The Feminist Encyclopedia of French Literature* (Westport, CT.: Greenwood Press, 1999).

Sonya Stephens (ed.), *A History of Women's Writing in France* (Cambridge: Cambridge University Press, 2000).


## Medieval and Renaissance


Barbara K. Altman and Deborah McGrady (eds.), *Christine de Pizan: A Casebook* (New York: Routledge, 2003).

Simon Gaunt, *Retelling the Tale: An Introduction to French Medieval Literature* (London: Duckworth, 2001).

Sarah Kay, *The chansons de geste in the Age of Romance: Political Fictions* (Oxford: Clarendon Press, 1995).

Sarah Kay, *The Troubadours: An Introduction* (Cambridge: Cambridge University Press, 1999).

Neil Kenny, *An Introduction to Sixteenth-Century French Literature and Thought: Other Times, Other Places* (London: Duckworth, 2008).

R. J. Knecht, *Renaissance Warrior and Patron: The Reign of Francis I* (Cambridge: Cambridge University Press, 1994).

Ullrich Langer, *The Cambridge Companion to Montaigne* (Cambridge: Cambridge University Press, 2005).

John Lyons and Mary McKinley, *Critical Tales: New Studies of the Heptameron and Early Modern Culture* (Philadelphia, PA: University of Pennsylvania Press, 1993).

Deborah McGrady, *Controlling Readers: Guillaume de Machaut and His Late Medieval Audience* (Toronto: University of Toronto Press, 2007).

Michael Randall, *The Gargantuan Polity: On the Individual and the Community in the French Renaissance* (Toronto and London: University of Toronto Press, 2008).

Jane Taylor, *The Poetry of François Villon* (Cambridge: Cambridge University Press, 2001).



## 17th and 18th centuries

Faith E. Beasley, *Salons, History, and the Creation of 17th-Century France* (Aldershot and Burlington: Ashgate Publishing, 2006).

Jean-Claude Bonnet, *Naissance du Panthéon: Essai sur le culte des Grands Hommes* (Paris: Fayard, 1998).

Peter Brooks, *The Novel of Worldliness: Crébillon, Marivaux, Laclos, Stendhal* (Princeton, NJ: Princeton University Press, 1969).

Robert Darnton, *The Forbidden Best-Sellers of Pre-Revolutionary France* (New York: W. W. Norton, 1995).

Joan DeJean, *Tender Geographies: Women and the Origins of the Novel in France* (New York: Columbia University Press, 1991).

William Doyle, *The French Revolution: A Very Short Introduction* (Oxford: Oxford University Press, 2001).

Anne E. Duggan, *Salonnières, Furies, and Fairies: The Politics of Gender and Cultural Change in Absolutist France* (Newark, DE: University of Delaware Press, 2005).

James F. Gaines, *Social Structures in Molière's Theater* (Columbus, OH: Ohio State University Press, 1984).

Dena Goodman, *The Republic of Letters: A Cultural History of the French Enlightenment* (Ithaca, NY: Cornell University Press, 1996).

Michael Moriarty, *Early Modern French Thought: The Age of Suspicion* (Oxford: Oxford University Press, 2003).
Michael Moriarty, *Fallen Nature, Fallen Selves: Early Modern French Thought II* (Oxford: Oxford University Press, 2006).
Orest Ranum, *Paris in the Age of Absolutism: An Essay* (University Park, PA: Pennsylvania State University Press, 2002).
Lewis Carl Seifert, *Fairy Tales, Sexuality, and Gender in France, 1690–1715: Nostalgic Utopias* (Cambridge: Cambridge University Press, 1996).

## 19th century

Tim Farrant, *An Introduction to Nineteenth-Century French Literature* (London: Duckworth, 2007).
Alison Finch, *Women's Writing in Nineteenth-Century France* (Cambridge: Cambridge University Press, 2000).
Cheryl L. Krueger, *The Art of Procrastination: Baudelaire's Poetry in Prose* (Newark, DE: University of Delaware Press, 2007).
Rosemary Lloyd (ed.), *The Cambridge Companion to Baudelaire* (Cambridge: Cambridge University Press, 2005).
Christopher Prendergast, *Paris and the Nineteenth Century* (Oxford: Blackwell, 1992).
Debarati Sanyal, *The Violence of Modernity: Baudelaire, Irony and the Politics of Form* (Baltimore, MD: Johns Hopkins University Press, 2006).
David Wakefield, *The French Romantics: Literature and the Visual Arts 1800–1840* (London: Chaucer Press, 2007).

## 20th and 21st centuries

Lucille Frackman Becker, *Twentieth-Century French Women Novelists* (Boston, MA: G. K. Hall, 1989).
Victoria Best, *An Introduction to Twentieth-Century French Literature* (London: Duckworth, 2002).
Dorothy Blair, *Senegalese Literature in French* (Boston, MA: Twayne Publishers, 1984).
Patrick Corcoran, *The Cambridge Introduction to Francophone Literature* (Cambridge: Cambridge University Press, 2007).
Edward J. Hughes, *Writing Marginality in Modern French Literature, from Loti to Genet* (Cambridge: Cambridge University Press, 2001).

Ann Jefferson, *Biography and the Question of Literature in France* (New York: Oxford University Press, 2007).
Shirley Ann Jordan, *Contemporary French Women's Writing: Women's Visions, Women's Voices* (Bern: Peter Lang, 2005).
Michael Lucey, *Never Say I: Sexuality and the First Person in Colette, Gide, and Proust* (Durham, NC: Duke University Press, 2006).
Christopher L. Miller, *Nationalists and Nomads: Essays on Francophone African Literature and Culture* (Chicago, IL: University of Chicago Press, 1998).
Charles Sowerwine, *France since 1870: Culture, Politics and Society* (Basingstoke and New York: Palgrave, 2001).

## “牛津通识读本”已出书目

古典哲学的趣味
人生的意义
文学理论入门
大众经济学
历史之源
设计，无处不在
生活中的心理学
政治的历史与边界
哲学的思与惑
资本主义
美国总统制
海德格尔
我们时代的伦理学
卡夫卡是谁
考古学的过去与未来
天文学简史
社会学的意识
康德
尼采
亚里士多德的世界
西方艺术新论
全球化面面观
简明逻辑学
法哲学：价值与事实
政治哲学与幸福根基
选择理论
后殖民主义与世界格局

福柯
缤纷的语言学
达达和超现实主义
佛学概论
维特根斯坦与哲学
科学哲学
印度哲学祛魅
克尔凯郭尔
科学革命
广告
数学
叔本华
笛卡尔
基督教神学
犹太人与犹太教
现代日本
罗兰·巴特
马基雅维里
全球经济史
进化
性存在
量子理论
牛顿新传
国际移民
哈贝马斯
医学伦理
黑格尔

地球
记忆
法律
中国文学
托克维尔
休谟
分子
法国大革命
民族主义
科幻作品
罗素
美国政党与选举
美国最高法院
纪录片
大萧条与罗斯福新政
领导力
无神论
罗马共和国
美国国会
民主
英格兰文学
现代主义
网络
自闭症
德里达
浪漫主义
批判理论

德国文学
戏剧
腐败
医事法
癌症
植物
法语文学
微观经济学
湖泊
拜占庭
司法心理学
发展
农业
特洛伊战争
巴比伦尼亚
河流
战争与技术

儿童心理学
时装
现代拉丁美洲文学
卢梭
隐私
电影音乐
抑郁症
传染病
希腊化时代
知识
环境伦理学
美国革命
元素周期表
人口学
社会心理学
动物

电影
俄罗斯文学
古典文学
大数据
洛克
幸福
免疫系统
银行学
景观设计学
神圣罗马帝国
大流行病
亚历山大大帝
气候
第二次世界大战
中世纪
工业革命